# THE DARK SORCERER'S ASSISTANT

# THE DARK SORCERER'S ASSISTANT

## GAVIN BROWN

Podium

Cover design by Mike F. Miller

ISBN: 978-1-0394-7558-8

Published in 2025 by Podium Publishing
www.podiumentertainment.com

Podium

# THE DARK SORCERER'S ASSISTANT

**MAGICAL SECURITY AGENCY**

**SUPPLEMENTAL THREAT ASSESSMENT BRIEFING—
TOP SECRET**

**TO: MSA DIRECTORS AND ABOVE**

**FROM: SPECIAL AGENT ANGELICA CRANE**

A significant security breach has occurred at the Guiana Space Centre launch facilities, which was formerly operated by Lukas Volker in cooperation with the European Space Agency. Lukas Volker, a persona fabricated by "Demon Duke" Vulkatherak, had been funding the construction of a rail gun capable of launching satellites into orbit. The rail gun project created a satellite launcher capable of accelerating objects to orbital escape velocity by using electromagnets over the course of a three-mile track.

After Mr. Volker was revealed to be a demon, local authorities seized his assets and facilities, and the European Space Agency assumed control over the rail gun construction project. Unfortunately, the demon Vulkatherak appears to have infiltrated the facility with the combination of inside knowledge and the use of a demonic ally, believed to be a succubus. The demonic entity reportedly seduced the director of the space centre with what he described in questioning as "*des seins vraiment, vraiment incroyablement parfaits,*" (translation from French: "really, really, unbelievably perfect boobs"). He has been taken into custody, and the centre is providing surveillance video evidence both for use in the criminal charges of negligence and his wife's divorce filing.

After gaining access to the facility, the demon duke used demonic magic to supercharge the rail gun's magnetic coils, and he used it to launch himself into space. Our contacts at NASA have analyzed the trajectory data, and they believe that on his current flight path, Vulkatherak will land on Mars in fifty-nine days.

Video and audio recordings show the demon Vulkatherak boarding the rail gun launch accelerator capsule and interacting with the French armed forces security staff on site, who were attempting to prevent his departure. Transcription follows:

**SERGEANT DURAND:** Unknown intruder, you are in violation of French and international law, step away from the accelerator capsule immediately, or we will open fire.

**CORPORAL MOREAU:** Sergeant, that's not a man!

**VULKATHERAK:** I am indeed no mortal man, I am Vulkatherak, one of the four dukes of the red wastes! Stay back or be incinerated.

**SERGEANT DURAND:** Monsieur Demon, please do not activate the rail gun. If you do, you will be subject to the full retribution of the United Nations Arcane Threat Committee.

**CORPORAL MOREAU:** Sir, I don't think he's stopping. Projectiles inbound! It's some sort of lava! Get down!

**VULKATHERAK:** Pitiful human, you think I care the least bit for your petty governments? I wanted to bring my demonic forces here to rule your world and renew the prismatic prison. I would have saved you all, you know that? But you had to steal the arcane conduit and ruin my plans. So now you will get to deal with *him*. Good luck with that! The glass is already cracked on all but the outermost layer. I would have let most of you live! Probably more than half, at least.

[Further dialog was masked by a high-pitched whine as the rail gun engaged and the capsule began accelerating down the track.]

Damage to the rail gun apparatus was minimal, but the project has been put on hold while a team of academic wizards from the Sorcerbonne have been dispatched to investigate the demonic magical enhancements applied to the device.

While the broader media has not been made aware of this incident, information about it has leaked online to some magic enthusiast groups.

# CHAPTER 1

As I walk out onto the sand, I give a friendly wave to the guy in a suit and dark glasses. He looks utterly out of place here at the beach, but in fairness to him, when he started tailing me this morning, he had no way of knowing where I was headed. It's early September now, and with summer fading away, I could be headed anywhere in flip-flops and carrying a canvas bag. The swim trunks should have been a giveaway, but I doubt they issue these guys swimming gear to be ready for a day at Orchard Beach.

And, after all, this is New York City, so *Let's go to the beach* isn't the first thought of the Magical Security Agency employees who are tasked with following me any time I leave Zambrano's warehouse in Queens. Though I have come here about once a week for the past couple months since I really haven't had much else to do. They don't dare follow me into the warehouse—no one wants to provoke the wrath of the last living dark sorcerer. Zambrano disputes the "dark" part of the "dark sorcerer" title, but honestly I can see both sides of the argument. He's not exactly a Boy Scout.

I toss my bag down, lay out my towel, rub in some sunscreen, put on my shades, and lie back to relax. I love the beach, but I have to admit, New York City does its best to make it tough. I bet a lot of people don't know NYC even has beaches. With not much else to do this summer, I've been trying out as many of them as I can. There's Coney Island, the Rockaways, Brighton, and if you're feeling adventurous, you can take a ferry over to New Jersey for the nude beach. I have to admit I haven't had the nerve to try that one, yet. No, the beaches on Staten Island don't count, because . . . is anyone sure it actually exists? Has anyone actually ever been there?

For Orchard Beach, I have a little slogan. "You may be at the beach, but never forget that you're still in the Bronx." When I looked it up online, they called it "The Riviera of New York City," and while I haven't ever actually been to the actual Riviera in the South of France, somehow I don't think it quite compares.

It's too hot in the sun, too cold in the shade, and the wind blasts you with sand. The refreshments are overpriced, there are screaming kids and bits of trash everywhere, and if you leave your stuff unattended for any amount of time, it will disappear. It's definitely not like those commercials for Corona or similar beers. But it's got sun, sand, and surf, so I love it.

But a few months ago, Zambrano and I defeated a demon duke, shut down the arcane conduit that would have opened a portal to Earth for all the demons on Mars, then had the government shoot it into the sun in a spaceship. I think I deserve a little rest and relaxation, even if it's at imperfect beaches.

After an hour of lying in the sun, I'm overheating and ready to hop into the water. I check my phone to make sure Zambrano hasn't texted me, as if that were likely to happen. And then I stand up, take off my shirt, and toss the rest of my stuff into my bag. Ignoring the kids yelling, I walk over to the guy in the suit, who's sitting on a bench.

"Hey there, Derek," I say, plopping down next to him. "What's up?" These guys never say their names, probably due to some MSA policy. So I just make up names for them. Today it's the really buff Pacific Islander guy with the slightly longer buzz cut than the other ones, who I decided last month looked like a Derek.

"Mr. Alexander," he says with a nod, tight-lipped and careful as usual.

"You can call me Bryce," I answer, knowing that he won't no matter how many times I say that. It's a fun little ritual that we have—can you tell that I'm bored?

At first, they didn't talk to me and tried to stay away and blend in while they tailed me. But I made a game of finding them and saying hi, so after a certain point they relented and started acknowledging my existence. I don't have many other people to talk to, and I feel bad for them just having to follow me around all day. Though I guess they probably get paid pretty well to do it.

After Zambrano and I saved the world from the demon duke almost three months ago, the MSA started taking a real interest in me. Now, they could have talked to me about it and worked something out, but in classic government fashion they didn't consult me at all and just started sending some poor low-level employees to trail me around anywhere I went, day or night. And my MSA contact, Agent Crane, has gotten a promotion and is too busy to text me back that often. After the battle of Yellowstone she was very responsive for a while, but I think at a certain point she realized that I didn't have any information and was just bothering her because I was bored.

So I make it my job to mess with the security detail. Or at least use it as an opportunity to vent. Which they probably count as valuable intel, or at least it gives them something to write up in reports and justify their salaries.

"Another beautiful day at the beach," I say. "Thanks for coming to hang out with me, it's great to have company when nothing is going on."

"Any time," Derek says, a ghost of a smile on his face.

"Any time that you're on duty and the MSA sends you to follow me, right?" I say. It's not that I mind, I just like bringing up subjects he's not allowed to talk about.

"Maybe I just enjoy the beach," he says with a shrug. "Such as it is."

"You told me you were going home to Hawaii a few weeks back," I point out. "Does this really compare to that?"

He looks out across Orchard Beach, which is a little semicircle of sand that doesn't even open onto the ocean. It's on the Long Island Sound.

"Okay, Bryce, you got me. This isn't a beach, it's a piece of water-adjacent land with sand that was probably brought in on a truck."

"I looked it up, it came on barges," I say. "If you're bored, would it make things more exciting to have a sea monster attack or something?"

He looks at me, suddenly alarmed. "Is that going to happen? Are you going to make it happen?"

I laugh, amused to have gotten a rise out of him.

"No, no," I say. "I don't have the power to do that. I can't ever learn or do actual magic. Which is why I keep taking you to dumb tourist destinations around the city. I'm supposed to be Zambrano's intern, but I can't actually do any magic. So he's off trying to figure out how to get into . . . some place that will help us save the Earth from demons." I keep it intentionally vague. Zambrano and I haven't told the MSA about Merlin's Vault in the Challenger Deep yet. We don't need them snooping around until we can get in there. The vault is in the very deepest part of the Mariana Trench, and we definitely don't want company when we go down there. If I let anything about that slip, Zambrano *probably* wouldn't kill me. But he would certainly find a way to make my life miserable for a while.

Derek purses his lips but doesn't say anything.

"Look, I'm sure you think I'm just wasting my time doing all this stuff. And I'll admit, there's only so many times you can go to minigolf or expensive meals before it all starts to feel pointless," I say. "Zambrano isn't letting me in on what he's working on, so I'm just waiting around until he needs me to break into somewhere or spy on someone. It feels like I'm a one-trick pony, you know?"

Derek stares at the water with a furrowed brow. He's acting like he's ignoring me, but he's definitely remembering all of this for his reports. Or more likely his phone is recording all of it.

"It's just frustrating. I'm so bad at magic that I'm actually undetectable to magic spells. Which is cool, but it means that Zambrano really only needs me to help out sometimes. And so I'm just wasting time here. Days at the beach feel meaningless, especially with the possibility of the world ending from a demonic invasion or something at any time."

Derek keeps looking at the horizon.

"Okay, look," I say, deciding to answer the question that I tell myself he's not asking. "Zambrano is often kind of a dick to me. He doesn't respect me and doesn't bring me in on the key decisions. If he was my friend, I would have blocked him months ago."

The MSA agent gives a noncommittal shrug. I'm sure this is all part of their strategy, to get me talking. But I don't really care.

"The thing is," I continue, "we worked together to stop the

demon duke from summoning an army of demons from Mars. We prevented a huge war and saved a ton of lives. And there are other threats out there. If there's even a small chance he needs me to stop the next demon invasion or whatever, shouldn't I be able to tolerate having a boss who says mean things to me sometimes?"

Derek nods in appreciation.

"And okay," I admit, "free housing, food, and other stuff is kind of nice too."

I will admit that it is nice having the iPad that's hooked up to an Apple Pay account that appears to have no credit limit. I started taking it out of the warehouse and using it around town, and Zambrano doesn't seem to care. I did ask about where the money comes from, because knowing Zambrano he might be stealing it from the UN Earthquake Humanitarian Emergency Response Fund or something like that. But it's not magic, he said that he's so old that investments from centuries ago have made him rich enough that he doesn't notice if I buy a two-hundred-dollar steak on a Tuesday night. It sort of makes up for the deadly peril in which I often find myself.

"Is there . . . anything you want to say about that possibility? The demonic invasion thing?" Derek asks.

At first the MSA agents would just sit there and pretend to ignore me, but I think at some point they realized that they might as well pump me for information.

"I've heard the rumors about Volcanose fleeing the planet," I say, referring to the reports I saw on the WizardWatch chat group about Demon Duke Vulkatherak taking a one-way trip to Mars. "Do you know anything about that?" I read the transcript that supposedly leaked from one of the European spy agencies, but I'm not sure what the prismatic prison is, and I don't want to reveal that I got ahold of it from my buddy Parth. Since I'm Zambrano's intern, world governments will probably leave me alone unless I really cause a problem, but Parth is a student at the Indian Institute of Magic, so he could really get in trouble. He and I know each other from the WizardWatch Discord server, which helped fuel my passion for magic over the past few years.

I look at Derek. He looks at me.

"You can't tell me anything about it, can you?" I say.

Derek shrugs.

"I can't say what I know about it either," I admit.

Derek nods. He gets it.

"So I'm just sitting around, waiting for Zambrano to need me to be magic-undetectable guy," I say with a sigh.

Derek raises his eyebrows in a sympathetic way.

I don't mention that I learned that I have that special ability not because of genetics, but because my mother was a great sorcerer who locked away her magic to save her sanity, and she passed that trait on when she gave birth to me. The MSA doesn't know about that, and we can't have them snooping around.

I asked my parents about my birth mother, but it was a closed adoption through an agency, so they didn't know anything. So I let it drop. I figure they're already potential targets for someone who might want to get to me, and through me to Zambrano, so I didn't want to give them information that could make them even more vulnerable. Luckily, the government has kept a lid on letting pictures or videos that would identify me out to the press yet. I'm hoping it can stay that way as long as possible.

We sit there in silence for a few minutes, looking at the wimpy little Long Island Sound waves lapping at the barge-sourced sand. And then I remember why I came over here in the first place.

"Watch my stuff while I go for a quick swim?" I ask.

Derek rolls his eyes but gives me one of those shrugs that says "sure, fine," without actually saying anything.

So I leave my bag next to the MSA agent who's tailing me and walk down to the shore to take a dip.

# CHAPTER 2

Eventually my phone's battery dies, so I head back to the warehouse. It's quiet when I get back. It used to be that Seraphex, the demon queen trapped in the form of a duck, would have greeted me with some sort of insult. But she's been gone ever since she offered to unlock my magic in exchange for letting her return to her full demonic power.

That was a pretty cruel, manipulative thing to do, right? It was especially hurtful from someone who I thought was becoming my friend. So it's messed up that I still miss her every time I get home.

It's not just her little sunny nook by the window that's empty. Zambrano has also been gone for the past week. After the battle of Yellowstone, we did go on a couple of trips, but since we got stuck on the project to enter Merlin's Vault, he hasn't been around much. He says he's doing research, and maybe he is, but I have no way of tracking him.

Even the birch butlers have seemed bored. The little wooden servants usually clean up all the messes that Zambrano, Seraphex, and I leave around, but with no one but me here, they've seemed to focus on deep cleaning the whole place over and over again.

I go to the wall of teleportraits, a vast collection of individually painted scenes from around the world. Each one is magically tuned to the place that it shows and allows Zambrano to instantly transport himself and up to a couple other people to that location. Research wizards from around the world have been trying to replicate the process for decades, but they don't seem to be able to paint the portraits with the right combination of intuition and artistic finesse that Zambrano has, and they have only succeeded about half the time . . . the other half, a hapless magician or wizard ends up turning themself inside out or teleporting with the bottom half of their body merged with some rocks.

They just can't figure it out, which Zambrano is quite smug about. I'd say it's one of his less appealing characteristics, but to be honest, there are a number of worse ones. Still, he's my friend. Well, kind of.

The thing with teleportraits is that when Zambrano uses one, he takes it in his hand and it teleports with him. So it only takes a second for me to look for the familiar blank place on the wall. It's his painting of a cute little alley in Barcelona, right around the corner from a small nightclub that he likes to go to. And yes, he pronounces it "Barthelona" with the pretentious lisp. But he is actually from Spain originally, so I guess that's allowed.

He actually took me there a month ago, after I bugged him about it for a week. But he said I "spoiled the vibe," "got in the way of his game," and "had no idea how to dance."

His first two complaints seemed unnecessarily mean, but the third felt kind of fair. I have no idea how to dance properly. Or even how to learn. I mean, you can sign up for classes in swing, tango, hip-hop, and everything else all over the city. But if you try to bust those moves out in a club playing deep house or pop music or techno, you look even worse than you do just standing there with your drink, bobbing your head. There's no class that teaches you how not to look like an idiot dancing to live DJ mixes.

Shrugging, I head upstairs. I know I've been lazy this summer, but I did make one promise to myself that I'm keeping. I may never learn to cast spells or dance at a Spanish discotheque without looking like an idiot, but I am working on myself in one key way.

After Seraphex left, Zambrano immediately cleaned out a room down the hall from me that I hadn't even known had existed. I wouldn't have been so quick to throw out her stuff, but forty-eight hours after she was gone, the room was empty, and when I asked if I could turn the empty space into a gym, he shrugged and told the birch butlers to reinforce the floor. So I ordered a bunch of equipment, and I've been lifting weights, running, and now that I'm at a baseline of fitness, I've just joined a climbing gym and started taking jujitsu classes.

I head to the mini gym and start my workout.

It's weird. I was always the super skinny kid who was more into reading about magic than doing any sort of sports or physical activity. To be honest, the closest I ever got to a gym was the gyms in Pokémon video games. "I wanna be the very best" didn't really involve much physical fitness. Charmander and Squirtle did all the actual work for me.

And now, a couple months into being forced to work out because of the ever-present threat of demons and magical beasts trying to crush or eat me, I've gotten . . . well, I don't want to mislead you. I'm not Dwayne "The Rock" Johnson.

As anyone who's spent time in a gym knows, the most important piece of equipment isn't the weights or the treadmill or the kettle-bells. It's the big-ass mirror where you can "check that your form is correct," which I've come to understand is code for "look and see if you've gotten any hotter since Tuesday's leg day." And I look slightly less like a stiff breeze would knock me over. It's nice.

I finish my workout, take a shower, cook myself a meal. Over the past months, I found a kitchen and learned to cook three different meals. Are you proud of me? And I'm not even counting scrambled eggs, toast, or cereal as a meal. I've just landed in my room, firing up the TV that I installed, and settling in with my plate of pasta and meatballs with red sauce—I know, I have a sophisticated palate—when I hear loud footsteps in the hall.

"Bryce!" Zambrano yells.

Without asking, he flings the door open. I'm sitting there in nothing but my boxers, a full plate of food balanced on my chest, and the intro to the latest season of *MILF Manor* (I've watched everything good already, okay?!) playing on the screen.

"Bryce, where have you been?" he demands. He's clearly been drinking, but Zambrano never actually gets drunk, probably due to his magically supercharged body. He just gets a manic gleam in his eye. Which might be more terrifying than if he started slurring his words or passed out.

"Um, here?" I say. "And I was at the beach earlier. You have my phone number, you know."

I glance over at my phone. I can see that he actually texted three times and called twice—but it's all been in the past six minutes.

He gestures at the phone, as if it somehow proves his point, but then drops the subject entirely.

"I figured it out. I was flirting with this gorgeous Portuguese linguist at the bar, and, okay, I'll spare you all the tongue-themed innuendo as it doesn't translate well, but we got to discussing dirty talk."

I look down sadly at my plate of pasta, take a single bite, and put it aside. That's clearly not happening for now.

"I really don't need to hear about your dirty talk or your seduction of yet another brilliant and beautiful European," I say. "We've talked about this before . . ."

"Oh, yes, that's fine," Zambrano says. "She was better with her hands than her tongue, anyway, to be honest. People underrate just how important fingers can be in—"

"Zambrano, that's exactly what we talked about!"

"Okay, okay, I'm done. There's an important point here. She was saying how dirty talk isn't so much about the actual content. And I was saying that yeah, it's about how you say it. Your tone of voice, intention, body language—it's like magic. You have to be in tune with the harmonies. I could give you some examples," he continues, but I glare at him.

"Okay, okay. Boundaries. So anyway, she says that, yes, all of that is true, but equally important is who is saying it. It doesn't matter how seductively you phrase something if you're just not the right type of person. Which might be hurtful for someone like you, I know."

I purse my lips and stare him down, and he moves on.

"Anyway, it got me thinking about the nature of passphrases and code words, and how that goddamn demon duck screwed us over. She gave us the passphrase, and it should work, but for some reason it just doesn't. So I've been looking at all sorts of possible ways to say it differently, pronounce it more correctly, imbue it with magical energy."

I glare at him, but he's not paying attention, so I stealthily grab my plate of pasta back and take another few bites while he rambles on for a minute or two about all the things he tried and failed. As he's finishing up, I put the plate back on the bedside table.

"But in the end," he concludes, "none of that was the issue. The problem was that neither you nor I was the right person to say it. That's an extra layer of security—Merlin must have known that the passphrase would get out eventually."

"So who needs to say the passphrase?" I ask. Zambrano is being as frustrating as usual, but this is pretty exciting. Zambrano says that all sorts of powerful artifacts are supposedly locked in Merlin's Vault. Maybe there's even something in there that will make me useful for something other than stealing and sneaking. Something that will make me a partner valuable enough to get Zambrano to take me more seriously.

"We need some water magic. In the year 500, Merlin had mer-folk allies who lived in that area, and he entrusted them to be the ones to open his vault after he went to Mars to lure the demons off Earth," Zambrano says, grabbing my fork and taking a bite of the spaghetti for himself. I start to object, but what's the point? He paid for it, and literally every other thing I've eaten for the past two months other than a couple dinners at my parents' place. "But the last of the merfolk were driven extinct in the late 1900s, and with them went their ocean-based magic. So with them gone, the password will need to be said by an old friend of yours, actually."

"Seraphex?" I guess. "I don't think we were ever really friends though." She used me and tried to get me to betray my whole species and help her become a full-fledged demon queen again. How was I dumb enough to think a demon could be my friend?

"Right species," Zambrano says with a gleam in his eye and a mouth full of meatball. "Wrong type. Seraphex may be in the form of a duck, but ultimately she doesn't have oceanic magic."

"Oh god, no," I say. "Not him again."

Zambrano smiles.

"The only other creature with powerful enough water magic on the planet is the Leviathan, which is trapped and sleeping in a cave off the coast of the Philippines. It escaped in the 1920s, and it took half a dozen sorcerers to put it back in its cage, one made by Merlin, from which escape is almost impossible. Which is lucky, because you would not believe the carnage of the battle of Tokyo Bay, before the Sorcerers' Circle was able to assemble and lock it away. I don't think we want to awaken that mythic monster, now do we, Bryce?"

I do. Honestly, risking the Pacific Rim under threat of a Dread Leviathan seems like a good alternative to having to deal with one of the grossest beings that I've ever encountered. Especially since he has a disgusting little crush on yours truly.

But I've been harassing Zambrano for most of our relationship about not risking people's lives for dumb reasons, to the point that it's become "my thing." And I read up on the Leviathan after Zambrano first told me about the battles that he and the Sorcerers' Circle fought against it. It was apparently a truly terrifying threat, a gargantuan sea serpent with tentacles, indestructible to conventional weapons and most magic.

So I just groan and shake my head.

"Slickwad?" I complain. "That nasty abomination? With the terrible smell and overly familiar seaweed limbs?"

"Slickwardinaeous! The same!" Zambrano grins. "I'm sure he'll be thrilled to help."

"Really?" I ask. "Isn't he mad that last time we used a lava cannon to blast open his menagerie, set it on fire, and free most of his prisoners?"

"Well, he doesn't know that we did it," Zambrano says. "We used illusion prisms and a lava-spewing Caldera Cannon. And then the demon duke, a lava demon, was very publicly defeated. I'm hoping he connects the dots there."

I take a deep breath. "Can we use a voice synthesizer or something? An AI fake? Hire one of those people online who does accents really well to impersonate him? Another demon who can do perfect voices like Seraphex used to?"

Zambrano shakes his head, continuing to raid my plate. There's plenty of pasta left, but the meatballs are all gone now. What a dick.

"It's not like some wimpy technological security system," he explains. "The magic recognizes the pattern of the particular entity. It has to be a seawater demon to open the gate, though we'll only need him for the initial unlocking. We're lucky it needs to be a seawater demon—if it was looking for a demon of tree or ice varieties, we'd be out of luck. There are none on Earth, and a field trip to Mars is out of the question."

"Well that's good, I guess," I say.

"Though theoretically the latest Mars probes did send back imagery accurate enough to make a teleportrait of the Martian land-scape, I'd just need to use an external arcane power source strong enough . . ."

"No!" I interject. "We don't need to do that. And it sounds like a *terrible* idea. We don't need to poke the demonic hornet's nest."

"Well, sure, it's just a very interesting theoretical concept, there would be a lot of work needed to deal with the distance and relative velocities . . ." Zambrano mutters, and I can see his eyes glazing over as the calculations start twirling around in his head.

Suddenly, dealing with one single demon doesn't seem so bad. Slickwad the seawater demon pervert is a hell of a lot less dangerous for me—and the entire planet—than all the armies of demons that have been trapped on Mars for millennia.

"Okay," I say, trying to interrupt his train of thought. "So how do we get Slickwad to agree to help us?"

"Right, right," Zambrano says. "Well, we want to make a good impression on our seawater friend. And for that, in my experience it all starts out with a nice gift. Something thoughtful, appropriate, rare, and fresh. Well, not fresh in the traditional sense. Or to human senses. Luckily, I've placed a hold on just the right thing at a local small business."

"This is going to be utterly disgusting, isn't it?"

"Well, that's a very human-centric viewpoint, isn't it?" Zambrano chides, an evil twinkle in his eye.

# CHAPTER 3

The next day, we suit up and gather our things and prepare to meet with Slickwad. Apparently, the wealthy seawater demon did agree to meet with us in his newly renovated menagerie in Istanbul.

Unfortunately, I got assigned to pick up and deliver the "nice gift" for Slickwad. Which turns out to be two buckets of the absolute stinkiest fish ever, sourced from the fish markets of the Queens Chinatown. Zambrano explained that the more famous Chinatown in Manhattan apparently was too gentrified to carry this sort of stuff—even in the Queens Chinatown, there was only one small shop that had it in stock, and they seemed relieved to get it out of the fridge in their back room, having held it there for Zambrano for the past week as it "ripened."

After realizing that no Uber would ever let me in, I ended up having to take the buckets of stink home on three subway lines, watching as my car mysteriously stayed almost empty even as the ones I could see through the window were packed with commuters.

So by the time we were at the warehouse and ready to make the trip, I wasn't in the best of possible moods. Why had I so easily agreed to be the errand boy? Well, first off it didn't seem that unpleasant until I got there and the fishmonger fellows carried in two buckets, looking at me like I must be an idiot. They didn't haggle over price at all though, just shot each other looks and said things in Chinese that were clearly some variation on *Who is this sicko,* and *Is he really going to eat this stuff?* They did also mention the word "Zambrano" once or twice in a tone that wasn't very positive. That part I could relate to.

I agreed because I don't know how else I can contribute. Zambrano doesn't really listen to my ideas, and in terms of hard skills, I have one trick—being invisible to magic detection—that's only occasionally useful.

Zambrano, of course, traipses down, looking perfectly composed, and he's exchanged his usual modern three-piece suit for swirling blue robes, a very traditional look for a sorcerer.

"Oh, wow, that stuff does smell awful, doesn't it?" he says as he grabs the teleportrait from the wall that will take us to Istanbul. "I guess it makes sense. It's technically rotten."

"Beyond its FDA best-by date or, like, straight up rotten?" I ask.

"Oh, well those FDA guidelines are pretty much fake. But I'll put it this way—you know how you can tell if an egg is good by putting it in a glass of water?"

"Yeah," I say. "If it's good it sinks to the bottom, if it's bad it floats. Too much gas in it or something?"

"Yup," Zambrano says. "And if this fish were an egg, it would be hovering in the air above the glass. That's why I paid the owner of that fish shop to hold on to it until it was ripe and ready. Definitely couldn't have it here. Speaking of which, let's get going before the smell gets into my books or something. I don't think any of the sentient ones have the ability to smell, but I can't be sure."

I grab the two buckets, he grabs me by the neck, and a moment later we're magically whisked away to Istanbul. We're met by a guy in an SUV, who straps the buckets down in the back seat and drives us through the crowded streets. Teleportraits are great, but even with Zambrano's big collection, you end up having to take local transportation to get to wherever you're going most of the time.

"Okay," Zambrano says as he buckles his seat belt. "Let's go visit our fishy friend."

He makes a pointed look at my seat belt, raising his eyebrows in a disapproving way. I roll my eyes and buckle mine as well.

"You know, Bryce," he says. "I like you. We're friends now. If I saw you flying through the air about to crack your skull open, I would very likely cast a spell to slow you down so you wouldn't splatter yourself all over the car. Also, it would ruin these throwback sorcerer robes I pulled out of storage to impress Mr. Slickwardinaeous."

"That's . . . very touching," I say.

"Sure," he replies. "But if we get in a car accident or get hit by some sort of kinetic spell while we're driving, that will all happen in fractions of a second. There's nowhere near enough time for me to understand what's happening, let alone decide what to do and invoke a spell phrase and perform the gestures. So . . . buckle your seat belt."

"If we got in a car accident, would you die?" I ask. "Just from randomly being T-boned by a big SUV?"

"Oh, no," he says, "I've got all sorts of magical reinforcements and protections. It'd take more than one little car crash to kill me. Don't take that as an invitation to try anything stupid though. When explosions start, you never know what will happen—sometimes great wizards and sorcerers can die from really stupid causes."

"Could you, like, do any of that for me?" I ask hopefully. "You gave me that helmet in New Zealand, but it only does so much." Being able to do a few push-ups is great, but this is a very dangerous world that we live in.

"Huh," he says, as if he hasn't thought of that before. "Yeah, maybe. It would need to be some sort of artifact, maybe. Most human-protective spells are keyed in to someone's magical essence. Bound to their soul, as it were."

I roll my eyes again. "And I don't have a soul because my birth mother did whatever magic-binding nonsense she did to save herself from the insanity that always comes with being a sorcerer."

"I can't say whether souls are real in some grander religious sense, but basically, yes," Zambrano says, ignoring the clear implication about his own sanity or lack thereof. "You're some sort of weird philosophical zombie without the spark of magical life. You seem . . . fine though, I guess?" He stares at me in that way that makes me feel like a slab of meat on the butcher's block. "I'll try to figure something protective out for you though. What about just installing some airbags in your shoulders? Or putting you in one of those giant rolling hamster balls? I could magically reinforce the plastic, for sure."

I glare at him, but I can tell he's actually thinking about real possibilities as well, so I don't interrupt him.

As we talk, we drive past giant malls, traditional mosques with gorgeous minarets, and gleaming new apartment buildings. Soon, we're in the affluent district where the menagerie is located.

"So what's our plan here?" I ask.

"Just follow my lead," Zambrano says, continuing his months-long streak of constantly frustrating me.

"Surely there's more to it than that?" I prod him.

"Yes, yes, of course," he says. "The plan is to offer him a thoughtful gift, make nice, convince him that we had nothing to do with the previous destruction of his property, and offer him an opportunity that his greedy little seaweed heart can't possibly resist."

"Okay, that sounds good. Why did you want me to come along?"

Zambrano shrugs. "Well, technically, you're still supposed to be on display in his hall of lesser curiosities. We'll have to promise to give you back once this mission is over."

"I am *not* agreeing to go back into that box," I protest. In our previous interaction with Slickwad, Zambrano sold me at auction as a specimen to sit in a slow-time glass display case in his menagerie of curiosities. He auctioned me in exchange for a fancy magic toilet from the 1800s, but I'm not mad about that, except for any time that I think about it.

"Oh, of course," Zambrano says, as if he didn't literally just suggest that. "We're going to double-cross him. He's a demon, after all. Messing with them is what I *do*, you know?"

I take a deep breath. "Okay, but I'm not going to pretend to be into him. He's gross."

"Can't you flirt with him just a tiny little bit?"

I groan. "Okay. Just a tiny little bit." When I said I wanted to be useful for something other than being magically invisible, that wasn't what I had in mind. But this will have to do, since we're trying to save the world, after all.

Though now that I think about it, *are* we trying to save the world?

"What's the *point* of getting into Merlin's Vault? What do we think is in there?" I ask as the car pulls up to Slickwad's menagerie building.

"Oh, there could be goodies of all sorts in there. Who knows what kind of cool stuff Merlin had himself buried with? Artifacts, key knowledge, powerful spells, demonic items," Zambrano says. "Powerful demons like Seraphex have been trying to keep me from getting into there for centuries. Plus, it's *locked*. I hate things that are locked and I'm not allowed to see! Don't you want to know what's inside?"

"If there's stuff in there that will help protect humanity from demons, then I'm on board."

So it's *arguably* part of saving the world. That's good enough for me, given that I really want to find out what's inside for the purposes of satisfying my curiosity as well.

We leave our phones behind in the car, since Slickwad won't let anyone take photos of his precious exhibits. Zambrano makes me grab the buckets of fish, complaining about not wanting to get his robes messed up. I am already covered in little bits of seawater from the ordeal of bringing them to the warehouse, so I grab them and follow the sorcerer up to the main entrance. I nod in appreciation at how well all the damage has been repaired. If anything, the exterior of the place has been remodeled and is even grander and more ornate than before. It's impressive.

We knock at the door and are ushered inside by a butler. He runs some sort of wand over us to check for phones and leads us inside. The interior restoration is just as impressive as the outside. There's not a single sign of the lava damage to the walls or the rugs wrecked by the fire suppression systems when I was last here. We're ushered through the main hall, where it appears to my dismay that most of the trapped people and beasts that I freed have been returned to their slow-time cases.

The glass cases line the hall, large enough to hold people and creatures, each caught in a different pose in the slowed-down time that's magically maintained inside. I remember being inside one of them, watching the world around me move around in a blur. I guess in some sense it's more humane and less dangerous than a typical zoo. The subjects in the exhibits only feel like they've been there for a few days as years pass, and they don't have time to plot an escape.

"The magical process of using rare element–infused glass to slow time was actually invented by Merlin, you know," Zambrano says as we pass a case containing a rockhide demon similar to the ones that work for Volcanose. And then I glance closer, at the plaque, and see that it's actually Bronk, one of the rockhide demons I'd encountered before.

Bronk looks *pissed* but luckily is mostly frozen in time, so I look away and hustle after Zambrano. I feel a tiny automatic tug of sympathy, but however he managed to get himself here, it's probably a good thing. He missed the kindergarten lesson about playing well with others, and him being on ice is definitely for the best.

"Merlin was a master of the manipulation of time," Zambrano continues, "though his 'lesser' areas of expertise would probably be as good or better than many of the latter-day sorcerers like the ones from my Sorcerers' Circle."

We're led upstairs, then turn a corner and enter a large dining room. My stomach twists itself into a knot as I see Slickwad standing by a large window, looking out on the grounds of his little estate. His body looks like a combination of seaweed and eels, with two snakes for eyes. His seaweed hair is moving as if it's blowing in the wind, but the air in here is completely still.

In the center of the room is a large dining table, though it only has one chair and place setting.

In the corner, a small and terrified-looking string quartet is huddled, dutifully pumping out music. The four musicians look stressed and sweaty, their boredom somewhat masked by the more surface-level fear. They are, of course, playing Pachelbel's Canon, which is Slickwad's preferred music, and as far as I can tell the only thing he listens to. The poor group looks like they've been playing it on repeat for quite some time.

"Mr. Dark Sorcerer," Slickwad says as he turns, his voice fairly squelching as it comes out of his seaweed mouth. "You are looking charming and powerful, like the sorcerers of old. Oh, and I see you've brought a delicious morsel for me," he continues, looking over at me holding the buckets of fish.

"Yes, where would you like these?" I ask.

"Oh, and the delicious morsel has also brought buckets of fish along as well," Slickwad says, chortling at his own disgusting joke.

He heads over and looks at the buckets, coming behind me and putting a seaweed hand on my back as he leans over my shoulder to look down in a completely unnecessary way. I try to hold myself still despite wanting to pull away from his touch, and I take a deep breath to calm myself down. Taking a deep breath turns out to be a big mistake, given the smell of the fish, but I tough it out anyway.

"Ah, yes, silver pomfret, a very fine culinary delight." Slickwad takes a long sniff, the seaweed on his face wiggling with delight as he takes in the rotten stench. "From the Guangzhou fish market, I detect?"

"Yes, I believe that's correct," Zambrano says, giving me a wink.

I glance down at the sides of the buckets, which are labeled SILVER POMFRET, SHANGHAI FISH MARKET, 5 KG, but I'm not about to tell the demon he's wrong, and I guess neither is Zambrano.

"It appears aged to perfection," Slickwad says.

"It's aged to rotten," Zambrano says under his breath, but Slickwad ignores it. Or maybe seaweed doesn't make for good ears, and he doesn't have great hearing? Hard to be sure. Loudly and clearly Zambrano says, "Thank you for agreeing to see us."

"Yes, yes, very well," Slickwad says, finally backing away from me and gesturing for me to place the buckets at the head of the dining table in the center of the room. "You've brought me a nice gift, Mr. Dark Sorcerer, but you have been holding this delicious morsel from me since he escaped during the outrageous home invasion incident that resulted in so much property damage early this summer. I don't suppose, with all your magical powers and knowledge, that you would know who would do such a thing? Blast a hole in my beautiful menagerie with lava and attempt to free all my prized exhibition pieces. Several of them were never recovered . . . at least, not yet." His snake eyes ogle in my direction.

Zambrano shrugs. "It's hard to say for sure. But there was a powerful lava demon who was discovered to be active on Earth not long after that. Perhaps he is the one to blame? If it makes you feel any better, I fought with him not long after your unfortunate break-in. And I believe that caused him to flee the planet."

It's a good thing that Seraphex isn't here, with her demonic inability to lie. Because Zambrano is laying down some real whoppers, and she would be unable to cover for him.

Slickwad laughs at Zambrano, and I tense up. Does he know that we were responsible for the break-in?

"You think Vulkatherak fled the planet because of you, Mr. Dark Sorcerer?" Slickwad shakes his head, and the swirling seaweed flings little splashes of salt water on both of us. "I don't know the details, but my understanding is that he is afraid of being a small fish," he says, meaningfully flipping one of the fish from the bucket into his mouth and slurping it down, "in a small pond."

"What do you mean?" Zambrano asks, his brow furrowing in concern. "Is there another supernatural force on the move?"

"For some reason," Slickwad says, heaving his mass into the single chair at the dining table, "the other demons don't share much information with me. I'm not sure why that is, since I have such sophisticated taste and impeccable manners." His tentacle hands grab another fish, and he slurps it down. "But they're all concerned about something very powerful coming into play."

"I've been hearing the same," Zambrano muses.

I'm guessing he's referring to the report of Volcanose fleeing the planet, but I worry that there's something even worse that the sorcerer hasn't shared with me.

"In any event, you didn't come here to speculate about how humanity's reign over Earth will almost certainly come to an end," the seawater demon says.

I try to comfort myself with the fact that, while demons like Slickwad and Seraphex are incapable of lying, they can be deceived, misinformed, or just plain wrong about their predictions and statements. Still, this overall thing seems . . . bad. Not a fan of powerful new enemies who want to take control from humanity.

"So what brings you here? Are you going to return this tasty treat"—he waves his seaweed fingers at me—"to fulfill the contract that you entered? This silver pomfret puts me in a good mood, but I'm not going to forget your obligations. Why didn't you turn him back in after he ran off?"

"I'm terribly sorry about not returning him sooner," Zambrano says. "It was poor form on my part. And I'm happy to return him to your custody now."

My fists are starting to ball up, but this is all part of the plan. I try to focus on listening to the music, which is still Pachelbel's Canon, and I think that we're now getting it for the third time in a row.

"Indeed? How pleasant!" Slickwad says. Noticing me glancing at the musicians, his seaweed rustles in pleasure. "You like my performers? They are very fine, and quite consistent."

"You . . . really do like just that one song, huh?" I say.

"There's none finer! It's the perfect balance of melody and harmony. There's really no point to any other music, once you've heard it." He tosses another fish in his mouth, chewing it noisily. "In the 1990s, I did briefly engage with the fine musical offering called 'Cotton Eye Joe,' but it was a brief flirtation. I know where my musical home is."

"Such wonderful taste," Zambrano flatters him. "But I did want to discuss my intern more, if I may."

"Oh?" Slickwad's eyes look at him questioningly. "And what would you say of my delectable exhibit?"

"I believe that we might be able to use his unique talents in a shared project. With my magic, his ability to move undetected, and your particular demonic seawater nature, taste, intelligence, and other skills," Zambrano says, laying it on thick, "we could both gain a number of powerful artifacts."

"You have my interest," Slickwad burbles. "What sort of powerful artifacts are you speaking of, in particular? I could use such currency for some upcoming auctions that have very fine items on offer."

"I can't say exactly," Zambrano answers. "But I'm sure you've heard the rumors. I have the passphrase to Merlin's Vault, and Bryce here can bypass the type of magical traps that a sorcerer like Merlin would have left behind."

Slickwad drops the fish that he had halfway to his mouth.

"That is . . . ambitious. You really think you're going to be the one to open the vault?"

"Who else?" Zambrano says as a wide grin lights up his unnaturally-handsome face. "As the last living sorcerer, I could argue that I have a legitimate claim to inherit whatever artifacts Merlin stored in his vault."

"I want half the artifacts that we find. And I want an additional ten years of rights to display this young morsel in my menagerie," Slickwad says. "Since his involvement in your defeat of the demon duke in the battle of Yellowstone, his historical value has increased. I'm going to be moving him to the main display hall. And his increased musculature makes him even more sexy. I have a fun new outfit planned for him now that he'll be in the premier exhibit."

Why is this seawater demon the only entity in the whole world who has ever referred to me as sexy? It's infuriating.

"One out of three of the artifacts, and five years of display rights to the boy," Zambrano counters. "As you say, his value has increased."

"Oh, don't be so upset," Slickwad says, seeing the look of anger on my face. "I won't make you stay in the slow-time case all the time—I'll take you out to play with you periodically!"

I elbow Zambrano, but he ignores it.

"Do we have a deal?" he asks.

Slickwad consumes two fish as once, somehow chomping on them as he stares at me with his slithering snake eyes.

"Oh, very well! It's a good deal. I would have liked more, but you drive a hard bargain, Mr. Sorcerer. The other demons here on Earth won't be happy that I'm working with you, but none of them came to my New Year's Eve gala this year, so who cares? Let's rob a grave!"

Zambrano and the seawater demon go back and forth on a few more terms and plans, and within a few minutes we're being ushered out. I glance back in sympathy at the string quartet. As we walk out, we pass the two chimpanzees in tuxedos that I remember from my last visit here. They're carrying platters holding more stinky seafood, and the looks in their eyes are pure sadness.

We walk to a nearby side street that's deserted enough to teleport out from. Zambrano doesn't like to use his teleportraits in public when it can be avoided.

"I know you miss Seraphex," I say as he takes the painting out from his wizard robes.

"I do not miss that feathered traitor," Zambrano mutters in a tone that reminds me of exhausted kids who say they don't want to take a nap despite barely being able to keep their eyes open.

"But," I continue, "we cannot replace her with this stinky bastard. You can't do that to me."

"Oh, no," he says with a laugh. "Don't worry, I'll get rid of him as soon as we've got what we need. But I don't know why you had to drive Seraphex off. I'd grown rather attached to her."

"She did try to trick me into helping her regain her demonic powers so that she could take over the planet and turn it into a living hell," I point out.

"She's been trying that for decades, I guess I just got used to it," Zambrano admits. "Okay, that's somewhat fair."

He grabs my neck, and we return to the warehouse.

After a week of waiting, arranging travel, and gathering magic ingredients, Zambrano teleports us to Guam, where we catch our boat and head to meet Slickwad above the Challenger Deep in the Mariana Trench.

# CHAPTER 4

The sea breeze whips across the deck of the small yacht that Zambrano borrowed from some rich guy who owes him a favor. I've been texting with my buddy Parth, who's at his university in India. I'm using the boat's satellite connection to catch up with him and let him know where I'm headed. I don't say it, but I'd like at least someone to know where I am if I don't make it back.

The brisk wind is blowing a mist of salt water in my face and setting my hair to waving. Does the wind make me look cool and heroic, or goofy and messy? I honestly have no way to tell, and I'm sure as hell not going to ask Zambrano, who's standing next to me.

He, of course, looks charming and debonair, dressed in a wetsuit that really outlines his unreasonably perfect body. Do most wetsuits show a six-pack through the rubbery material? Somehow, his does. Mine certainly doesn't, but I also don't actually have a six-pack. And with a jawline like Zambrano's, it doesn't matter how wildly your hair flails around, it always looks stylish.

I can also see Slickwad standing on his own ship a few hundred feet off, the only other visible object on the North Pacific, which is otherwise empty and glittering in every direction.

I tame my sea-swept hair by putting on the helmet that Zambrano gave me when we went to New Zealand to rob a harpy's nest earlier in the summer. It says "Intern" on it in the worst combination of fonts imaginable, but I've come to love it anyway. That New Zealand trip was where we got the magical feathers that are currently suspended in amber in a large circular slab that Zambrano gave me. In addition to the feathers, there are several other objects hanging in the yellow substance.

"You wouldn't believe the lengths I had to go to in order to get all the ingredients of these amber nexuses," he says, affixing it with straps that go around my chest and over my shoulders. Once they're pulled snug, the amber circle is close and tight against my body. "Harpy feather for pressure resistance, Norwegian eternal coal for heat, a tiny ship in a bottle for watertightness, and an evergreen sprig imbued with druidic magic for oxygen. It also has some iron for weight—that's not magic, it's just heavy. In the old days I would have needed something for light, but I realized you can just use your phone for that. Don't worry, the magic will protect it."

I roll my eyes at that. Magic sure hasn't protected my phones so far.

"Couldn't we have just hired a submarine or something?" I ask. "Or use a teleportrait?"

"Hah!" Zambrano shakes his head, smiling condescendingly as if I just suggested he skip his skin-care routine or something equally ridiculous. "Merlin's Vault is shielded from any sort of teleportation, like most places of great magic power. As for a submarine . . . You really think I would trust our lives to a tin can and some flimsy electronics? As if!" he says as he finishes strapping this bizarre collection of totems to my chest. "We'll use nice, safe, reliable magic."

I want to point out that I haven't personally found magic to be so perfectly safe and reliable, but Zambrano is already strapping on his amber nexus, stepping to the edge of the deck and motioning for Slickwad, who gleefully leaps into the air and dives into the ocean. A moment later Zambrano follows, arcing from the ship in an elegant dive. Of course he would be a skilled swimmer.

Taking a deep breath—that I realize may or may not be necessary given the magic in play—I step to the edge of the ship and dive in.

For a split second the water is cold and wet, and then I feel a steady heat on my chest as the amber nexus kicks in. I can sort of feel the water around me, but it's dull and distant. And the heat suffuses my whole body, which on the one hand is really nice, and on the other hand feels like the part of the pool where somebody peed, but everywhere. I shake off that thought, letting myself sink fully into the ocean, just below the choppy surface.

I hold my breath until I can't anymore, my body unwilling to do anything else. But at least I blow out some bubbles and can convince my panicking lungs to try taking something in—and I'm surprised to find that I can actually breathe normally. It takes several careful breaths in and out to calm my pulse and my panicky brain, but fairly soon things settle down, and I can focus on what's happening in the water around me.

Zambrano is floating nearby, grinning as he's been watching me acclimate. He gives a thumbs-up as he sees me able to breathe, and points downward. Then he grabs me by the wrist, makes a movement with his hand, and lets some bubbles out of his mouth as he speaks a spell. I suddenly feel my stomach lurch as we begin descending. The water rushes past, feeling like a constant waterfall. The magic of the amber nexus protects me from the worst of it, but I can feel the raw power of the water as we accelerate.

Zambrano casts a few more spells, and we surge farther, gathering speed and plowing through the water. I try to point my feet straight down to take the worst of it. As I'm struggling, I see Slickwad next to us, his seaweed and eel body moving through the water with ease. He grins at us, and then dives faster, moving ahead of us.

The sorcerer keeps adjusting the spells, and our speed levels off, though it's fast enough that we need the magical protection that holds off the worst of the water—otherwise it would tear the skin off our bodies.

We descend, and the light has long since completely faded away. I feel and hear the rushing water, but in total darkness. My instinct is to pull out my phone, but I'm pretty sure it would get ripped out of my hand. I've been able to go the last couple months without needing a new one, and I'd like that streak to continue.

The water goes by for long minutes, roaring over us in complete darkness. I know from my research before this adventure, that this is going to take a while. The Challenger Deep is the lowest point in the deepest trench in the ocean, almost seven miles down. Even with magical protection and the speed boost, water is really hard to move through.

Eventually, I feel Zambrano let go of my wrist, and the rushing of the water slows down. Once it stops, I can feel the pressure around me. Again, the magic is keeping it from being fatal, but it's still intense. I did my research here too—at this depth, the pressure is a thousand times as much as on the surface. Without the amber nexus, it would probably pop my head off. Or crush it into a pin. I didn't do my research on that part. I don't need to look it up to know that fourteen thousand pounds per square inch would be instantly fatal to a surface dweller like me. I'll skip the science lecture on what exact shape my body would splatter into, thank you very much.

Suddenly, I'm blinking as a bright light illuminates the area. My eyes have to adjust after the long darkness of the descent, but soon I'm able to see Zambrano and the rocky background around him. I try to speak, but I can hear the sound deadened, not even reaching my own ears through the water.

He's holding up his left hand, and magic light is shining out of it, illuminating the area around us. I recognize it as the same *Handlicht* spell that one of the security mages in Peru used, which I looked up after that disaster of a mission, where Zambrano let me get taken captive by the demon duke's mages. I nearly died several times, and I almost walked away from the whole Zambrano situation.

But I didn't get out then, so now I'm here at the bottom of the ocean, at the center of a long ravine. Looking up, I can see only the walls of it going up forever and curving outward. Below, the ravine continues down into the darkness.

Just below us, Slickwad is sloshing his way around, seemingly completely at home even in the incredible pressure down here. Demons are just built different, I guess.

Zambrano taps me on the shoulder and passes me a familiar object, a silver spyglass. I smile as I turn it over, remembering that initial outing with Zambrano. My very first international magical crime! It's somewhat nostalgic, now that I've done so many other things that that one theft in Japan is just the tiniest bit of my rap sheet. I was forced to throw the spyglass away in Chicago, but he must have somehow tracked it down and gotten it back. I guess it's lucky that powerful artifacts are very hard to destroy.

The sorcerer smacks me on the head, making a "get on with it" motion and an even more annoyed expression on his face.

He raises his other hand, and it starts to glow as well, doubling the illumination. I put the Spyglass of Spinoza to my eye and start scanning the area. The spyglass detects magic and should light up anything that's emanating arcane energy. After several minutes and several glances at Zambrano to see his impatient scowl, I'm about ready to give up. But then I see, far off and below us, an orange glow coming from the cliff wall.

I excitedly point to the area where I saw the glow, and Zambrano raises an eyebrow. I try to make a movement with my hands for "glowing" with some sort of jazz hands and waving fingers. Zambrano, of course, makes some motions with his hands that look to me like American Sign Language. Or maybe International Sign Language. Or maybe Ancient Sumerian Sign Language. I honestly have no idea which one, because for all I know he is probably fluent in all three of them.

Zambrano leads the way, and we swim toward the spot where I saw the orange glow. It takes a lot longer than I expect for us to reach it, not just because we're swimming but also because it's so far away. I periodically use the spyglass to check, and as we get closer I'm amazed at the intensity of the glow. It's invisible to the naked eye, but through the spyglass it's as bright as day.

Eventually, we reach the glowing area, and I put the spyglass away because it's too bright to look through. Nestled into the rocky cliff face, there are carved pillars, walls, and what looks like a large open central door, a yawning darkness.

Zambrano turns off one of his glowing hands and motions for both Slickwad and me to wait as he swims around, inspecting the architecture, casting small spells, and generally looking concerned. Finally, he nods and leads the way into the central door.

As Zambrano and his light move to the threshold of the door, I see that there's something different about the water ahead. And as he half swims and half steps through it, I see his boot land on the ground, and he's standing rather than floating. He steps farther in, motioning for us to follow. There appears to be a transition from water into air, which is reinforced when Slickwad lurches through the doorway and lands on his feet with a squelch, water dripping off him and seaweed once again pulled down by gravity.

I follow after them, eager to get out of the water, but rather than effortlessly transitioning from swimming to standing, I somehow fall forward, tumbling into a pile on the floor at their feet. With water streaming off me, I stand up, avoiding eye contact with both of them. It's my first time passing through a magical water/air boundary, I'm sure everyone flops on their initial try!

I jump up and brush myself off, standing in a growing puddle.

Slickwad looks at me, seaweed rustling thoughtfully. "I thought I would like him better all wet like that, but . . . the morsel just looks soggy. I'll have to dry him out for my exhibit."

I was sure he was going to say something gross, but instead I'm left both relieved and annoyed. Is something wrong with the way I look wet? I ignore him and follow Zambrano as he advances.

"Let's get this open," Zambrano says, leading the way into the cave, his hand casting shadows on the walls.

The interior of the cave is neatly hewn out of rock, a flat smooth floor and a curving arch of dark stone overhead. We proceed about fifty feet deeper, where we come to a massive set of double doors made of dull and rusty metal. The rock is emitting a glow of its own in a deep blue hue, and Zambrano drops the *Handlicht* spell, the glow fading from his fingers.

"How is all this maintained, the force field or whatever that is, holding the water out?" I ask.

Zambrano frowns. "I really wasn't expecting to find an enchantment so large still active down here, fifteen hundred years later," he admits. "I figured it would be the size of a small house, maybe the size of our warehouse at the largest. But it's much bigger than that. It's quite a lot of water pressure to hold back. You would need a good reason to build a protective arrangement as complicated as this. A locked door and various small protections that don't use a lot of power and could last more or less forever. But this air bubble must be drawing from a power source."

"Is it geothermal, like when the arcane conduit was connected to the Yellowstone volcano?" I ask.

He shakes his head as he places his hands on the metal door, examining it with senses that I can only guess at.

Slickwad smiles as the eels that form his eyes dart back and forth eagerly. "There's demonic magic in the air. My demon senses can smell it."

How he can smell anything over his own stench, I have no idea.

The sorcerer nods slowly, closing his eyes and holding the pointer finger of his unilluminated hand in the air like a golfer checking the wind direction. "There is," he says. "There's a hint of demonic magic. That may be the power source."

"So there's a demon in there? Or, like, a demonic artifact?" I ask. "Maybe a cool lithium-demon battery? Can it be that, and not a demon who's going to murder us?"

Zambrano chuckles. "Most likely it's a trapped demon of some sort. Though how you could trap a demon for that long without active efforts to maintain it, I have no idea. But Merlin was devious and powerful."

"He's not in there himself, is he?" I ask. As if the fear of being at the bottom of the ocean in an ancient vault full of traps weren't making me nervous enough already.

Zambrano shakes his head. "I don't believe so, but so much from that time is lost. Merlin built this vault to store his precious possessions and knowledge. As far as we know, he set up one end of the arcane conduit on Earth and went to Mars with the other end. Liao Ling built an alliance of sorcerers and wizards with a plan to trick and force demons into passing through it, with a clever magical barrier that kept them from returning. Sadly, Liao Ling died before the conduit was finally put into use. But there's no geothermal energy on Mars to power something like that. So Merlin had to open it with his own stored power. It could also be opened with demon magic, which was how Volcanose was powering the other end a few months ago when we stopped him and shut the Earth end down."

"Could Merlin have come through? Escaped somehow?"

"There shouldn't have been any way for him to come through and hold it active at the same time. Sorcerers at the time claimed that after most of the demons had passed through, Merlin was under attack from demons on the other side. The portal failed. As far as we know, he was trapped and died on Mars."

"As far as we know?"

Zambrano shrugs. "Even a great sorcerer can't stand against an army of demons. He died on Mars fifteen hundred years ago—and Seraphex confirmed to me once that she and other demons believe that as well."

"Do you know what happened to Merlin?" I turn and ask Slickwad.

He bobs his seaweed head back and forth, considering for a moment. "Demon lore says that he was slain by Demon Duchess Typhoria, mistress of hurricanes. But I was not there at the time. I was not invited to the Tragedy of the Conduit, as most demons call it. That worked out well enough for me because it left me as one of the few demons left to play on Earth for all this time. I would not have been here to assemble my menagerie or nurture the talent of Johann Pachelbel to create the greatest piece of artistic expression that this world has seen. Still, my lack of invitation was hurtful at the time."

Wow. This guy is hated, even among demons, the premier assholes of the solar system.

"Shall we open up our little present," Slickwad burbles, "and see what treats await inside?"

"Why yes, indeed," Zambrano says. "Let's see what Merlin left for us." He hands Slickwad a piece of paper with some runes written on it as well as a phonetic pronunciation below it.

Stepping closer, I see that it's the same phrase that Seraphex sent us after the battle of Yellowstone, when Zambrano won the bet that he could keep me alive long enough to foil Demon Duke Vulkatherak's evil plans. I like to think of it like the classic trope where someone asks someone else out on a bet, but then they fall in love. Though in Zambrano's case it's not really love, more like grudging tolerance.

Stumbling over the syllables, Slickwad slowly and haltingly reads out the words in Old English.

"What does it mean?" I whisper, sidling over to Zambrano.

"It translates roughly as 'I know I am probably making a mistake, but I command the vault to open despite the danger within.'"

"That sure makes it seem like this is a really great idea, doesn't it?" I say.

"I know," Zambrano says, suddenly talking quietly and dropping his bravado. "I have to try this, Bryce. Yes, I'm curious to know what's in there. That temptation is very real. But I need an edge. We need an edge. Every other sorcerer is dead and gone. And for some reason, new ones aren't being created. It's just me. Demons and other threats just keep coming, and I can't beat them on my own."

"I get it," I whisper as Slickwad concludes his reading of the long Old English phrase. "Did it work?" I ask.

"We're about to find out," Zambrano says, and he holds his hands out in a blocking motion. *"Raksha karana,"* he intones, and a sphere of blue energy appears around us. "Just a precaution, in case there's some sort of trap. Merlin was known for them."

We wait, and there's a low rumble. Then, slowly the doors begin to slide apart, revealing a wide set of glowing rocky stairs leading down into the depths.

"This is *so* cool," I say under my breath. Sure, we might be unearthing some sort of super dangerous artifacts that imperil the world. But still, it's the secret vault of the most powerful sorcerer of all time. It's awesome, and I can't wait to tell my friend Parth about it.

Zambrano holds the protective sphere up while I tensely wait for something bad to happen. Slickwad isn't covered by the magic shield, but his demon body is much tougher than our frail human ones. I'm glancing around, expecting an explosion or flight of poisoned arrows or something, but nothing comes.

With a shrug, Zambrano drops the shield. "Let's see what the old bastard left behind for us, why don't we? He was famous for loving traps and for jealously protecting his things. *Wǒ fāxiàn xiànjǐng,"* he says, holding his hand out in front himself with his fingers continuously flexing slightly, as if feeling something invisible. "This should detect any traps that he's set for us."

The sorcerer leads the way, walking down the broad staircase and continuing to hold his hand out in front of him. The wide stairs and walls all glow blue, illuminating the space in an unnatural, shadowless way. Zambrano tells me to check the walls and stairs with the spyglass, which I do frequently, but I don't see anything but the light already coming from the stone around us. The staircase goes on and on, taking us ever deeper into the Earth. I wonder if at this point we're below even the lowest level of the ocean.

I look back as we get farther away from the gate and see with relief that the large stone doors have stayed wide open. At least we won't need Slickwad to get in or out now that the passphrase has been used.

"How much do we really know about them? The legendary old sorcerers, Merlin and Liao Ling?" I ask as we walk slowly and carefully down the stairs.

"They invented many powerful spells, learning a great deal from the demons, elves, merfolk, and other magical creatures who were still available and cooperative in that time. So much knowledge has been lost since then, things that could only be learned by direct instruction from beings with that knowledge. Liao Ling herself created the magic trap detection spell that I'm using right now. I would have no idea how to create something so specific—the rumor is that she actually originally created it to detect traps that Merlin would leave around."

"In college, I remember reading papers debating the existence of races like elves and merfolk. So they're real?" Whole academic careers were made proving one way or another from circumstantial evidence whether they really were separate groups or just human cultures that had been mythologized over the centuries.

"As real as demons," Zambrano says. "But not as strong. After the banishment of the demons, there were unintended consequences, throwing the balance off. The merfolk went extinct, and the elves went into hiding."

Another thing that humans ruined. As if driving the dodo, Tasmanian tiger, and woolly mammoth extinct weren't enough.

"Here, walk along the right-hand wall," Zambrano says, and we follow him in moving to the right and walking down in single file. "There's a trigger to the left, and I don't think we want to find out what it sets off."

"In hiding?" I follow up as we walk down and he directs us to cross the stairs and move to the opposite wall as we continue. "Elves could still be around somewhere?"

Zambrano shrugs." Seraphex knows, but she won't tell me. Stupid duck."

I glance over at Slickwad, who has been following along with us. He is absolutely not going to replace Seraphex on our little team. But, still, I would normally ask her. So I try asking him.

"Do you know where the elves are?"

"I only ever met one elf," he says. "I ate it. It was rather stringy and not delicious. I didn't pay attention to them after that. I would love to have one in my menagerie if you do ever find one."

Groaning, I keep walking down the stairs and checking the areas ahead with the spyglass. I occasionally glance back behind me, nervously wondering if a giant boulder is going to come rattling down on our heads at some point.

"Hold on," Zambrano says, and the seawater demon and I both stop. Peering ahead, I can see in the dim light far down that the stairs seem to bottom out.

We advance slowly at first, carefully checking the open landing at the bottom of the stairs. Unable to help himself in his burbles of anticipation, Slickwad gets ahead of us. He reaches the bottom of the staircase with us hurrying to catch up.

There we reach a large open room, lit more brightly than the stairwell had been by a flickering blue flame coming straight up from a hole in the center of the floor. Around the room are three pedestals, each holding a single item. A cloak, a staff, and a coin.

Zambrano carefully walks the room, hand held out with his trap-detecting spell, feeling the air with his face screwed up in deep concentration. He spends an extra-long moment at the flame in the center, walking carefully around it in a slow circle. The sorcerer then takes his time to examine each of the three items on pedestals.

"I want them!" Slickwad says, moving toward the pedestal with the staff on it. "These must be incredibly powerful and valuable."

Zambrano motions Slickwad back with a firm gesture, and he stops, but he is clearly salivating at the idea of getting his hands on them. The seawater demon looks ready to pounce on the artifacts. So much so that his gross leering at me has stopped and his focus is entirely on the objects. Should I be jealous? No, no I should not.

For my part, I use the spyglass to scan the room. The walls, ceiling, and floor are all glowing with a low level of magic, but the power is clearly concentrated in the three artifacts on pedestals and the central flame, which glow brightly through the spyglass's magic-detecting lens. They're not quite as intensely powerful as the arcane conduit was, but the glow is still striking. I also notice a square outline of power below the flame, on the blank piece of stone that the flame rises from.

"Are they trapped? Can we touch them?" Slickwad demands, his seaweed curling in anticipation.

"They're safe," Zambrano says, finally dropping his hand and letting go of the spell. "Merlin must not have expected anyone to get down this deep, so he didn't create traps."

"So we can just take the artifacts?" I ask. "What do they do?"

"It would take much more study to determine their functions," Zambrano says. "They are immensely powerful, but they should be safe to take. And there are three of them and three of us. Seems perfect."

"I get one?" I say, surprised that I don't even need to fight for it.

But Slickwad laughs, his seaweed mouth shaking and his eel eyes gleaming with delight. "You'll be getting none of them. I will be taking all three of Merlin's treasures."

Zambrano raises his hands, ready to cast a spell, but Slickwad hisses at him.

"I'm not actually the only seawater demon left on Earth. While I decided to join you humans on land where all the interesting baubles are, my annoying brother, Diquardinaeus, quietly stayed in the watery depths. He followed us down into this trench and is waiting just outside the entrance with an explosive device. He is prepared to trigger it, burying this place under thousands of tons of rock. Will the magic hold, in that case? Will this place be destroyed? I am virtually indestructible and am very much at home underwater. How long will you survive? And this place is shielded from teleportation, so your usual tricks won't work."

Zambrano glares at him. "You've double-crossed us!"

Slickwad cackles, seaweed wiggling. "I have, how delightful! Do you think I didn't know that you are responsible for wrecking my menagerie? Do you think I didn't realize that you are the only logical culprit for that crime against my property?

"It would be a shame to bury the last living sorcerer at the bottom of the sea. I do rather hope to add you to my collection one day. Both of you, in fact. But in the interest of not having a battle that might set off the ancient sorcerer's traps, I'll take these three little trinkets for now."

The sorcerer takes a deep breath and then nods. "Very well," he says, "Let's negotiate."

I'm shocked that he's not putting up more of a fight. Are we that vulnerable down here?

"Very good, you're a good little sorcerer," Slickwad says, gurgling with pleasure as he enjoys his sense of power. I can only hope that Zambrano is charging up some devastating spell that will blast him away. But instead of melting the pile of lecherous seaweed, he launches into a rapid-fire negotiation.

"I'll let you leave with those artifacts," Zambrano says, "and you will share the mystic identification of those artifacts and any other arcane research that your staff is capable of doing. Which you will undertake within the month. You get the items, but we both get the research. And you will leave us unharmed here, free to exit and unhindered by you or your allies."

"You can leave right now," Slickwad says with a shrug. "My allies and I will not strike at you as you depart unless you strike at us first."

"You leave first and promise that you have done nothing to stop our safe exit. And your forces will not directly attack my facilities or my . . . minions," Zambrano says with a gesture toward me.

"Minions?!" I object, but they both ignore me.

"For how long?"

"In perpetuity," Zambrano demands. "You're getting three artifacts of incredible power."

"I have the upper hand, you're trapped here," Slickwad says with a sickening grin. "One year of non-aggression. And you stay here for at least an hour before you leave."

"Two years," Zambrano counters. "Who knows how much those are worth? Or what powers they might have?"

The two go back and forth for a few minutes on more details like lawyers haggling over a particularly nasty divorce. I am pleased that Zambrano holds the line on throwing me into the deal. Luckily Slickwad is so focused on the artifacts that he no longer has much interest in me. Should I feel insulted?

In the end, the basic deal is simple enough. Slickwad leaves with the artifacts, we get a safe exit, and nobody starts a fight for the next two years.

Zambrano is glowering, Slickwad's eels are gyrating in pleasure, and I'm furious. We're just giving up the artifacts?

But before I can figure out anything to do to stop an indestructible demon, Slickwad has grabbed the cloak, the staff, and the coin and is traipsing up the stairs, humming the seventeenth century's most annoying ditty.

I turn on Zambrano immediately.

"How could you do that?" I complain. "We find the cloak, staff, and coin of Merlin—and you just give them to a demon? Those might be the most valuable and powerful artifacts in the world! Who knows what he'll do with them? And we won't even be able to fight against him if he starts using them to cause trouble!"

Zambrano raises a single finger to his lips and gives me a playful wink.

I glare at him, waiting in silence as we listen to the seawater demon's footsteps and humming disappearing into the distance. I stare daggers at Zambrano as he ignores me, quietly looking around the room, moving his hands in small gestures and whispering the incantations of spells.

Finally, he stops and nods.

"Okay, Seaweed Breath is gone," the sorcerer says, "it's safe to talk."

"What the hell is going on?" I demand. "Why did we just give a demon some of the most powerful artifacts on the planet or something?"

Zambrano grins and rears back, laughing. "You really think I would just roll over like that and give up powerful artifacts? The thing that demons often forget is that, while they can't lie, I tell fibs all day long and still go to bed and sleep like a baby at night."

"So what?" I demand, still furious. "So you don't have to abide by the treaty? What's going on? Maybe one of those artifacts could have been something I could use, even if I can't directly use magic. Did you think about that?"

Zambrano shakes his head, leaning against a wall as he laughs. "No, no, Bryce. That wasn't the lie. I fully intend to abide by the treaty with Slickwad. I negotiated that so that he wouldn't be able to strike back, once he realizes what I've done."

"What you've done? What was the lie?" Then I start to get it. "Were those artifacts not actually powerful?"

"Oh, they're powerful enough," Zambrano says, still smiling like a kid who's found his mom's stash of the nice candy. "They're just not useful. I used Liao Ling's spells to carefully detect what they are, but when normal identification spells are cast on them, they'll disburse all their arcane energy by bouncing around and breaking everything in sight. All three at once. It's one of Merlin's traps. Don't worry, it'll just wreck things, shouldn't cause too much collateral damage beyond Slickwad's estate."

I breathe a slow sigh, still pissed at Zambrano but also relieved. "So . . . no demon with powerful artifacts? And I never had a chance to use any of them?"

Zambrano nods. "Precisely. Also, sometime in the next few days, Slickwad's home will probably be destroyed again."

That thought improves my mood. "Okay, I've got to hand it to you on that one," I say. "So, what do we do here now that the artifacts are gone? Is there anything left?"

"Oh, yeah, that," Zambrano says, casually walking to the center of the room. "Secret door under the magic flame. It'll take a few minutes to disable that trap and open it up."

Zambrano goes into magic concentration mode, slowly casting a series of spells around the flame in the center of the room. I want to ask him more questions, but I give him space as he works. I want to find out what's in the real Merlin's Vault, below the fake trap one.

First, various mystic barriers appear around the flame and then, slowly, it shrinks and eventually winks out. Zambrano drops the barriers and approaches close, putting his hand on the stone below where the flame had been burning.

He stands there deep in concentration for a long minute. And then he steps back.

"Gotcha," the sorcerer says as the stone makes a grinding sound, and a hole appears with what looks like the beginning of a spiral staircase below.

I jump in surprise as Zambrano whips around, looking behind me.

"God damn it," Zambrano says, pointing an angry finger. "*Now* is the time you choose to bother me again?"

A pair of webbed feet hop down the final few steps, and a feathered head with a sly grin on its duck bill comes into view.

"Hello, boys," Seraphex says, her regal tones echoing in the stone chamber. "Did you miss me?"

# CHAPTER 5

The goddamn demon duck is just standing there primly, beaming up at us like she just came home with pizza and Popsicles.

I really, really want to kick her again, like I did the last time I saw her in Yellowstone when she tried to tempt me to betray humanity. Just charge forward, swing my foot in a big old arc, and send her flying against the wall in a flurry of feathers.

I want to, but I don't. Mostly, to be honest, because she's actually quite spry, and I'd probably miss entirely and look like an idiot.

Zambrano glares at her, and I can see his fingers twitching. I can tell he's thinking about blasting her with magic. Which would be fine by me.

"What are you doing here?" Zambrano demands. "Haven't you caused enough trouble?"

"Oh, come now, surely you've been incredibly bored and lonely with only Bryce here to keep you company," she says. "And young Bryce, haven't you missed me explaining our eccentric sorcerer friend's tricks and helping you to navigate the magical world?"

"I . . . don't really remember you doing much of that," I say. "I remember mostly mockery, confusing hints, and then you tried to tempt me into helping you return to your full demonic form." Since the demonic code means that Seraphex can't lie, the odd thing is that she must genuinely believe that she was helpful.

"We'll have to agree to disagree," Seraphex says, "about exactly what degree of wrong you are about all that."

"Okay, enough games, demon," Zambrano says. "What are you doing here?"

"Why . . . I'm here to help you save the world," Seraphex answers.

"A bold claim," the sorcerer says, "but everything you do is a trick of some sort. What's in it for you? Why would you help us?"

Seraphex points her beak at the open trapdoor. "Because of what's down there. I think you're going to be glad to have my help. You're going to need it."

I glance over at the door in the floor, which feels like it's beckoning us forward. I really do want to know what's hiding down there.

"Give me one reason why I shouldn't just lock you away in a slow-time case for the next century—or just a regular old metal case so you have to suffer every agonizing moment of it," Zambrano says, lip curling in snarl.

"I believe that I just did," Seraphex says. "Maybe we should go down and see what we're up against before making very rude threats at each other."

"We would be idiots to trust you again," I say. "He should lock you up for good."

"Why are you both so angry at me, really?" Seraphex says, hopping forward. "Just because I tried to make a deal that would have been good for all of us?"

"I thought you were my friend," I say, pointing an accusatory finger at the duck. "I trusted you."

"Oh, Bryce," Seraphex says. "You always think everyone is your friend. Me, Zambrano, probably even the birch butlers. They no longer have the independence to think that sort of thing, you know, since Zambrano gave up his oppressive ways and got rid of the sentient ones years ago."

"I . . . well, yes, I actually am his friend," Zambrano says, almost as if he's just deciding it at that moment, largely to spite Seraphex. "And I freed the birch butlers as soon as I realized they were sentient."

"Good for you. If I remember correctly, you told them, 'You're free! Go away! Do whatever you think is best! I never want to see you again!'" she says, using her uncanny ability to perfectly imitate Zambrano's voice. And since she can't lie, I know it's a perfect quote. "In any event, shall we proceed down into the depths so you can see why you're going to want me on your side?"

Zambrano leans on one of the now-empty pedestals and screws up his face as he stares at Seraphex.

I stand and watch, not saying anything. I'm incredibly curious about what's down those stairs, but I hate to give Seraphex the satisfaction.

"Okay. Fine," Zambrano finally says. "This had better be good. Or bad, I suppose."

He goes to the stairs and begins using his fingers to sense traps again. He pauses for a moment at the edge of the stone staircase and then leads the way down. As he disappears down the stairs, Seraphex waddles up to them.

"Such a silly spell. He looks like he's trying to feel up an invisible person," she says with a glance at me.

I don't give her the satisfaction of reacting. All is not forgiven so easily. I follow along behind, watching the duck in demon form. I stay close as she hops down the stairs. If she tries anything, my kicking foot is still very much ready to go.

We proceed slowly down the stairs, the stone itself still radiating light. The stairway is narrow and straight for the first couple minutes, but then we reach a point where the right-hand side opens into a vast chamber. The staircase continues down the wall to the floor a hundred feet below, a narrow set of stone steps along the wall. Walking down it is terrifying, as there's no railing, but in Merlin's time there was no OSHA to ensure proper safety standards. Though in a reasonable world, I would need to wear a hard hat any time I was in Zambrano's presence. It'd be a hell of a lot more useful than the "Intern" hat he enchanted to stay on my head when we first met.

As the full chamber comes into view from the stairs, I gasp. The large room is dominated by a massive glass cube. The glass doesn't look smooth and perfect like modern windows, but is instead clouded with impurities and splotches of color like some handcrafted tchotchke that your mom bought on Etsy. Inside of the large cube is another one, set at diagonal angles within it. And inside that is a third glass cube set at angles to the one that it's inside of, but parallel to the outermost. In the fourth and centermost cube, which is parallel to us, there's . . . something horrific. All I can make out clearly is dark smoke, fire, and sparks, all of it frozen perfectly still in time. Deeper in the smoke, I can make out the back of some sort of massive figure with a spiked back, two horns on his head, and a claw raised in the air. As I look longer, I also see the tip of a tail, with vicious-looking spikes coming off it.

"What is that?" I whisper. "Are those slow-time cases?"

"Yes, nested slow-time cases," Zambrano confirms. "Each one multiplies the temporal slowing of the one inside it."

"The existence of a demon queen and a demon duke imply what?" Seraphex asks, and her authoritative regal tone is way more annoying now that I kind of hate her.

"I don't know, a demon baron? Demon count? Demon stable boy?" I say, already realizing with a creeping sense of dread where this is heading.

"Your ex," Zambrano says. "Damn it."

"Yes, my former husband, the tyrant of Mars—the demon king," Seraphex declares. "And a real proper bastard."

"That sounds bad," I say. "Really bad."

"I told you you'd want my help," Seraphex says primly. "Wait until you see the other side."

I gulp, eyeing the back of the giant demon with a sense of pure horror building in the pit of my stomach as we proceed down the steps.

As we descend, Zambrano points out several steps that we skip.

"Nasty traps," he says, pulling out a small bottle of spray paint and marking each one with an X. I would have expected something more magical, but it gets the job done. I gingerly step over each of the trapped steps, and don't breathe easily again until we make it to the bottom without triggering anything.

And then I look up at the massive scaled and spiky back of the demon king, and my breath catches up again. The smoke and fire is all contained in the innermost slow-time case, I'd guess because the others were installed around it after the demon king was initially trapped there. Along his back, I can see through the smoke what looks like a glowing dagger stabbed into his back, right between the shoulder blades.

"Does he—does he have a name?" I stammer, not knowing what else to ask. The demon king himself looks to be about ten feet tall, and merely one of the spikes on his back looks like it could go straight through me.

"Rexhalarkhart," Zambrano says, and then he starts to slowly walk around the perimeter of the outermost case, alternating casting his trap detection spell with what I'm guessing are other detection spells. "I had always thought that he was trapped on Mars, lured there by Merlin fifteen hundred years ago when the wily bastard tricked most of the demons on Earth to pass through the arcane conduit."

"And what's that in his back?" I ask. "The glowing dagger thing?"

"I'm not sure," Zambrano says. "Some sort of magical weapon. Not enough to kill him though, I'd guess. There's no known artifact that could do anything worse than slow him down for a while. He's a nasty big beast though. I had hoped to never know what Rexhalarkhart really looked like."

"We're calling him Rex for short, right?" I say, walking closely behind Zambrano. "Please?" I'm suddenly feeling very vulnerable, though the demon king appears to have been trapped in these nested cases for many centuries.

"It's not as deliciously insulting calling the demon duke Volcanose, but sure, why not?" Zambrano says. "His name is actually the source of the Latin word 'Rex' meaning king, from the earliest days of Indo-European languages."

"So how long has Rex been down here? How much do these cases slow time down?"

"He's been in the prismatic prism for fifteen hundred years," Seraphex says, padding along behind us on her little duck feet. "Since Merlin and Liao Ling trapped him in there. Merlin masterminded the forging of the arcane conduit, which could create a portal to Mars once he took the other end there. Liao Ling created an alliance of sorcerers and wizards from across the world to push all the demons through the portal once it was created. But they knew that my former husband the demon king was too powerful to be forced through the arcane conduit portal. So Liao Ling created a magic weapon to weaken Rex, and Merlin constructed this temporal trap to bind him in place."

"Merlin and his traps . . ." Zambrano says, looking at the giant glass edifice with admiration.

"What happened after they captured Rex?" I ask.

"Merlin claimed that Liao Ling was killed by the demon king in the battle," Seraphex explains. "She wasn't seen after it. Merlin took over leadership of the alliance in her name, and then he went to Mars with the far end of the conduit while the allied magic users forced demons through it, one by one, including me."

"That must have been terrible for you," I say, rather relishing the thought of human sorcerers and wizards casting Seraphex and all her demon friends from Earth.

"We got our revenge when Merlin died on the swirling claws of Typhoria, mistress of hurricanes," Seraphex says primly, "and never made it back to Earth."

"Why are they arranged like that?" I ask, pointing to the geometric placements of the cubes of glass, each nested with some edges and corners touching the one outside of it. "Why not just have them all at the same angle?"

"Temporal geometric waveform collapse," Zambrano says. "Not that Merlin had that language or the mathematics to express it. He must have figured it out purely by feel. It's . . . pretty damn impressive. Since him, no one was able to build something like this until the mid-twentieth century. I'd read some references to a 'prismatic prison' in arcane scrolls, but I had no idea something existed on this scale."

As we round the corner, we see that the front of the innermost case is covered in so much smoke it's hard to really make out Rex's face or body. But there is one part that is very clearly visible. One of his claws is pointed at the glass of that innermost chamber, and a bright fiery bolt is touching the glass. The glass is cracked and broken, and I can see, frozen in time, shattered pieces exploding from the breaking point.

"Shit. If the glass is cracked, then the innermost layer has already failed," Zambrano says.

"Then . . . he's going to get out?" I say, suddenly even more horrified and scared.

"Each case slows time by roughly a factor of three hundred and fifty. With four cases nested, roughly . . . ." he calculates in his head.

"Three seconds," Seraphex interrupts. "It took him three seconds of his subjective time to realize what was happening and that he would be trapped and time slowed down. He immediately cast a flaming bolt of energy to break the glass, but it's taken fifteen hundred years to break through the first section."

"Then he would have sped up by a factor of three hundred and fifty since the glass fully cracked," Zambrano says, casting an annoyed glance at Seraphex.

"So he's going to get out," I restate.

"Indeed, he's going to get out," Seraphex says. "You didn't think I lured you down by giving you the passphrase so that you'd have a nice educational field trip, did you? I was hoping to escape to Mars, but I'm stuck here, and time is running out. So I tempted you with the secrets of Merlin's Vault in order to get you down here in time." Seraphex asks. "It's only a matter of a fraction of a second for the flame bolt to blast through the three remaining cases, in subjective time inside the center."

"You knew about this all along?" I demand. "How long do we have out here?"

"Yes," Seraphex says, a sulky tone in her voice.

Seraphex and Zambrano start batting numbers back and forth, discussing the speed of the flame bolt, the nested factors of time dilation, and various other temporal mechanics. It's hard for me to follow, so I just keep examining the scene in the innermost case. Most of the massive demon is obscured by smoke and fire, but if I look closely, I do see a shape on the other side from the one we walked around, slumped up against the glass.

"We've got about three weeks, give or take," Zambrano finally says, and Seraphex bobs her little duck head in agreement.

"That magical dagger in his back is a good sign, however," Seraphex adds. "I didn't realize he had been wounded like that. I'm not sure what sort of weapon it is, but it appears to have harmed him. Most impressive, even to wound him. He won't be at full strength when he gets out."

"That's good," I say.

"Don't mistake me, he will still be stronger than we are, by a wide margin," Seraphex adds. "But it's good news for the world. He will need some time to recover from a wound like that once he escapes."

"And what happens when he escapes?" I ask, dreading the answer. Just the glimpse of the spikes, claws, and demonic muscle through the smoke and fire is enough to be terrifying.

"Hell on Earth," Seraphex says. "Eventually. But he won't strike at first. He'll need time to recover from his injury. And immediate direct action isn't his way. He'll seek to use trickery and pawns to remove his rivals and destabilize the world, triggering disasters and pitting one group against another. Then, finally, when everyone is exhausted by disaster after disaster, he'll seize power."

"Can we make more cases, buy ourselves even more time, keep him trapped in there?" I ask, as I walk around the glass to get a closer look at the shape.

"Three weeks is nowhere near enough time to make more slow-time cases, not at this scale. They get far more difficult to construct and require far more arcane energy the larger they get," Zambrano says. "I'm shocked that Merlin was able to build the largest one here—I've never seen a slow-time case of this size. He must have given magical assistance to glassmakers in the Byzantine Empire in order to get this size and scale." Zambrano is somehow ignoring the giant terrifying demon at the center and instead is examining the rough-looking glass panes that make up the cases.

"What are you looking at?" Seraphex asks, hopping along toward me.

I squint, trying to make it out. There's something in there down at the base of the smoky wall. I keep walking around and get a slightly better view past some of the smoke, and I can see what I was starting to suspect.

"It's a person, I think," I say. "Pressed up against the glass. I can see a face. Has someone been trapped in there with Rex for over a thousand years?"

Seraphex stops in her tracks, staring at the figure.

"Well," she says quietly, "that's a surprise."

# CHAPTER 6

What is?" I ask. As I examine the case more thoroughly, I can see that it's definitely a body, pressed in the corner with their face and mouth smooshed against the glass.

"Is there a corpse in there?" Zambrano asks, looking into the Prismatic Prison with suspicion.

I draw out the Spyglass of Spinoza to try to get a clearer look at the body, which appears to be a young Asian woman. It's bright as hell from all the magic, but the spyglass adjusts, dimming things so that I can use it just as a miniature telescope.

I can make out all the details on the woman's face, twisted in an expression of pain, and what looks like several nasty wounds on her arms, body, and forehead. Peering through the spyglass, I see that on the glass in front of her face, a small smudge of fog is on the transparent surface.

"Are we sure that she's dead?" I ask. "That looks like condensation from breath on the glass." It's hard to tell with them frozen in time, but it looks like a small trickle of fresh blood flowing out of the cut on her forehead. "And the wounds may be fresh. That poor woman."

"That's not just any random woman," Seraphex says, hopping as close as she can to the glass and peering in. "That's Liao Ling herself."

Zambrano gives a low whistle. "Is this where she ended up? None of the historical writings seemed to know where her body went, only that she died in the battle against the demon king."

"Well, that is fascinating," Seraphex states. "Crafty old Merlin was able to trap both of them in there. Removed both of his rivals in one move and took over leadership of her alliance."

"Maybe he didn't have any choice," Zambrano points out, walking up next to us. "In the chaos of the battle, he had to seal both of them in there at once as he sprung the trap. It might have been too risky to try to get her out."

"Why are you defending him? He was an egotistical maniac," Seraphex shoots back, "who appears to have betrayed and abandoned his ally."

"A *brilliant* egotistical maniac," Zambrano says. "We're not so bad, are we? And I'd think you could relate—you're in that club as well."

Seraphex preens slightly. "We all share a certain love of the game. Even if I find his obsession with traps very tiresome."

"I have to say this particular trap has worked out pretty well for humanity," I note, gesturing at the massive glass prism. "Merlin saved the world, it seems to me."

The demon trapped under glass in front of us is massive, larger than Volcanose by a significant margin, his back rippling and his claws gleaming in the dim glow from the bricks.

"I do appreciate that," Seraphex admits. "Fifteen hundred years without my dear ex-husband has been, despite this whole transmogrification situation," she says, flapping her wings to indicate her duck form, "quite pleasant."

"It's nice to finally know more of the history," Zambrano says. "The historical works that I've perused never stated where Liao Ling's body had ended up, only that she supposedly died in the battle against the demon king. And then Merlin went to Mars and never came back. So he never left any memoirs or records or anything. Just his traps, standing as testament to his works."

"You really have a thing for old Merlin, don't you?" Seraphex taunts him. "You wish you could read his diary, hear about all his mushy feelings?"

"Merlin's not also alive, is he?" I ask. That seems like a stretch, but the way this day is going, anything seems possible.

"Merlin is dead," Seraphex says. "Several demons were there when he died. I had the word from Typhoria herself. Demons can sense the moment when a living human becomes a corpse. It's delicious, that split second when the life goes out . . ."

"Gross," I say.

"You eat beings lower than you, like cows and pigs. What's the difference here?"

"Duck is also a common human dish," Zambrano points out. "I know a chef in Beijing who makes the most delicious Peking Duck . . ."

"Point taken," Seraphex says. "So how are we going to defeat my former husband and trap him again? At least another fifteen hundred years would be nice."

"So now this is a 'we' task, huh?" Zambrano asks, giving the demon duck a skeptical look. "Just like that, working together again? How do we know this isn't some sort of a trick?"

"I want to help keep him trapped. I have my various plans for the future, but I want the demon king off the field of play. I don't want him back."

"He's the ex you'd rather forget, is he?" Zambrano says.

I take a closer look at Seraphex. Something about her seems slightly off, and she's acting even stranger now that we're down here looking at the demon king. "You're scared, aren't you?"

"Scared? Me? A demon queen?" she retorts.

"You didn't actually deny it," Zambrano notes, a hint of a smile on his face for the first time since she's appeared. "Do you deny it? Are you not scared?"

"Why would I deny it?" she shoots back. "Do you really think a demon queen can be frightened of some other demon?"

"That's not a no," I say with a grim smile of satisfaction. "You're scared."

"Fine," the demon duck says, turning away from us to look down into the massive set of nested glass cubes. "I'm frightened. I don't want him to come back. Look, I'm a kind of creative and fun evil. Evil with flair and style. The being who I once considered my husband is just . . . *evil* evil."

"Plus, if he comes into power, your shot at ruling the planet is toast," I guess.

"That's also true," Seraphex says with a sigh. "Most of you humans would be dead within a few years, I would guess, if he has his way. I would likely be tortured for eternity, tormented endlessly, something along those lines."

Zambrano nods. "We've all had that sort of angry ex, haven't we? Those are the wages of love, in the end."

"Um, no?" I object. "I don't think we all have that. Exes who want to torture you forever is really not a necessary consequence of romance!"

"You're still very young, Bryce," Zambrano says as he gives me a fatherly pat on the shoulder.

Below, we can see the cracks in the innermost glass. Is it growing ever so slightly? The speed of it probably isn't visible to the naked eye, but I can't help but think it's getting worse by the second.

"If I'm going to work with you again, Seraphex, I'm going to need certain assurances," Zambrano says. "We'll need to negotiate the exact terms."

"As I expected," Seraphex says. "I'm willing to make some compromises. I can potentially agree to a limited term of full cooperation specific to the matter of defeating the demon king until he is no longer a threat, promising best efforts not to endanger Earth or create significant human casualties as a result, as I know you are ever so precious about that sort of thing—"

"No," I blurt out. "Your little mind game lawyer treaties aren't enough. You have to promise to . . . to . . ." My mind races as I think of what to demand. "To be our friend. *Actually* our friend."

Seraphex stares at me, her little duck eyes going wide. "You don't know what you're asking of me, Bryce," she protests. "That's not the sort of thing that a demon agrees to. Ever."

"No, the boy's right," Zambrano says, suddenly giving us both a wicked grin. "We want both. Everything you said and what Bryce said."

She looks back and forth between us, clearly panicking.

"You need me! You can't defeat Rex without me!"

Zambrano shrugs. "We'll find a way. We always have in the past. And we can't defeat him working with you if we're expecting you to sell us out at the first clever opportunity, can we?"

"You can't ask this of me," she says, taking a few steps backward.

"Eternal torture by your demon ex-husband—or our friendship. Your choice, demon."

"I don't want this!" she exclaims, hopping back and forth on her little webbed feet.

"Please," I say, taking a softer tone. "You can. I believe in you."

Seraphex stares up at us, her bravado and arrogance suddenly stripped away.

"Very well," she says in a soft and husky whisper. "I agree to all of it. Full cooperation to defeat the demon king, attempt to avoid human casualties, and . . . I'll be your friend."

"Well done," I say, feeling my heart suddenly go out to this strange demonic duck.

"Huh," she says, shaking her whole body as if she's trying to get water off her feathers. "Okay. That's not too bad so far." She nods slowly, then freezes. "Oh. Oh, that's quite invasive. That is not pleasant." For a long moment she breathes heavily, staring into the distance. She's lost deep in thought, ignoring everything around her. Then, at last, she gathers herself up and gives each of us a look.

"I hate you both," she says. "And yet, I'm still friends with you. How is that possible?"

"That's pretty much how friendship works in my experience," Zambrano says with a shrug.

"No, that's not true either!" I complain. "Have neither of you ever had a healthy relationship in your lives?"

"What do you think?" Seraphex says, poisonous rage in her voice.

Zambrano tilts his head to the side as if seriously considering the question.

"Oh, whatever," I say, turning back to the geometric shapes of the slow-time cases below us. "So we're all friends. Great. Now . . . how are we going to save the world?"

# CHAPTER 7

I have three weeks, I'll figure something out," Zambrano says. "Give me some time."

He turns and starts walking around the room, examining the prismatic prism from every angle. Periodically, he casts one of his detection spells, quietly muttering the words and moving his hands in small, controlled motions.

I watch and sit tight for a couple minutes, waiting for him to tell us what he's learning. But time drags on as he completely ignores us, muttering to himself and walking around the giant prism.

"What are we working with?" I ask, but he puts up a hand and then goes right on walking slow circles around the giant demon.

I wait expectantly for another minute, but he is clearly lost in thought and not going to clue me in on what's going on.

"Want to talk it through?" I ask. "Just say it out loud so I know what's going on?"

He ignores me, lost in his own thoughts. Typical.

Shaking my head, I decide to figure out what I can on my own.

As I walk around the prism, I notice how different angles and layers of glass seem to reflect and color the light differently. It's hard to quite understand the rules, but the hues of the light seem to be different depending on which exact combination of panes I'm looking through. I use the spyglass, trying to get more details, but it's hard to make anything out.

I look closely at the glass, where it's cracked and the flame bolt is breaking through. Has it moved since we last looked at it? If it's going to take three weeks to make it all the way out, I'm sure it wouldn't have moved an amount that human eyes could detect. And yet every time I look at it my pulse starts beating faster and it feels like it's coming out, ready to smash glass pane after glass pane, accelerating each time. And then, once he's out, how long before he recovers from his wound and his plans to destabilize and then destroy the world come to fruition?

I glance over at the demon duck, who has calmly sat plopped down on the bottom step of the stairs, rubbing her head against her tail and then her feathers.

"What are you doing?" I ask.

"Preening," she says, continuing to use her beak to clean her feathers. "There's a gland by my tail that secretes an oily substance that I can use to make myself more waterproof if I rub it—"

"Okay, gross," I say. "What I mean is, shouldn't you be helping him? Doesn't he need us to help figure this out?"

"Yes, my help would be critical," Seraphex answers.

"So why aren't you helping, then?" I demand. "The fate of the world hangs in the balance, and you're working on your weird water-proof coating!"

"Well, we're at the bottom of the ocean," the duck points out. "What if I get wet down here? I expect he'll ask for help when he has no other options. You know, sorcerers and their stupid pride."

I leave the duck to her preening, an activity that I never wanted to know the real definition of, and return to wandering around the large room. Examining what I can see of Liao Ling, I'm convinced that she's still alive. She's in the innermost layer of the time cases and looks passed out, but she's still bleeding from a few different wounds with a drop of blood falling from her forehead frozen in time as it falls. It's hard to tell if she's badly or even mortally wounded, but it doesn't look good.

Zambrano is stuck in his own world, examining and muttering calculations to himself, so I examine the room itself. He's focused on the demon in the case, so I figure maybe I can look at the walls of the room and find some other useful clue or tool. I look for a hidden message or a lever or a brick that can be pushed in. Maybe I can notice some key detail that Zambrano missed that allows us to reset the demon's cage or maybe turn the demon king into a hedgehog or something. And then we could have two fun demon pals!

But all I find is the neat geometric pattern of large bricks suffused in blue light that emanates from inside them. At least it's better than video games that have dungeons lit by inexplicable torches that have apparently been burning for hundreds of years since they were sealed off. But even with the spyglass I can't find any hidden compartments, secret levers, or illusion walls that can be walked through. I don't get to be the hero today.

I pull out my phone and take a lot of photos, pretending I'm one of those crime scene investigators. If we're all going to die at the hands of Rex the demon king, at least maybe before the end-times I can post the photos on social media and get a bunch of reshares. Probably not a whole ton of Likes, because who would press Like on their almost-certain doom? Well, actually the world is full of total maniacs so probably quite a few.

"All right, we're done here," Zambrano declares, finally seeming to notice that Seraphex and I still exist. "Let's go. I think we should be able to set up a teleportrait right by the entrance where the protection magic is weakest."

He starts walking back up the stairs, not even checking to see if I'm following behind him. I wait for fifteen seconds to see if he does, but he just keeps on walking up the stairs. Scowling at his back, I hustle along behind him. Seraphex flaps her wings a few times and lands on my shoulder, letting me carry her up as well.

"You're so lazy," I grouse. "Aren't you an indestructible demon? Shouldn't you have unlimited energy or something?"

"We're friends now," she says primly. "Doesn't that mean you like carrying me around and being nice to me?"

"It's supposed to be more of a two-way street," I growl.

"You weigh almost a hundred times what I do. If I ever get back my full body, which is much larger than yours, I promise that I will offer to let you ride on my back. Because we are friends."

"Huh," I say. "That's nice, I guess?" I have to admit, it does sound cool. But I have decided definitively, no way in hell are we going to let her get her body back. Even if we are "friends" now.

I catch up to Zambrano at the top of the stairs. I feel my stomach drop as we step back onto this level, back in the room where we found the fake artifacts that Slickwad ran off with. This whole place is just disappointment after disappointment.

And then I look at the three pedestals. One holds a cloak, one a coin, and one a staff.

"They're back," I say, pointing at the pedestals.

Zambrano freezes. "Don't move," he says, and I stay as still as I can.

"Did Slickwad return them? Or," I say, starting to get excited, "are these the real ones? The real powerful artifacts?"

"No," Zambrano says. "They're more of the same booby-trapped fakes. God damn it, Merlin. I was really hoping to avoid this."

"Avoid what?"

"Merlin was one of the most powerful sorcerers of all time. He invented some of the most powerful spells and innovated in fifty different ways. He may even have been a greater sorcerer than me."

"He definitely was," Seraphex interjects.

Zambrano doesn't react other than very slowly tilting his fist and extending one meaningful finger at the duck.

"He had all that power, and he could have used it to better humanity or end wars or raise great architecture. And he did do some of that . . . but his greatest creativity went to stupid shit like this."

"Like what?"

"Traps. Largely to mess with Liao Ling and the other great sorcerers of the day. Stupid, pointless traps."

"It was likely intended to make sure that if someone was able to break in and get past the other traps, they wouldn't get out," Seraphex points out.

"And so now we won't be able to get out and figure out how to save the world. Great work, Merlin," Zambrano gripes.

"What sort of trap is it?" I ask. "Will something bad happen if we move?"

Zambrano takes a long moment, using his trap detection spells, but moving his body in slow motion. Finally he relaxes and stretches out.

"It's too late, we're already fully stuck. It must have happened when we got out of the staircase."

"I did have an odd feeling then," I say. "What do you mean, stuck?"

"I'm guessing it's a classic pocket universe trap," Zambrano says. As if I'm supposed to be familiar with that? "Come on, let's check," he says, leading the way up the staircase the way that we initially came in.

"Is that as bad as it sounds? How does it work?" I ask.

"You know how some rich people use magic to make their buildings bigger on the inside?"

"Yeah, like banks and really expensive apartments on the Upper East Side," I say. One of my friends from NYU was from an old-money family that had a home like that—it was a narrow townhouse that was three times as big once you went inside. She only let us go there one time and swore us to secrecy because she was somehow ashamed to have so much money and something *so freaking cool* in her family. "Those form a pocket where reality and space are stretched, like an addition to a house that extends into another dimension and gives you some extra square footage."

"That's a wildly inaccurate simplification," Seraphex says.

"It's close enough . . . unless Mr. Alexander here has taken graduate courses in arcane topology?" Zambrano says, eyeing me skeptically.

"Uh, the simplification works for me," I say.

"Great. So it's like that, only in this case, once you step through, the trap is sprung. The entrance disappears, and you're trapped inside the pocket universe with no exit. It looks similar to Merlin's Vault," he says, gesturing to the large vault room that we've stopped in. "But we are in a totally separate little universe, trapped all on our own."

As he says that, we get to the top of the steps and emerge into the same room again, with the coin, staff, and cloak on pedestals.

"And so we're trapped. We dealt with another one of these back in 1929 after we returned the Leviathan to Merlin's cage. I was distracted then too—we had just battled the giant beast for days, and Ilyas Rahmani was losing his sanity. We didn't know it yet then, but the fight against that giant tentacled beast started Caravello down a dark path as well. I took a break from the rest of them, triggered the trap, and I was stuck in there for days."

"Oh, so you've escaped one of these before. So you know how to get us out of here, right?" I ask.

Zambrano sighs. "Well, not exactly. To be honest, I only got out before because Caravello and Zuzanna were on the outside, realized I had gone missing, and were able to track me down and help me from there. They were able to extend the pocket universe's small connection to the real world into something large enough to move through. Caravello had a brilliant understanding of the mathematics of pocket universes, teleportation, and the like before she became obsessed with death and trying to bring people back from the dead. She and Zuzanna were very close. When Caravello figured out the spell to activate the arcane conduit, Zuzanna was the only person she shared it with. The two of them worked together to figure out these pocket universes."

My heart seizes up at the mention of Zuzanna's name. "My birth mother helped get you out of the pocket universe?"

"She did," Zambrano says. "Once they figured it out, it was easy to open a bridge out. I know the spell, it's pretty easy. But I can't do it from inside the pocket universe, only from the real world. I think Caravello had to talk her into helping, to be honest. She didn't like me too much by then. She was a shrew and never really trusted me."

"I can't imagine why," I say with an eye roll. "So how can we get out of here, then? Any chance of a teleportrait or something?"

"That's a less completely stupid suggestion than one might think," Zambrano says as if he's somehow being generous. "Technically, we're no longer in Merlin's Vault, so those protections against teleporting won't apply. This particular spell creates a pocket that exists in . . . it's hard to describe it. A different arcane mathematical space, you could say. Okay, actually that wasn't that hard, that describes it pretty well," Zambrano says with a self-satisfied smile. "Pocket universe math is different, and the incredibly complex rotations and transferences required for teleportrait translocation will get messed up if we try to go from pocket universe rules to normal universe rules."

"So what, then?"

Zambrano shrugs. "I don't know. We stay here and starve to death, probably?"

"There has to be a way out," I say. "Seraphex, any thoughts?"

"If we wait long enough," Seraphex says from my shoulder, "the energy sustaining the pocket universe will run out, and it will collapse and drop us back in the regular world. If we're really lucky, Rex will figure out what happened after he takes over the world, and he'll come in and murder you and torture me. But the most likely outcome is that we will be trapped here until it collapses."

"How long will that take?" I ask.

"Oh, around three thousand years," the duck says cheerfully.

"We'll long since have died of thirst, malnutrition, or old age," Zambrano says.

"Don't worry, the violent transition back to the regular universe would crush your fragile human bodies to death, anyway," Seraphex says. "The pocket universe is tied to a specific point in the real world, usually an object of some kind. So I would pop out right at the spot since I'm basically indestructible."

"Oh, I'm worried," I say, desperately wanting to wring the little duck's neck. Same as it used to be. "There has to be a way out of here!"

"There's one other complication," Zambrano says. "Last time I was trapped in one of these, I wasn't alone."

"Who did you bring inside with you?" I ask. "Another stupid intern with more ambition than sense?"

"Oh, no, I didn't bring anyone with me. Merlin left something there to take care of anyone who was trapped. A beast. He always liked leaving something fatal in his traps—Merlin really was kind of a psychopath," Zambrano says with a note of reverence in his voice. "Last time, the beast wasn't there immediately, it only appeared after I'd had a few minutes to loop around and realize that I was trapped."

Right on cue, we hear a growling sound from somewhere down below us.

# CHAPTER 8

**Y**ou can kill it, right?" I say, glancing down the staircase. There's nothing but the soft glow of the bricks down there. For now.

"I did last time," Zambrano says nonchalantly.

"That's not a yes," I say.

"Well, I only killed it at the very end, right before I escaped," Zambrano says, "once the pocket universe lost integrity."

"So what do we do now? How do we make that happen, break the pocket integrity?"

"Well, to begin," Zambrano says as we hear the sounds of a growl and heavy footsteps on the stairs below, "I'd suggest that we start running."

He immediately turns and starts jogging up the stairs. I follow him with Seraphex the lazy demon queen still on my shoulder, balancing somewhat precariously now. Though she never seems to fall off—I'm not sure if that's a bird's advanced sense of balance or a demon thing.

I'm immediately glad that I've been putting in time working out. A few months ago, I would have been gassed within thirty seconds. Luckily, Zambrano also isn't running that fast.

"Why aren't we going faster?" I ask. "Is the beast that slow?"

"This pocket universe loops back in on itself. If we run too fast, we'll catch up to it from behind," Seraphex explains, "and then it would have the high ground on us."

As if to illustrate her point, we pass back by the open floor with the three pedestals and their artifacts on each.

"Our beast friend is fairly slow-moving," Zambrano explains, "but incredibly powerful. It draws its energy from the pocket universe that we're in."

"So this pocket beast," I say, "Why wouldn't Merlin make it faster? Or something that's more immediately deadly?"

"A combination of a murderous beast being a solid off-the-shelf component, and going for style points. I guess he wanted his victims to know how screwed they were before he got them. It's also a very tricky trap. It draws its life-force from the pocket universe's bubble of energy. Don't get me wrong, I *could* kill it. Blast it with enough different spells and destructive force, and eventually it would lose integrity."

"But it would drain the energy of the pocket universe," Seraphex says. "Every blow would take a few hundred years off the universe's existence. And when the beast died, it would be because the energy ran out. The pocket universe would collapse on itself, and that would be it for you."

"Okay, so avoid killing the pocket beast, got it," I say. Zambrano slows down to a walk, and I follow suit.

"It doesn't move too quickly," he says. "It's more of a persistence hunter. We just have to keep moving, for now."

"Okay, and then what?" I say.

"Let me think!" Zambrano says, so I shut up. We trudge up the stairs at a steady pace, periodically hearing growling from below.

I'm starting to feel the burn of all these stairs, and my huffing and puffing is making talking difficult. But being quiet is almost worse. Because I have no idea what's going on, or how screwed we are, or if Zambrano is coming up with a great plan or a stupid one.

Finally, I can't take it anymore.

"Okay, what are you thinking?" I demand.

He makes me wait for an answer, scowling as he climbs the stairs.

"I don't know. If we kill the beast, the pocket universe collapses. We can't teleport from here back to the real world. We can't make a bridge between universes without a sorcerer on the other side. We might be able to slow the beast down or trap it for a time, but that would be temporary. I don't know, maybe we do kill it and try to cast protective spells. At least if it doesn't work, we won't have to deal with Rex when he gets out," Zambrano adds. "That would be a small relief."

"Seraphex, a little help here?" I ask.

"Well, I'll be fine either way, you know," Seraphex admonishes me.

"But if we die, you won't get help against your ex."

"Well, yes, that's quite true. And also," she says and then falls silent, seizing up for a moment. "And also . . . I don't want you to die. I would prefer for you to live. This is quite an uncomfortable feeling."

Zambrano gives a wry smile. "The kid got you, demon. You should have made some sort of deal with fixed terms. Friendship can be a real bitch. It's caused me all sorts of headaches over the years, that's for sure."

"Quite," Seraphex says and falls silent. From the feeling of her perched on my shoulder, I can almost sense the wheels in her head turning as she works this situation over.

"There has to be something better than collapsing the universe and hoping we can somehow survive it," I say.

At this point my legs are burning, and we've passed through the full cycle of the looping staircase and the pedestal room several times. We just keep heading upward, keeping the beast below us as we pass through each loop.

"I don't know. Walking up stairs *sucks*," Zambrano complains. "Why not just take our chances? Who cares, really?"

"I care!" I say. "And you care too, I know that. Let's not give up so easily, okay?"

"Sure, if you insist," Zambrano says with more the air of a petulant child than a great wizard.

"We can't make a connection to the real universe without a sorcerer on the other side," I say. "But there is a sorcerer over there. Does that help?"

"You mean Liao Ling?" Zambrano asks. "That's no help. She's unconscious, trapped in a slow-time case, possibly mortally wounded, and has no idea that we're in here or that she should help us. And there's nothing we can do to contact her."

"Yeah, okay, that seems hard to make work," I admit.

Our pace has slowed down, and I glance back, catching a look at the pocket beast. My breath catches, and I barely avoid stumbling when I see it. This thing is nasty. It's got four legs and moves with the gait of a dog, and it has jet-black skin or maybe very short fur. But instead of a head, it just has a giant mouth with row upon row of teeth. No eyes, no ears, no nose, just a massive opening with way more rows of spiky teeth than could possibly be needed for any normal biological digestive purpose.

It's horrifying, and terrifying, and highly motivating. We speed up, and soon it disappears down into the gloomy light of this strange place.

"What are all those teeth for?" I ask.

"It can eat almost anything," Seraphex says. "Rocks, metal, flesh, bones, all of that."

"Not you though," I note.

"Well, it *could* eat me," Seraphex says. "But it wouldn't be able to digest me, if that's what you mean. Perks of being an archdemon. It could probably have shredded Slickwad though. He wouldn't have died, but he would have been out of commission for a while."

"Real shame we let the demon go," I say. "Okay, so we can't get help from the outside. And we can't teleport home. We need to at least buy some time. Is there anywhere that we *can* teleport to?"

"Oh," Zambrano says and stops walking. "Oh!"

I stop a few steps above him and look back.

"Huh," he continues, working his jaw as he thinks. "That . . . might actually work. I'd need time to draw, and it would take more energy than a normal teleportrait effect. But I am a ridiculously talented wielder of arcane powers—"

I see the beast emerging from the dim light of the stairs below, its rows of teeth gleaming in the dull blue glow from the bricks.

"Mr. Chompers is coming," I say, grabbing Zambrano's arm and pulling him up. "Let's walk and think, maybe?"

"Oh yeah, right," Zambrano says, climbing the steps with renewed vigor. "He does look like he could really chomp things with all those teeth, doesn't he?"

We speed up, gaining some breathing room again. Zambrano and I are both huffing and puffing, and my legs have never hurt this much. Seraphex is just chilling on my shoulder. If we survive this, I am going to be very sore tomorrow and very annoyed at this lazy duck.

"We can't teleport back to the regular universe because it's so different. But this is the same type of pocket universe as the one I was trapped in at the Leviathan's cage. We can make a teleportrait to there! And then we can use the escape route that we created back in the 1920s."

"Really? That's amazing!" I say, pumping my fist. "Let's do it!"

"It's not going to be quite that simple," Seraphex points out. "Zambrano will need to create an artistic teleportrait that represents the destination well enough for magic to be able to identify it and take us there."

The sorcerer pulls a notepad and a pencil out of his jacket pocket. "This universe is so small that the teleportrait doesn't need to be as detailed as one for the real world," he says. "A quick sketch should do it. But I'll need about ten minutes staying still to draw it."

"Oh, crap. Okay, can you use some sort of spell to trap Mr. Chompers?" I ask.

"This whole thing is designed sort of like quicksand," Zambrano says. "Merlin was a real bastard like that. Genius, but a real bastard. In his traps, the more you struggle and fight, the tighter it grips. If I started using magic to cage and hold the beast, it would draw power to overcome the cage, and we'd get into a pissing match. I would win, naturally, because I'm me, and it's a dumb beast. But it would draw all the energy from the pocket universe as it pushed against the cage holding it in."

"There's not something more elegant you could do?" I ask. "Trick the trap? Fool the beast?"

"With a week and my lab and library, I'm sure I could come up with something. Unless you have anything?" the sorcerer asks with an eyebrow raised toward the demonic duck freeloading on my shoulder.

"It's not demonic, I don't have any easy cheat codes. I never knew too much about Merlin's magic—that's part of how he was able to fool all of us demons. He had some tricks that no one else was able to figure out."

"What sort of tricks?" Zambrano demands. "Something that I don't know?"

"Focus! We need to slow Mr. Chompers down for ten minutes," I say. "If we can't cage it, we need to distract it. How long is this loop we've been walking on? A couple minutes?"

"Two minutes, eighteen seconds on average," Seraphex helpfully notes. "Demons have a very accurate time sense," she says as I glance over at her, or at least try to, given how close sitting on my shoulder makes her to my head.

"And how do you propose to distract it?" Zambrano asks. "I'll need to focus on drawing."

We walk on for a moment as I think. The idea that I have sounds really, really annoying. But it just might work.

"We'll pull the tiger's proverbial tail," I say. "I'll go faster and catch up behind it. See if I can get it to turn around and come after me."

"That will gain us a couple minutes," Zambrano notes. "But it'll just run into me going the other way."

"Well . . ." I say. "Seraphex, can you distract it from the other side?"

She opens her beak, gives a little squawk, and fidgets for a second.

"You leave me no choice," she says at last. "Against my better judgment. As your . . . . friend . . . I will help you. Damnation, this sucks."

"Okay. No time to waste. Let's do this," I say.

"One second," Zambrano says. "Stand still. Let's see if this works."

I stand still, and he puts his right hand on my forehead. He closes his eyes for a second. I can see him wince in concentration. Suddenly, I feel a surge of euphoria, energy, and adrenaline. I'd say it's like taking a hit of certain drugs, but I would never admit to having tried anything like that. Certainly not when I was hanging out with that one crowd junior year of college.

"What did you do?" I ask. My heart is pounding, and suddenly I'm ready to go.

"Natural magic. Wild magic. Druidic magic. They call it a 'blessing,' but I don't buy into their weird religion. Whatever you call it, it's the only trick I managed to learn from them. Should give you an extra boost of strength. The effects are unpredictable though. And you'll pay for it once it wears off."

"Whatever," I say, suddenly not caring about possible consequences. "Let's do this!"

First, we all charge up the stairs together, passing through the artifact room once and putting a bunch of space between us and Mr. Chompers.

"This is as good a place as any," Zambrano says, sitting at the bottom of the stairs and starting to draw.

Seraphex hops off my shoulder and begins stretching her little legs and wings like a duck track star about to run a race.

I turn and charge up the stairs, taking them at top speed like Rocky training on the steps of wherever it was in Philadelphia that had all those stairs he famously ran up. I go hard, and before long I can see the back of Mr. Chompers. Its hind legs are massive with big scary rippling muscles. I can see the rear view of its giant mouth, which is opening and closing in anticipation.

Beyond the beast, I can see Zambrano where I left him on the steps, drawing madly. I close the gap, moving less quickly now but still faster than the beast's steady, plodding steps.

"Hey!" I yell. "Beast!"

It continues to plod on, ignoring me.

"Here I am!" I shout. "Come on, eat me!"

The beast's steady progress up the stairs doesn't stop, or even slow. I yell some more and stamp my feet and slap my hands on the walls. Nothing.

Flustered, Zambrano stands up and starts walking again, keeping ahead of the beast as it continues toward him.

"I'm delicious! Nice, fresh human! Don't you want some? Way better than that ancient husk up ahead of you!" I yell, but it continues to not even appear to notice. "Can it even hear?" I say loudly.

"I suppose not," Zambrano answers, his voice carrying through the stairwell. "They were made, not evolved, so who knows how they actually work. You might need to touch it."

"I'm not going to get close enough to touch it!" I shout. "It'll devour me!"

"I don't know, throw something!" he says. "It may not have hearing, but it probably has some sense of touch."

I look around, but the perfect stone has no crumbling bits or random rocks. I pat my pockets, but all I have is my phone, which I really don't want to lose again. Instead, I pull off my belt. God damn it. "I really don't want to go through this whole stripping nonsense again," I yell, recalling unpleasant memories of the time I was forced to take off my clothes and throw them in order to course-correct while magically floating down from a skyscraper in Chicago. "How does this stuff always happen to me?"

"You became the intern of an ancient, reckless, and morally ambiguous sorcerer," Seraphex chirps from up ahead.

"Hey!" Zambrano yells. "I'm not morally ambiguous! I'm very . . . morally biguous."

I get in closer and toss the belt at the beast. It's not a great throw, and the first time misses. The beast keeps on climbing, so I catch up, grab the belt, and give it another throw.

This time it catches the beast, glancing off its side. The beast turns and snaps the belt up. Up this close, it is absolutely horrifying. Row upon row of teeth that gnash and grind and chop the belt into a thousand tiny chunks of leather and metal.

But instead of coming back after me, it turns and keeps up after Zambrano. We're reaching the point in this loop of stairs where we come into the open room with Merlin's three pedestals. As the beast crosses to pursue Zambrano, I grab the coin and hurl it, calling on my two years of little league experience to try to get a good throw. And it works perfectly, the coin bouncing off the right butt cheek of the muscly beast.

But the beast just stops for a second and then continues on.

Finally, in desperation, I grab the staff off its pedestal. With a war cry, I charge up to the beast and swing the staff at Mr. Chompers. Neither Shoehi Ohtani nor Tiger Woods would be impressed with my swing, but the staff connects with a loud thwack.

Gripping the staff, I quickly backpedal as the beast turns, hissing as its disgusting mouth of teeth leers at me. It starts to advance, and I turn and run. As I reach the stairs down, I glance over my shoulder. The beast is coming straight for me, but beyond that, on the bottom steps of the stairway up, I can see Zambrano has taken a seat, a look of intense concentration on his face as he starts to sketch.

Leaving Zambrano behind in the large open room, Mr. Chompers pursues me down the stairs.

My feet slap loudly on the steps as I run down. I was worried that the beast would be a lot faster going downstairs, but it's moving about the same speed as before.

"Bryce!" Seraphex's voice booms through the hallway, louder than I've ever heard it before. "I'm not going to be able to get it to go back up!"

"Damn it," I mutter, realizing that this is going to be a big problem. Seraphex was supposed to follow the beast down and taunt it into coming back up. But the beast can't hear anything, so Seraphex isn't going to have any way to get the beast to turn around. Taunting is her main skill. She definitely couldn't swing a staff with her little webbed feet or duck bill, even if she had one.

I mutter a few inappropriate words and start sprinting down the stairs at full speed. I'll need to loop all the way around to get behind the beast and stop it before it reaches Zambrano. Going downhill is actually really nice after what feels like an hour of hiking a literally endless mountain of stairs. The druidic nature magic he did is still going strong, and it's kind of a thrill barreling down these stairs at top speed, holding a magical staff. Not a cool or useful magical staff, but still. Merlin's staff! Well, a staff made by Merlin.

Going down is fairly easy, and I'm able to reach the beast well before it can attack Zambrano. I follow behind it until I'm about fifty stairs from it. Then I scamper down, and with a gleeful whack, I annoy Mr. Chompers enough that it turns around, facing its concentric circles of slavering teeth at me. Leaping back and turning, I charge back up the stairs.

"Great work!" Seraphex shouts cheerfully from her spot next to Zambrano. Apparently, she came to the same conclusion that I did and decided to do . . . nothing. We're going to have to work on this whole friendship thing.

As I run up the stairs, I've still got pumping adrenaline and the power of the druids in my body. It's not so bad, but I'm definitely breathing heavily by the time I catch the beast and give it a smack with the staff. I'm really hoping that the magic trap doesn't trigger from blunt force impact, but it seems to be fine so far. And with the reach of the staff, I can keep enough distance between me and the beast to feel a marginal amount of safety.

The next run downstairs isn't so bad, though I'm huffing and puffing by the time I catch up to the beast and give it a good thwack with the staff. It's the next climb up the stairs that really kills me. The magic boost I had is weaker and weaker, and the running I've been doing absolutely did not prepare me for this uphill marathon.

This time I just barely catch up to the beast in the big open room. I see him closing in, and Zambrano glances up and sees the approaching beast. At the last minute, he jumps up, jogging up the stairs. I put on a final burst of speed and catch up to the beast, giving him an exhausted swing from the staff. As I do, I feel the power of the druidic blessing suddenly drain from my body. And there is precious little energy of my own remaining. It's all I can do not to just collapse right here.

The beast spins around, mouth chomping and legs churning, and I stumble backward. I'm not sure if I trip on the bottom stairs or just my own exhausted feet, but I fall on my butt, just barely holding on to the staff as I slide across the glowing stone floor. Mr. Chompers lunges forward, and I roll to the side, barely escaping its jaws.

Its hind legs smash into me, and I'm slammed into the wall, hitting it with my left hip, and I hear and feel a sickening crunch. For a second I think my hip must be broken, but the pain isn't nearly that bad. Or maybe it's even worse. Are the nerves severed so I can't feel anything at all? My hand goes down to my side, and I breathe a sigh of relief. I dodge back from the beast, and my hip feels fine. I wiggle my toes, and can feel that they're still connected properly. Putting my hand to my side, I realize that I'm fine—it's just my phone, crushed again.

"Bryce!" Zambrano yells. And then "*Froststråle!*" And I see a blast of icy blue energy shoot down and smash into Mr. Chompers. But the beast has me in its sights, or whatever sort of senses it has, and I'm sent scrambling away as it makes another lunge.

I bump into the pedestal with the cloak, and in desperation I throw it at the beast, but it just shakes its head violently, flinging the cloak to the ground. This only buys me a few seconds, but I take them to use the staff to lever myself to a standing position and retreat from the beast. I make it to the stairs, but as soon as I start up them, I realize that I'm now on the other side of the beast from before, the upward path. Zambrano, Seraphex, and I are all on the same side of the pocket beast.

But there's no time to dodge around the beast as it advances, and I retreat upward. Glancing up, I see that Zambrano is standing up but holding the notebook in one hand and the pencil in the other, still sketching as he slowly steps up each stair.

The pocket beast takes heavy steps up the stairs, growling with a low fury. Seraphex hops back onto my shoulder.

"The staff!" she whispers. "Feed him the staff!"

I stab the staff, wielding it like a spear straight at the beast and into its jagged rows of gleaming teeth. I'm able to jam it right into the hole in the very center of its mouth, and about a third of it goes straight in. The teeth start gnashing wildly, and the whole staff starts feeding into its mouth slowly and steadily, like pushing a log into a wood chipper. As soon as it feels like the whole thing is going, I give it a final shove and leap backward, barely avoiding tripping and falling.

I watch as Mr. Chompers takes the whole staff in, grinding and growling like a printer with an absolutely epic paper jam. It holds its position for the first time since we've seen it, and I hear a loud rumbling. Its mouth jams shut, and it leans down. There are sounds like muffled fireworks as it crouches, shivering. The magic trap of the staff ignites inside Mr. Chompers, and for a moment I think maybe the whole beast will explode, and, as disgusting as that would surely be, we will be safe.

But instead, the noises quiet, the magic now fully discharged. The beast stands back up to its full height and shudders like a dog shaking water off after getting out of a lake.

"I just need thirty more seconds!" Zambrano shouts, pencil scribbling madly. "Almost there! Just hold him off for a moment!"

I'm breathing heavily, barely able to move my legs at this point. The staff is gone, and I doubt my phone or my shirt will slow it down. Turning around and running feels impossible. I don't think I can move faster than the beast at this point. My body is dead.

"We need to hold it off," Seraphex says.

"What about the amber nexus?" I ask.

"Not nearly powerful enough, it would only buy you a second or two," she answers.

I glance around but don't see the coin, and the cloak is lying on the floor on the other side of the beast.

The beast advances, slowly at first but then regaining its usual steady gait.

And that's when I get an idea that I'm really not proud of. Especially not for someone who is supposed to now be friends with Seraphex.

But she's invincible, as she's made it perfectly clear so many times. And she's a Grade A jerk, who has helped put my life in danger more times than I can count.

I grab the duck off my shoulder, and she must immediately realize what's going on because she opens her tiny beak.

"Bryce. NO!" she yells, and somehow the volume of it is massive, making my ears ring. I knew she could make perfect imitations of other people's voices, but not that she could make noises so incredibly *loud*.

Still, I have no other choice—I fling her at the beast. Squawking, she tries to flap her wings and fly away, but I put a little spin on her, and she tumbles helplessly through the air. Just as she rights herself, the beast reaches her, and its massive jaws close around her body.

I can't quite follow what happens next, but it's an explosion of feathers and whirling teeth, and a moment later the duck has disappeared into the beast, its mouth closed around her.

# CHAPTER 9

I wait for the beast to charge me, but it just holds still, making motions as if gulping and trying to swallow. The sounds are much louder this time, like a mix between a construction site and bubbling swamp. The beast whimpers, stumbling to the side and leaning against a wall. It stays there for almost a minute with an orchestra of disgusting noises coming from inside it, muffled by its jet-black hide.

"Okay," Zambrano says from behind me. "Done."

Just at that moment, as if on cue, the beast opens its mouth and Seraphex explodes out of it, like she's been shot from a cannon. With the reflexes of a hockey goalie, Zambrano reaches out and grabs her with one hand. She's completely featherless and has traces of gross black slime spatted on her naked light pink duck body. She is otherwise unharmed, but her beady little eyes are glaring at me with a look of absolute hatred.

Still holding the duck in one hand, Zambrano wraps his other arm around my neck, the hand holding his newly completed sketch in front of his face.

"I want to go to there," he says, and the world twists away.

I'm not quite sure how teleportation manages to avoid accidentally merging the people being transported into the local environment, but we've always appeared and disappeared from relatively flat areas. Occasionally, there's a slight jostle as we land, as if the teleportation magic doesn't quite know how to deal with two people standing on different steps at different heights. Zambrano and I both appear at odd angles and tumble to the ground. Seraphex jumps out of Zambrano's hand and flaps her wings, but without feathers her flying doesn't seem to work, and she also lands on the ground in an ungraceful heap.

Lifting my sore body up, I look around. The hallway that we're in looks to be made of similarly cut stone to Merlin's Vault, but it glows a soft red instead of blue. Looking down the hallway, I can see that at one end it turns left, and the other end branches into three passages in a distinctive-looking way that I guess may have been what Zambrano drew for the teleportrait.

Seraphex hops up to me and pecks at my arm, hard.

"Ow! Hey!" I yell and push her away. "What the hell?" I ask, but I know what she's upset about. I tossed her into the mouth of an ancient magical beast.

"The indignity! That was actually fairly painful!" she gripes. "I haven't felt pain like that since they turned me into a duck. Maybe not even since the bad old days when I would quarrel with Rexhalarkhart. What do you possibly think gives you the right to treat a queen like that?"

"You tried to trick me into agreeing to give you your demonic powers back, dooming the human race," I point out. "You manipulated all the events to set up that scenario, didn't you?"

"Why would you think that?" she protests.

"That's not a denial, or any sort of statement of fact at all," Zambrano notes as he brushes himself off and stretches.

I had also noticed that. I'm starting to get used to the logic of a demon's requirements to tell the truth. Maybe I should have gone to law school instead of becoming a sorcerer's intern. I mean, I definitely should have done literally anything other than that. But here we are. I was so desperate to learn magic that I threw myself at Zambrano. But now that I've gotten embroiled in all this, and the fate of the world might hinge on my being helpful, it's a level of stress and responsibility that, frankly, I never intended to sign up for.

"You set up that whole scheme," I say, pointing a finger at her as I shakily stand up, leaning against the glowing red wall for support.

"Not the whole thing," Seraphex says, sulking. "Only . . . a number of key elements that directed events toward my intended long-term goals."

"Well, there you go," I say. "That was not good. Bad duck. Naughty demon. And so, I think that it's only fair that you got tossed into the literal belly of the beast. But how about this?" I add with a kinder tone. "Let's call it even, now, shall we? We're friends now, officially. Let's have a fresh start."

"It's a good offer," Zambrano notes. "Better than I would give you."

She looks over at him, standing up to her full height and still looking quite silly with her featherless body. "Will you also honor this agreement?" she demands.

Zambrano shrugs. "Huh. Well, you did make a big commitment by agreeing to friendship, that I'll be fascinated to watch play out. Why not? A fresh start."

"Very well, then, gentlemen," she says. "A fresh start."

She holds out her wing, and I awkwardly shake it. I notice that the wing is slightly prickly—new feathers are already starting to protrude from her pink skin. It looks like at this rate she'll be back to fully feathered in less than an hour. She turns to Zambrano, and he shakes it as well, a bemused look on his face.

"Now, pick me up and put me on your shoulder," Seraphex demands primly. "I won't be able to fly properly for some time."

Shrugging, I pick her up and put her there. "All I need is an eye patch and peg leg and I'll be a really lame pirate," I mutter.

"Awk, Polly wanna Kobe beef sukiyaki," Seraphex says. Which is fair enough. She does love it when we order Japanese food.

"Or a nice glass of the blood of the innocent?" Zambrano asks with a wry twist to his lips.

"I'm telling you, it really does have a special flavor," Seraphex says. "Don't get mad at me, I'm not the one who made demons this way."

"Okay, okay," I say, interrupting their bickering. "So how do we get out of here?" I ask. "There's not another beast, is there?"

"No, no, I took care of that back when I escaped the first time. Do you think I'm some sort of amateur? Just follow along," Zambrano says, and he leads us down the hallway. It turns at the end, and then he leads us through a series of branches and turns, and I quickly lose track of where we are.

"This place is a labyrinth!" I exclaim as we come to another intersection and Zambrano leads us confidently to the right.

"Technically, it's a maze," Seraphex points out, using her annoying "well, actually" voice. "Traditionally, a labyrinth doesn't have branches, just one path in and out. Common misconception by humans," she continues, ignoring my exaggerated eye roll.

"That's nonsense," Zambrano says, shaking his head. "If a labyrinth just has one path, the original myth of the Minotaur in the labyrinth doesn't make any sense. Why would Theseus have needed a ball of string to find his way in and out again?"

"What do you know about it?" Seraphex shoots back. "Were you there?"

I stare at her. "Were *you* there?"

"It's an ancient myth. The story in your books didn't happen. There was no ball of string. Theseus was an egotistical jerk who made most of it up. And none of us knows how he actually was able to defeat the Minotaur. Even a young demon like that should have been much harder to kill."

"Oh, so the Minotaur was a friend of yours?" Zambrano asks, slightly mocking, but I can tell there's curiosity in his voice.

"Something like that. Certainly he didn't deserve to be trapped in that labyrinth for his entire life."

"It is certainly annoying, being trapped in a prison of this sort. I spent quite some time inside this maze, fleeing the beast, so I've got the whole place memorized at this point. And here we are," he finishes as we come to a halt at a nondescript spot in the middle of a hallway.

But then I see that on one of the walls, there's a single brick missing, about waist high. Leaning down and peering through, I see just darkness.

"Look closer," Zambrano says, and so I lean in farther, peering into the black nothingness. "There's a little trick that will help you see. Erasmus supposedly created it as a religious joke. Christian humor is so cringe."

I lean in even closer, getting my head pressed right up against the glowing brick, trying to see into the hole.

"*Facilius est camelum per foramen acus*," Zambrano says. And then I hear sudden movement, and I glance back to see him roundhouse kick me right in the butt.

The whole world twists and squeezes, but in a much worse and more painful way than using a teleportrait. I can feel every bit of my body compressed, and the hallway around me grows much larger. The force of the kick somehow propels me through the hole in the brick, though I can feel its cold force pressing against my body as magic forcibly scrunches me through the hole.

I land on the ground on the other side, screaming. I keep shouting for a few seconds, then realize that I'm sitting there completely unhurt. I stop, like a crying toddler who suddenly realizes that no one is around to come to their rescue.

I do a quick check of myself, and I'm utterly exhausted but basically unharmed. My hand goes to my pocket automatically, and my phone has fared far worse than I have. I can feel from the outside that it's cracked and shattered, and there are little pieces of glass crinkling in there. I don't dare put my hand in, I really don't want to cut my fingers on broken glass. When we get home, I guess I'll just toss them both out and order new pants and a new phone. Thank god for cloud backups and overnight delivery.

The room I'm in is cast in more of the same red glow. There are stairs leading up. Instead of being in a brick wall, I seem to have tumbled out of a little cube of darkness that hangs in the middle of the air, a total void of light in the dimly lit room. As I watch, a duck bill pokes out of one side of it, and the rest of Seraphex follows, wriggling out of the side. It looks like she just fit through, no magical shrinkage required. She pops through and flaps her way down to the ground, landing daintily. She looks haggard, but she's already mostly regrown her feathers while we were wandering around in the labyrinth—sorry, in the "maze."

Next, Zambrano blasts through, expanding from several inches wide to a full-size human in a burst of light and weird lensing effects. Unlike me, however, he lands gracefully, dropping into a stupid superhero pose on one knee with his fist hitting the ground even though my jujitsu classes taught me that it's a terrible way to actually land.

"What was that?" I gripe. "You just shove me through with no warning? I'm not a kid getting a shot at the doctor's office, you don't have to trick me."

"That," Zambrano says, "was Erasmus's spell 'camel through the eye of the needle.' I don't know, on second thought, maybe the biblical reference is funny, actually," Zambrano says with a chuckle.

"I was certainly amused by the effect of the spell," Seraphex says with her usual prim air. "Though certainly I could have gladly skipped some of the earlier indignities that were visited upon me by your Mr. Alexander."

I shrug and stand up, smiling as I dust myself off. I guess taking a tumble and getting a couple bruises seems a lot less bad in comparison to being digested by an ancient magical beast whose stomach looked like an uncountably vast number of rows of teeth.

Glancing around the room, I realize that it might actually be quite countable. Because there's a giant skeleton lying against the far wall, clearly the same size and proportions of the pocket beast that we faced in the other tap. Only this one has decomposed over the decades until nothing is left but pure white bones—and a truly enormous pile of teeth.

"Wow," I say, stepping over to take a close look at the skeleton.

"After I escaped, I was able to pull the beast out here where it couldn't tap the power of the pocket universe, which made it possible for me to kill the nasty thing," Zambrano says, following me over and giving the giant rib cage a kick, causing a bunch of the delicate ribs to collapse.

"Why did you do that?" I ask. "Were you worried it would get out and attack people? Or others would get trapped in there?"

"Um, yeah. Exactly. Can't have someone else getting caught in there with a dangerous beast!" Zambrano says.

"It was spite, wasn't it?" I ask.

"I would describe it as 'a fit of pique,'" Seraphex says. "But it's very subjective."

"You weren't there. How would you know?" Zambrano snaps. "And call it what you want, but I escaped and got back to my awesome life, and the pocket beast is nothing but a pile of bones and teeth now. I was hoping the tooth fairy would leave me a big chunk of cash, but no such luck. Now let's get out of here."

"Sounds good," I say, following him toward the stairs that lead up. I'm incredibly grateful to see light not too far above since my legs feel like jelly and can't handle more than a few steps. "Hold on a second. Is the tooth fairy—"

"Ugh, no," Zambrano says with a scoff. "Of course the tooth fairy isn't real, you idiot."

"There is a demon from South America that steals children's teeth, but that's not an inspiration for your human 'tooth fairy' myth as far as I know," Seraphex chimes in. "The teeth are taken from their living mouths, and no money is left in return.

"You have such a very a lovely species, Your Majesty," I say.

We emerge onto a tiny island, really just a rock jutting twenty feet up out of the ocean. There's nothing around us but empty sea in every direction. But as soon as we're out of the red glowing bricks, Zambrano is able to pull out a teleportrait, and after one awkward neck grab that makes the physical connection needed for us to teleport together, we're back on the first floor of the warehouse.

I'd like to say that I immediately jump into trying to help figure out how to save the world from an ancient demon king, but instead I collapse into one of the reading chairs by the library section, finally letting my body relax. As soon as I'm down, I feel the massive weight of fatigue on all my limbs, almost as if Zambrano has cast his "eye of Jupiter" spell on me. I'm not sure if I could get up if I wanted to.

"Ah yes, these things do come with a price," Zambrano says as he opens a small box that fluorescent lights come out of, and he reaches in, pulling out a sandwich that looks neatly wrapped with labels from the deli at our local bodega. "That druidic blessing uses up your body's own energy reserves to power incredible strength. Kind of like PCP. There's no such thing as a free lunch!"

"Well that's just swell," I say, glaring at him through eyelids sagging closed under the weight of extreme fatigue. I see his perfect hair and body, and his stupid smile as he unwraps the sandwich on his lab bench and takes a bite.

He sees me looking at the sandwich and cocks his head to the side. "I meant there's no such thing as a free lunch in terms of arcane physics and thaumaturgical dynamics," he says. "Obviously, if you have space-time bent in such a way that you can reach up from underneath the local deli counter and grab a buffalo chicken and cheddar on a hoagie, it's possible to get a lunch that you didn't actually pay for. Oh, did you want me to grab you one?"

Too tired to eat or debate metaphysics, I just shake my head and melt back into the chair, letting the magical exhaustion take over.

Stupid sorcerer. Stupid demons. Stupid druids.

I'll try to save the world . . . after a little nap.

# CHAPTER 10

Hours later, I wake up to the sweet, sweet sound of Zambrano and Seraphex arguing. I have no idea how long I've been out, but I'm hungry, I have to pee, and my back is sore from the awkward position I've been in.

The sorcerer and the duck are going at it at a fairly moderate volume—for them—so I take a minute to let my senses come back to me, knowing that everything is basically normal, at least for the moment. I also grab the backup phone that I bought on Zambrano's dime and start loading up my info, installing my apps, and signing in to everything while I listen to the two of them argue. Luckily, my old phone wasn't entirely broken, just a busted screen, so my photos of the bottom of Merlin's Vault uploaded automatically.

Do I really need to replace it and not just have someone replace the screen and live with a few dents? I guess not, maybe. But what would *you* do if you had access to infinite free phones?

"It's not improbable, it's impossible," Zambrano is saying. "How can we directly defeat the most powerful demon there is? With just over two weeks to prepare and only one sorcerer on our side?"

"You're incorrect," Seraphex says.

"I am completely correct!" Zambrano sputters.

"Simple existential proof, basic logic," Seraphex replies. "Merlin and Liao Ling did it, so it clearly is possible. It has been done in the past, therefore, it can be done in the future."

"Okay, that's technically true, but you know I'm right in the ways that count."

"I'm a demon, it's literally impossible for me to say things that are not technically true," Seraphex replies. "So that really is the way that counts."

"Pointless sophistry!" Zambrano cries. "The point I am making is that *we* are unable to defeat Rex. He's a demon king, my most powerful spells will barely slow him down."

"How can you hope to make a plan when you use words so loosely and callously?" Seraphex says. "If we fail, it will be because of your sloppy thinking."

"Sloppy? Because I don't obsess over the nitty-gritty details of every dictionary definition? Words have changing meanings! Contextual nuance! Words belong to us, they mean what we say they mean," Zambrano argues.

It goes on like this for another minute while my bladder starts complaining more and more. Zambrano and Seraphex get deeper into an obscure philosophical debate about language and truth with a side of demonology.

"When Wittgenstein said that 'the meaning of a word is its use in the language,'" Zambrano is saying as I stand up, "he clearly demonstrated that linguistic meaning is a transitory construct of—"

He stops, and they both look over at me.

"You're awake," Zambrano says.

"You look quite pale," Seraphex adds, completely unhelpfully.

I shrug. "I was tired. You haven't made much progress while I was out, have you?"

"I have suggested several valuable potential approaches," Seraphex says with a snooty air. "We should take a subtle approach to gain the advantage over my former husband in what will surely be a protracted battle. We have already lost half a week of our time thanks to that trap."

"Almost a week?" I explode. "What did that druid thing do to me? How long was I asleep for?"

"Don't be so dramatic," Zambrano scolds me. "You're fine, and you only slept for twelve hours or so. The lost time is due to the pocket universes. Time runs faster there, sort of the reverse of a slow-time case. Everything is smaller there . . . It's hard to explain. Anyway, four days have passed since we entered Merlin's Vault."

"We need to hit Mr. Demon King aka. Rex your terrible ex with maximum force the moment he comes out," Zambrano says. "If we had a full Sorcerers' Circle, maybe we could catch him by surprise and trap him again. But we don't. So . . . we'll just have to nuke him."

"Nuke him?" I say, flabbergasted.

"Yeah," Zambrano says. "If there's one thing I learned from the battle of Yellowstone, it's that modern technology can be quite useful and change the balance of power between demons and humans. It's clear that you have some sort of shady government connections—which is sketchy as hell, Bryce—but the Sorcerers' Circle rules are that we don't ask questions when someone brings valuable help to the table. So can you get us, like, a suitcase nuke or something?"

I open and close my mouth in shock. Sure, I was able to get the MSA to call in an air strike on the demon duke, but that's a pretty big step from getting a nuclear weapon.

"I . . . I really need to get to the bathroom," I say and flee upstairs to take a piss and think things over. It's lucky that I really need to go, because otherwise I don't know how I would convince my legs to go up more stairs with each step burning more than the last.

An epic leak and a quick shower later, I grab some leftovers from the fridge and head back down to the workshop with no better idea of what we should do.

"Look, just leave me alone, I've got a couple weeks," Zambrano is saying as I walk down the stairs. "I'll figure something out."

"Okay, so where are we," I say, rolling my shoulders and stretching out my back.

"*We* are nowhere," he says. "I'm going to figure this out myself, like usual. Just give me some time. I'll let you know when and if I need you. Maybe we'll have to steal an artifact or something."

"Sure you don't want to talk it through? Bounce some ideas around? Make sure your plan isn't going to, I don't know, trigger a tsunami and obliterate Guam?"

"Really, you think you can help me? What background do you have in arcanology?"

"Well, none," I admit.

"Demonology?" He demands.

"Not that either."

"Have you ever done a mystical binding?"

"No, I have not."

"Do you understand the spatial geometry of slow-time cases? Even basic temporal flow mechanics?"

I sigh. "No, I don't."

"Didn't think so," he snaps. "So you're not going to be much help to me, are you?"

"I feel like I can be helpful here," I insist. "We've made a good team so far, haven't we?"

Zambrano shrugs. "Look, I like you. You're a good kid. If this was some fun little mission to save a city, I'd make it a lesson and walk you through every step. But we're on a tight deadline, and literally everything hangs in the balance. So let me think and plan this out. Besides, I already told you what your job is. Go get us a nuke."

I sputter for a second. "I-I don't think I have that pull," I say. "The government isn't going to just give me a nuke."

Zambrano shrugs. "Is spying on me for them even worth it, then? If you can't even try to help, then go order more stuff that I pay for. I'll let you know when we need to sneak past magic traps or auction you off as a curiosity."

I want to punch him, but I just ball up my fists and stare hatred at him. "Okay, fine," I say. "I'll try." I turn and walk out the front door, which I almost never use.

I walk out into the street, which is fairly deserted, as it's early evening in an area that's mostly industrial. I do see in the one apartment building nearby, a couple windows with curtains that seem to close as soon as I walk out. I'm pretty sure various intelligence agencies have agents who've taken up residence in that building. In particular, there's a very buff-looking Asian man who's always walking his dog around the warehouse, and a pair of white women who are always jogging through the area when I happen to walk out of our secret second door, and who I've caught speaking what sounds like Russian or German or something.

But I'm not here for them. I step out into the middle of the sidewalk and start walking at a leisurely pace. That's the only pace that I can really manage at this point, as my legs are incredibly sore and barely cooperating. After a few blocks, I turn a sharp corner around a large building, and I stop and lean up against the wall and wait. About a minute later, I'm rewarded with a large man in an ill-fitting suit barreling around the corner, breathing heavily. I really have the feeling that the top MSA agents are not the ones assigned to maintain 24/7 surveillance of Bryce Alexander.

"Hey, Derek," I say as he pulls up in surprise. "I was hoping it would be you. Expecting me to pop out of the other door? Have to hustle to try to catch up?"

"Mr. Alexander," he says. He stares at me in annoyance, then gives a noncommittal shrug.

"How have you been?" I ask the beefy MSA agent. "Been up to anything fun this summer? You didn't go to the beach without me, did you?"

"I'm good," he says, starting to catch his breath and staring daggers at me. "How are you?"

"I've been better," I say. "Chased through a glowing blue nightmare by a nasty beast, discovered that we're all under threat from a monstrous demon, trying to build a genuine friendship with a murderous duck, dealing with a sorcerer slash internship boss who is a real egotistical prick and won't listen to my ideas. And my legs hurt from walking up too many stairs."

Derek opens his mouth to say something, but then closes it and just looks at me with interest. I'm guessing he's been trained that if someone he's surveilling is talking, he's supposed to just let them keep going.

"Anyway," I continue, "I think that summer vacation to a nice upstate Airbnb will have to wait. Things are getting perilously real. Which is why I came out to have one of our pleasant little chats. I need to have a meeting with Agent Crane as soon as possible."

He opens his mouth as if to deny that Agent Crane exists, then closes it. Finally, he just gives a shrug. "Very well, Mr. Alexander," he says. "Just hold on for a minute."

He walks off and starts talking into his sleeve. He goes back and forth for a couple minutes. Finally he nods and walks back over.

It feels weird going to the government for help about this when so often we're trying to stay under the radar. But at the battle of Yellowstone, Agent Crane was able to arrange a fighter jet to blast the Demon Duke Volcanose with an air-to-surface missile, so I figure she's not so bad.

"You're in luck. Agent Crane is actually back in the city. I've been authorized to bring you in for a face-to-face. They're sending a car to pick you up. Just hold on," he says.

And then he just stands there, calmly staring around at the city, clearly scanning for threats and saying absolutely nothing. Like some antisocial psychopath. Finally, it's too much for me.

"How are things at home?" I say. "The wife good? Looking forward to getting the kids back to school next month?"

He stares at me in shock. "How did you know— Have you been stalking me?" His face is turning red, and I feel like he's about to tear me in half.

I crack up and hold a hand up in a conciliatory gesture. "Dude, chill. It was just a stab in the dark. You're wearing a wedding ring, and you're about the right age to have kids in school. That was a total guess."

He takes a deep breath, but I can see he's still pissed.

"Also, pretty rich of you to get upset about someone being followed around, huh?"

He rolls his eyes.

"How long is this car going to take?" I ask.

He shrugs. "It's about twenty-five minutes away. Traffic is really backed up on the BQE."

"Oh my god, Derek, you were going to have us just stand here in silence for *twenty minutes*? Wow," I say. "Couldn't we just have called an Uber or something? That's way too long. I'm going to go back inside and grab a snack. Have my MSA Uber pick me up back at the door in twenty minutes."

He shrugs, probably relieved to not have to babysit me any longer.

I head back inside, get myself cleaned up, and head back out to the street where a giant gleaming black SUV is waiting. I hop inside, and the driver gives me a curt nod. Derek is already sitting in the front passenger seat. I try to start a conversation with the driver, but unlike Derek, this guy doesn't take my bait.

Clearly neither of them want to talk, so I pull my new phone out, telling myself I'm going to do some research into demonology and arcane theory, and whether there has been any strange demonic activity in the past day. But instead I end up watching funny reels for most of the ride.

Come on, like you've never done that before?

Before long, we're off the highway and driving through one of the nicer Brooklyn neighborhoods, tree-lined streets with lovely brownstones that a smoothie-slinger like me would never have a chance of owning, even if I had somehow gotten a graduate degree in magical studies and found a career in arcane theory.

We turn off at the end of one of the streets and pull up to a Whole Foods. The car turns into the parking lot, and I lean forward in my seat.

"Why are we stopping? Did Agent Crane ask us to pick up some kale salad and kombucha for the meeting or something?"

Derek shakes his head, and I can see the slight twist of a smile at the corner of his lips.

"No, no kombucha. This is the MSA's New York City headquarters."

"A Whole Foods?" I ask, but the big SUV swings through the parking lot, around the back of the store, and up to a garage door by the loading dock. The garage door opens, and the SUV drives down a ramp.

"That's right," Derek answers. "They actually have pretty good hamburgers at the deli if you don't feel like a kale salad. It's not the worst lunch option."

"But why here?" I ask.

He just shrugs. His last sentence was the closest thing he's given me to expressing a real opinion yet, so I let it slide.

We drive down through a parking garage level and then to a lower level where the car pulls up next to a large glass door. The whole thing reminds me of the airport spots where they send you to meet cars that you called from an app. I get out and head through the doors where they put me through elaborate security, also like an airport but in this case the guards actually are quite thorough and seem to genuinely care.

Once I'm inside, I go down an elevator and emerge into a huge room. We must be several stories down, but there's a big open atrium with a water feature in the middle and a big map with some collection of hotspots mapped out around the globe. MSA employees are hustling around in and out of offices and conference rooms.

It's spectacular. I thought secret bases like this only existed in Marvel movies. I really want to check out the map, but Derek hustles me through the atrium, down a hall, and into a small conference room. Inside, Agent Crane is hunched over what looks like a turkey wrap, the wrapper clearly indicating it was purchased upstairs. I'm guessing in a rush.

"Right in there, Mr. Alexander," Derek says as he ushers me in and stays outside, closing the door. It glides home with a slight suction noise, as if it's a hatch on a submarine sealing airtight. As soon as the door is closed, the noise of the atrium fades away and is replaced by a low-pitched, steady hum.

"Ah, Bryce," she says, eyeing me with her sharp features looking even more gaunt than usual. "I'm sure you're wondering—"

"Why the headquarters of the MSA is underneath an overpriced grocery store for people who don't realize that the organic option is the same product with a different label and higher price?" I say in a rush. "This place is kind of awesome."

"That actually wasn't what I was referring to. But if you must know, the MSA needed an elaborate build-out for arcane safety and privacy from magical surveillance, and getting new construction approved in New York City is incredibly slow, especially if you want it to be covered up. So we just piggybacked on the basement of this new store that was already under construction. Mr. Bezos was very cooperative in exchange for helping him with some troublesome supply chain issues in the Eastern Hemisphere."

"You know you don't exactly sound like a hero, right?" I say.

Agent Crane shrugs. "Nevertheless. We aren't here to debate the ethical merits of the MSA's approach to corporate politics and international labor relations, I hope. What I was going to explain was why I invited you here in the first place rather than meeting you at one of the city's delightful restaurants. There are several I've been meaning to try."

I shrug. "Um, I figured you just were busy and didn't want to have to make the trek up to Queens to visit me."

Agent Crane smiles. "If only. I invited you here because these conference rooms are secured from essentially every form of surveillance. From foreign governments, arcane eavesdropping and scrying, anything of that type. And nothing is recorded, so we're secure even from . . ." She trails off, gesturing at the broader MSA headquarters around us. "So you can tell me the truth. What's really going on?"

I sit down, looking across the table at Agent Crane. Her brow is furrowed with worry, and there are bags under her eyes from lack of sleep.

"Is everything okay?" I ask.

She shrugs. "Making the snap decision to deploy heavy munitions on American soil without pre-approval did *not* go over well with the secretary of homeland security and our friends on various congressional committees. Every senator and congressperson thinks they could have come up with an alternate solution that didn't shoot a missile at a national park. So my authority has been restricted. I've been instructed to observe only, and I'm not allowed to deploy any significant resources."

"Oh, okay," I say with a gulp. That's not going to make this any easier. But I have to try anyway.

"So what's going on?"

I'm not totally sure I believe her about us not being recorded, since this could all be an act. But I don't really care about that. So I tell her the whole story about Merlin's secret vault at the bottom of the Pacific Ocean and the demon king lying in wait there, about to break out of his prison. I even show her the pictures that I took in Rex's chamber.

Agent Crane shakes her head, and her shoulders slump. "There's no way they'll buy that. Even with the pictures—those could have been faked several different ways. Sorry. I'll have to take it up the chain, but it's going to take a while. Reports, committees, probably talking to some idiot senator or other to convince them to even authorize the navy to get some ships there. But I'm guessing that you and the dark sorcerer are going to be taking actions on your own. So I don't think you came here just to give me a heads-up and a whole slew of reports to write. What did you want?"

I take a deep breath. "I, um . . . well . . . I sort of was going to ask for a nuke."

Agent Crane's jaw drops, hanging open for several long seconds. "You really think I'm going to just hand over a weapon from our nuclear arsenal? To not just a civilian, but a dangerous rogue sorcerer who has a long history of leaving destruction everywhere he goes? Who would be in jail if we thought there were any chance of either capturing him or holding him without massive collateral damage? And even if we wanted to give you a nuclear weapon, how would you even use it? Do you have a submarine capable of carrying a Trident warhead?"

"We were sort of hoping there would be, like, a suitcase model, maybe with a timer or something," I say lamely. How did I let that pompous jackass sorcerer talk me into making a fool of myself like this?

Agent Crane stares at me for a moment, silently shaking her head. And then she puts her head in her hands and starts laughing. Or maybe it's crying, I can't quite tell. Let's call it laughing but with that distinct undertone that crying is definitely available right under the surface.

"I'm sorry," I say. "I know it's crazy."

"There is no way I could get you a nuke," she says. "Not a single person in the chain of command would authorize that, right up to the president."

"Yeah," I say, fidgeting nervously. "I figured. Is there anything you can do? Mobilize the military? Get MSA wizards to research the problem?"

Agent Crane shrugs. "I'll file a full report on everything that you said. The problem is Zambrano's credibility at the MSA and with world governments in general is just . . . let's just say he is not rated as an ally. And by extension, since you get your information from him, you are not classified as a reliable intelligence source."

"We saved the world from being invaded by the demon hordes!" I complain. "Just a couple months ago!"

Agent Crane steeples her fingers in front of her face.

"I believe you, Bryce, I do. Trust me, I've reviewed all the evidence and reports front to back. But there's a problem with saving the world."

"A problem? With preventing the whole country from being overrun by demons? Sorry we inconvenienced you!"

"No, no," she says. "The problem is that when you successfully save the world, it's very hard to prove that it was actually in danger. The United Nations Arcane Threat Committee and the MSA have made the judgment that what we saw in Yellowstone was a turf war between a dark sorcerer and a demon. They believe that it was a magical pissing contest and we were tricked into firing an AGM-65 Maverick in a national park by a wily dark sorcerer and his clever intern."

I open and close my mouth, dumbfounded. Then I slam my fist down on the table. Agent Crane waits patiently while I take a few deep breaths. Finally, I just shrug.

"They think I'm clever?" I say quietly. "That's nice, at least."

"Why do you think you've been tailed for the whole summer? The latest intelligence assessment referred to you as a 'dangerous rogue asset.' They think you tricked them, and they're pissed."

"Ugh, now I know how Zambrano feels," I say. "You just can't win with these people!"

"I'm sorry, Bryce," she says. "I do believe you. I advocated for you. That's partly why I'm out of the loop and can't do much to help you. That's why I brought you here, to a shielded conference room. I wanted you to hear the full situation directly from me, I think you deserve that much at least."

"I understand," I say. "So there's nothing at all you can do to help me?"

Agent Crane eyes me for a long moment, her lips pursing in different positions as she mulls it over.

"The world is really in danger again?" she asks. "Existential threat?"

"Yeah," I say. "That's what Seraphex says. She can't lie."

She nods. "Okay, fair enough. There's one thing I can do. Luckily, a lot of us here in the New York MSA branch think maybe we owe you one. The security guards who monitor your warehouse in Queens are armed with FGM-148 Javelin shoulder-launched missiles in case of a possible conflict."

"Wait, so you have missiles pointed at us twenty-four seven?"

Agent Crane ignores me and continues, "These missiles are fairly straightforward to operate, but they do occasionally fail safety inspections and are declared unserviceable. Then they're sent to be repaired or sent for recycling and disposal. If one of the missiles in active duty were to fail inspection, let's say later tonight for instance, I could probably make sure that the paperwork for its disposal got delayed, and then maybe the records got lost in the shuffle. Everyone here at the MSA is so very busy and overworked these days, mistakes do happen."

"You can just make it disappear like that?"

Crane shrugs. "In the Iraq War, the US lost nine billion dollars in cash. We have a lot of equipment, and it's very hard to keep track of it."

She goes on to explain the basics of how to operate the missile, and that the full user manual will be included and that I should *really thoroughly read it, like, several times* before trying to use the thing. I also promise to use it only somewhere that the government isn't likely to see.

After that she sends me out to the car, where I wait for a while alone with the driver. Talking to him is like talking to a brick wall, so I just sit there and wish my phone had any sort of service. Finally, Derek comes back to the car, gives me a nod, and we start the drive home, riding in silence.

The SUV finally comes to a stop outside the warehouse, and as I get out, Derek goes to the rear door and pulls out a big heavy backpack, which he lugs as we walk to the front door.

"Hey, uh, Mr. Alexander," Derek says, stopping outside the door like it's the end of a very awkward first date.

"What's up?" I ask, pretty curious to see what he has to say since this is the first time he's ever started a conversation with me.

"Don't tell me any of the details, I'm not allowed to know. But I have to ask. How bad is it? Should I be worried? Get my family out of the city?"

I shrug. "I don't know. I don't think New York in particular is that much more in danger than anywhere else."

He looks at the ground. "You're going to save the world again though, right? You and the dark sorcerer and whatever the heck that duck is? You've got a plan?"

I take a deep breath. No point in telling him that no, we definitely don't have a plan yet.

"Yeah," I say. "We've got it. Zambrano's in there working on it right now." He'd better be, and not in there arguing with Seraphex about the deeper meanings of words or whatever they were doing before.

"Thanks, Mr. Alexander," Derek says, smiling with tight lips.

He hands over the big backpack, which is exactly as heavy as it looks.

"One more thing," he says as he helps me into the straps and shows me how to connect it all. "How the heck did you know my name was Derek?"

I freeze for a moment with my mouth open. I had no idea whatsoever that his name was Derek. It just seemed funny. I want to tell him it was a lucky guess, which it was, but that wouldn't be any fun.

"I'm just a 'dangerous rogue asset,' aren't I?" I say.

"That you are," he says with a chuckle. "Have fun with the Javelin, Mr. Alexander," he adds as he turns and walks back to the SUV.

I walk inside, straining under the weight of the big case and struggling to get it through the front door as it pokes up above my head. I'm going to have to up my weightlifting routine if this is going to become a regular thing.

# CHAPTER 11

Inside, Zambrano is leaning low over his workbench, tapping his fingers nervously against the pages of an ancient-looking tome.

"I wasn't able to get a nuke," I say as I walk up.

Seraphex hops over, curiously eyeing the heavy package on my back.

"Oh," Zambrano answers, not looking up from his reading. "I didn't expect you to have any success. I just wanted you out of my hair so I could try to figure out how to save all of humanity from hell on Earth."

"At least Bryce didn't come back empty-handed, it would appear," Seraphex notes, approaching closer and looking up at my oversized backpack. It's a plain black pack, which I imagine is more conspicuous than the standard military packaging. Still, it's heavy.

Zambrano looks up, squinting at me as his vision refocuses from what he was reading.

"No, he didn't, did he? All right," the sorcerer says, turning in his chair to face me and raising a skeptical eyebrow. "What did you find out there in the world of technology?"

Straining, I carefully pull the backpack off and gently lean it up against the wall, then walk over and sit down at the table nearest to Zambrano.

"Oh, well, it's not a nuke," I say. "I'm not sure they actually have small suitcase models of those, anyway. Sorry about that. But I did get a Javelin anti-tank missile that I can fire from my shoulder. So that's pretty cool. I'm not so helpless anymore, I guess."

Zambrano smiles. "You only get one chance with those things. I know several spells that would kill you before you could get a shot off. And I'm working on one that would divert most of a blast of that type."

"Well, but you and I are best buds who never disagree on anything," I say, "so I'm not too worried we're going to get in a fight. The question isn't whether *you* have spells that can handle modern armor piercing missiles. It's whether our friend Rex would have that sort of knowledge. And given that he's never seen a rifle, let alone a missile launcher . . ."

"Oh," Zambrano says. "Good point."

We both instinctively look at Seraphex.

"It wouldn't kill him," she says, fluttering up and landing on the table I've sat at. "I don't think even a nuclear weapon would actually kill him. But a direct hit with something like that . . . He would have no idea what was happening. No context for it, really. And certainly no time to figure out what it was and stop it. It would both hurt and embarrass him. I like it."

"Okay, sure," I say. "But how much would it hurt him? Would it stop him?"

"He has a strong heat signature, so it would be able to go right for him," the duck muses. "And it would probably crack him right open and throw him back. He would be incapacitated for at least a few minutes."

"That sounds really useful!" I say, thrilled that I might actually be able to contribute something here.

"The one thing to keep in mind is that this will only work once. My former husband is not as clever as I am, but he is *very* powerful and resourceful. His demon body and magic will adapt as it heals, and the next time it will be a lot less useful."

"What will he do if he escapes?" I ask. I don't really want to know the answer, but we need as much information as we can get.

"He is vastly powerful, but he will be caught unprepared for how much the world has changed. He has no concept of technology or the modern world. He won't try to take on the whole world at once. He will take some time to learn the ways of twenty-first-century civilization—and then he will start to cause disasters that will set him up to take control of the world."

Zambrano scowls. "Why didn't he do that originally? I never understood that part of the story. Rex was on Earth for thousands of years before Merlin and Liao Ling trapped him under the Mariana Trench and banished most of the rest of the demons to Mars."

"Paper," Seraphex answers with a sniff.

"Paper?!" I explode. "The demon king decided to destroy us because he doesn't like paper? Is he some weird environmentalist who doesn't like us cutting down trees?"

"No, don't be absurd. For most of recorded history, demons viewed humans as a source of food and amusement. We enjoyed letting you build up your little kingdoms and cities, and then we knocked them down. We liked toying with you, and enjoyed the fun we could have tormenting you. But then, despite our best efforts, you started to develop. Agriculture, weaponry, domestic animals, simple machines, arcane lore, and spellcraft. It happened slowly, over millennia, and we didn't worry about it too much."

"But it turned out the little mortals with their short lives developed things you couldn't even dream of," Zambrano says with a self-satisfied grin as if he's taking credit for inventing fire and the wheel.

"You're not wrong," Seraphex admits, clearly slightly peeved. "We had immense power due to our nature but not the drive to create that you humans have. And so when the Chinese invented paper, and it started spreading, my former husband, terror that he is, decided that it had gone too far. Suddenly ideas, mathematics, architecture, and especially spells and other arcane knowledge could be easily written and transmitted. He knew that if he didn't do something, there would be an explosion of technological and arcane progress and he might lose control. Rex moves slowly, manipulating events to his liking. He does not attack immediately. But he was preparing a plan to destroy humanity's technical advances, a cataclysm that would return you to Bronze Age technology."

"But we stopped him!" I say, joining in Zambrano's humanistic hubris. "We trapped him and banished his demon armies."

"*You* didn't do anything," Seraphex answers. "But Liao Ling had some friends among the demonic horde—she was a great expert in demonic magics—and they told her what was happening. She reached out to her great rival, Merlin. The two competitors made peace, and Liao Ling recruited around a hundred other sorcerers in the world to help them in their quest. Humanity's magic was at its peak of power then."

"I never got that," I interject. "Why were there a hundred sorcerers in the year 500, and then fewer and fewer over the years? They lose their sanity, sure, but shouldn't new ones be born to replace them? How is there only one left now?"

"Merlin created more spells in his lifetime than anyone else did, before or after," Zambrano muses. "But that level of creation stopped after he went to Mars. Creating new spells has become harder and harder over the years. Magic has become increasingly more difficult to train, taking more patience and skill with each passing century."

"And why is that?" I follow up. "I read plenty of papers about it in school. They speculated things with sunspot cycles, or recessive genetic traits being bred out over time, or some magical resource being depleted, or some sort of interference from technology. But none of it checked out scientifically."

Zambrano shrugs. "No one knows. Even in my lifetime, I've noticed that magic has gotten less responsive, less willing to learn new tricks, as it were. Things that I was able to do sloppily when I was first learning now take my full level of skill and technique. That's probably why no one new has been able to learn sorcery in so long—it's gotten harder to start. If even the basic stuff requires advanced skills, you'll never develop the touch and instincts for it."

"Do you know?" I say, turning to look at the demon duck.

Her little duck bill opens and closes a few times. "I *really* want to say something mysterious and unclear to keep you thinking you need me," she says. "But . . . I don't think that's something that a friend would do, is it?"

I grin. "Regretting that friendship agreement, are you?"

Zambrano leans forward, eyes blazing. "What do you know? If you're truly my friend, you would know how important this is to me. We need more sorcerers." His voice is suddenly tight, holding back intense emotions. "I shouldn't have to defeat Rex without other sorcerers. Without a Circle. What happened to magic in the 500s? Damn it, *I shouldn't have to do this alone.*"

I pull back, gulping nervously. Is this flash of anger something I need to be worried about? Is his sanity starting to slip under centuries of use of magic combined with the pressure of this situation?

Seraphex looks at him with a sort of pity that I haven't seen from her before. "I'm sorry, I don't know. In the year 526, Merlin and Liao Ling defeated my former husband, Rexhalarkhart. Magical knowledge had grown up to that point, with more great wizards and sorcerers in each generation. After a great battle at Antioch, causing an earthquake that killed a quarter million people, Rex was trapped in the prismatic prison. The demons were driven through the portal created by the conduit. Merlin was stranded and killed on Mars, and we now know that Liao Ling was trapped in the prismatic prison. From that point on, creating new spells through sorcery became more and more difficult over the next fifteen hundred years, until today when no one manages to learn the art. That's all that I know, I'm sorry."

Zambrano nods, leaning back with a long sigh. "Okay. So I'm alone. And none of this academic discussion really helps with our current problem. Rex is going to escape and then start triggering disasters to tear the world apart."

"Do you have any potential solutions?" I ask, worrying as soon as I say it that I'm putting too much pressure on him.

But Zambrano just shrugs. "Not really. I don't have the knowledge of demonic arts required to defeat Rex when he breaks out. I could probably fight him briefly, but it won't go any better than it did when I tried to go toe-to-toe with Volcanose. For raw power, the higher-level demons are unmatched."

"You know," I say, "maybe you don't have to do this alone. And without demonic knowledge. You may not be the only sorcerer still alive, technically."

"What do you mean?" Zambrano asks. Then he rocks back in his chair. "Oh, right. But she's . . ."

"Yeah, Liao Ling is trapped inside the prismatic prison," I finish for him. "What if we're thinking about this wrong? What if this is less of a combat mission to defeat Rex, but instead a rescue mission to save Liao Ling? Then we get her to help us make a plan."

Zambrano bites his lip for a moment, then gives a slow nod.

"Okay, that's a more approachable problem."

"We're not going to come up with a plan to defeat and destroy him immediately?" Seraphex asks, a sudden tone of fear in her voice. "If he gets a foothold in our world, he will be very difficult to eradicate."

Zambrano raises an eyebrow at her. "And do you have any plan or strategy for defeating him right there? A special enchanted weapon, a secret vulnerability, a very personal insult that will hurt his feelings so badly that he surrenders on the spot?"

The duck glowers at him. "No, I don't know of any artifacts or weaknesses that we can exploit. I know plenty of biting insults, though they would certainly just make him angry rather than discourage him." She screws up her little duck face in thought for a moment. "Though I could certainly distract him temporarily, possibly long enough to get him away from the injured sorcerer long enough to grab her. You would need to turn me back into my regular demon self, however."

Zambrano cocks his head to the side. "Well we're certainly not doing *that.*"

"One demonic monarch is more than enough trouble for one planet," I add.

"Oh, the battle between us would almost certainly annihilate your species. You wouldn't like that," Seraphex says nonchalantly, like she's reminding us not to put a new red shirt in the laundry with the white sheets.

"We could simulate it though," Zambrano muses. "With an illusion prism and me channeling some of your energy to give it the right arcane vibrations. It would take preparation and testing. And you would need to promise to cooperate and not try any funny business," he adds pointedly.

"I would let you channel enough energy for the illusion, and would not try to take advantage of your channeling to cause you harm or return to my natural, proper, and true form," Seraphex agrees. "Though that is the way that I belong. During this specific encounter, I won't attempt to trick or fool you for my own advantage. I'm your friend, remember?"

"A friend from whom I need to extract a binding magical oath not to betray me, yeah," Zambrano says, making a sour expression. "Such a great friend."

"Okay, so we have a distraction to pull Rex away from Liao Ling, and a nice modern weapon to temporarily stop him while Bryce grabs her, and then we get out of there."

"Um, I can't both shoot a Javelin missile and grab Liao Ling at the same time," I point out. "Not even with your super-speed druid charm."

"Oh, huh," Zambrano says as if mystified that his plan weren't complete. "So we need another pair of hands, then. But few enough that we can all travel out by teleportrait."

"You can't teleportrait out of there," Seraphex notes. "You need to make it up and out of the vault before you can teleportrait."

"Is that pocket universe trap still active?" I ask, seeing around the room that the other two are coming to the same conclusion.

"It won't hold him for all that long," Zambrano says, but all of us are already plotting. "He's wounded but still stronger than all of us put together. So Seraphex and I need to distract him while you hit him with the missile. Meanwhile, someone else pulls Liao Ling to safety, and we all run for it."

"Okay, that could be workable," I say.

"Okay, so who are you going to get?" Zambrano asks, eyeing me. "Some government spook or something?"

I shake my head. "The Javelin is all they can do for us right now. What about you? Have anyone who can help?"

Zambrano shrugs. "That I would trust with this? Nah."

"You don't have *any* friends?"

"Do you?" he asks, glaring at me.

I think for a moment of who I actually know. Agent Crane already told me she can't do anything. None of my college friends would have any idea about this. Carla from Samba Smoothies is an obvious nonstarter. Mei Song helped us defeat her employer, Demon Duke Volcanose, but she wasn't ever a real ally, and I have no idea where she is now. There's really only one option.

I shoot my buddy a text and then have to wait a few hours until it's morning in India, and a couple minutes later I'm on a video chat with Parth, who looks like he just stepped out of the shower.

"Hey, Parth, how are you doing, man?" I ask.

"I don't know." He shrugs. "Tons of classwork. I'm good with the pronunciation of the words, but I can't figure out a lot of these hand motions. My TA for Mantras and Mudras is a real jerk about it—they all come so easily to her. And we're only a few weeks from the end of the semester. Sorry," he adds, "I know I'm complaining about something that's your dream."

"Oh, I'm fine," I say, realizing that I actually am pretty fine about it. "Sorry you're having a tough time. Um . . ." I pause for a moment, then dive in. "Is there any chance you want to travel to the deepest part of the ocean to risk your life trying to save the world against incredibly steep odds? We'll pick you up."

He pauses for a beat, blinking at me. And then he grins. "Dude, I was starting to think you'd never ask! Hell yeah!"

"That's amazing," I say, glad I don't have to try to talk him into it, or go to my second choice—one of my college friends who's fast and smart but has been kind of condescending since he got a job at a hotshot DC law firm and I was mixing smoothies. "I really appreciate it, and it's super important. I've got to warn you, it's going to be very dangerous. This plan is maybe the most dangerous thing I've done yet. Are you sure you want to do it?"

"Rad, dude, you know I'm in," he answers. "So what's the big plan? How am I going to die?"

# CHAPTER 12

The next two weeks are a blur of preparation, discussion, and training. I spend a lot of time watching videos and reading the manual to learn how to use the Javelin missile, and feel like I have a pretty solid grasp on how to use it, at least on a point-blank target that won't be moving fast and has a supernaturally warm heat signature. Zambrano confirms that even the magic of Merlin's Vault shouldn't interfere with the missile, and the air pressure down there is the same as at sea level, so no issue there either. Other than that, the sorcerer largely ignores me, spending most of his time in the lab with Seraphex, working on their spell to trick Rex into thinking she's there in her full demon form. I try to avoid the lab as much as possible because, to be completely honest, she's terrifying.

So with a few days to spare before we expect the glass to break, Zambrano teleportraits to Hyderabad, India, to grab Parth, and then the four of us teleport to a new yacht that Zambrano apparently won in some magical card game he teleported to in the Philippines a week ago. He claims he didn't cheat, but I have my doubts—the whole thing is way too convenient.

Meeting Parth for the first time is awesome—the enthusiasm and energy he has over text and video chat is even more intense in person. But it's really cool to actually be there in person with the guy who has kind of become my best friend over the past year.

We make the nerve-racking descent again, this time with Parth grinning like an absolute maniac while my pulse is pounding a million miles an hour. He genuinely doesn't seem to appreciate how much danger we're in down here. Instead he just chatters about how awesome the magic is. But I guess that he'll figure it out before long. Probably when he sees the demon, or when the first thing goes terribly awry . . . as it inevitably will, with Zambrano involved.

We reach the glowing blue underground entrance and discuss the plan a couple more times. Thankfully, with the stone door open, we don't need Slickwad's help again. Zambrano wants to go over it as many times as possible, constantly quizzing me on my part as if he thinks I haven't been absolutely obsessing over every detail for the last two weeks.

Parth walks down the stairs behind me, helping to carry the heavy case for the Javelin missile. He's not dressed in his usual smart collared shirt, instead he looks like an extra from a Bollywood historical epic, though maybe plainer and more realistic than who they would cast in a movie. He's wearing simple, loose cotton pants known as a dhoti paired with a basic tunic. The idea is that he'll resemble a common soldier from India in the year 526, which won't alarm or draw attention from Rex since he's accustomed to encountering people from all over the globe during that era.

"Hey, man," I say to Parth as we're walking down the stairs into Merlin's Vault. "Sorry I get the cool job with the missile. Seraphex says that since I'm not detected by magic and Rex isn't familiar with modern weapons, he'll ignore me and my strange contraption."

"No problem, dude," Parth answers. "I get the best job of all—saving the sexy damsel in distress."

"The 'sexy damsel' in question is one of the most powerful, dangerous, and vengeful sorcerers of all time," Seraphex points out with a haughty air.

"Are you kidding?" my friend answers. "What other type of damsel do you think I would be in to?"

"Just don't get distracted," Zambrano cautions, though he's smiling slightly. "We need you to get her out of danger with no delay. She could likely disembowel you with the flick of her little finger. She's the only one who can save the world. Frankly, the rest of you are expendable in comparison."

"Hot," Parth mutters as we continue down past the empty pedestals that held Merlin's fake artifacts the last time we were here.

"I know what you mean," Zambrano says with a wistful look on his face. "I once knew a woman like that. I would have done anything for her."

"Alix," I say, without realizing that I'm saying it, but Zambrano just nods. Alix was the great lover of Zambrano's life, another sorcerer of incredible power. But she was driven insane channeling demonic energy in the battle against Seraphex that trapped her in a duck body. Eventually, Zambrano had to kill Alix to protect the rest of the world from her madness.

"Sorry you lost her, I read about her in one of my classes," Parth says. "She must have been something. I feel ya, Mr. Z." Parth sticks out his fist for a fist bump.

"Don't ever call me that," Zambrano says, ignoring the fist. For a moment, I see a flash of anger, and I have a momentary worry that he's going to lash out, but he takes a breath and continues walking.

A few minutes later, we're down in the bottom of the vault, staring at the giant demon, with his massive horns, spikes, and barbed tail. The projectile that will break out has made clear progress since we first found the prismatic prism, and it's incredibly close to the outermost layer of the time-slowing glass.

"Wow, that is a serious demon," Parth remarks as we set up for the plan. "Scary stuff. Big boy, lots of scary horns and all that." He's extra peppy, which makes sense given that Zambrano gave him the same druid strength charm that he gave me in the pocket universe trap. Apparently, it's too soon for my body to safely use something like that again, so I'm just stuck with the old standard-issue human body. At least I have a missile though, right?

"That is the most powerful demon in existence," Seraphex points out. "And also the rudest and the worst relationship material of any that I'm aware."

"Worse relationship material than Slickwad?" I ask, just to needle her. "You did marry him, after all."

"A demon like Slickwad will disappoint you, but with him you know that you're getting a salty scoundrel with no real value. A partner like Rexhalarkhart will show you the most incredible, powerful things, opening up your mind and exciting the darkest recesses of your soul. And after universe-altering interactions that mortals like you can only imagine a glimpse of, only *then* will he disappoint you."

"Sounds like you're not quite over him, girl," Parth says as he takes his position at the closest point to Liao Ling. He lies down to make it look like he's injured and even less of a threat. "Are you sure you're not going to drunk dial him after he's out?"

"You know, I didn't promise to be this rude young man's friend," Seraphex says to me as she takes her position in front of the giant demon king, though it's as far back as she can go in the room. "I'm sure I could arrange to have him meet with some unfortunate accident at his school if I wanted to." She's set up just off-center from her former husband, so that the bolt of energy that he's shooting out through the layers of glass will miss her.

Zambrano stands directly behind her, holding a large illusion prism customized with complicated spells to make it powerful enough to fool a demon king, even if briefly. I take up my position high on the staircase, looking down on the scene from above. I shoulder the Javelin missile, using the sight to aim it down at the demon below me.

We wait for a long minute as Zambrano gets ready, performing spellcasting motions and saying incantations that I can't hear from up here. The missile digs into my shoulder, and I can feel sweat starting to drip down my forehead.

"How much longer will this be?" I ask when there's a break in the casting. "Or should I put this thing down?" The weight of the missile on my shoulder is frustrating, but part of me hopes this takes as long as possible. As soon as the illusion is created, we're going to free the demon king, and from there I have a really hard time imagining this going well.

"Yes, yes," Zambrano says. "It's not simple to create the illusion and also channel demonic energy to fool a demon king, okay? But here we go."

He finishes casting the last spell, and suddenly smoke and light are swirling around him. For a moment, they rush around him in chaos, and then they coalesce into a figure as the sorcerer and the duck disappear into the illusion.

Seraphex's demon form illusion, which I've started calling the Sera-fake, is not as huge as Rex himself, but it still stands about eight feet tall. She doesn't have any of the fire and brimstone of Volcanose, or the many spikes of Rex, but she is instead more sleek, shiny, and inky black with rainbow light reflecting off her like the mixture of black pavement, motor oil, and water on a road after a rainstorm. She does have small horns and sharp edges at every joint. And, yes, I know what you're wondering—she's hot in an alien sort of way. But before Parth or anyone gets too excited, remember that only a few specific types of demons are interested in people—the succubi and incubi whose main thing is seducing hapless humans.

"Everyone ready?" Zambrano shouts once the illusion is in place.

"Ready!" I call out, though really I want to toss the Javelin down and just run for it. All this waiting has only increased my anxiety.

"Let's do this!" Parth shouts from his position lying over on the side of the glass cube near Liao Ling.

"*Shattershot!*" Zambrano's voice calls out, speaking a brand-new spell that he made for this occasion, and a shotgun blast of small particles of energy shoot out from within the Seraphex illusion, flying into the glass case and crashing through the successive layers of it. I have to be honest, it's cool to see the very first use of a totally new spell.

That said, the bottom drops out of my stomach as glass explodes across the room and the prismatic prison falls apart, mostly dropping down in tiny fragments as Zambrano's spell takes it down like the controlled demolition of a building.

The air is suddenly filled with swirling smoke and sparks as the demon king, having been frozen in incredibly slow motion for so many centuries, comes to life with a roar. The bolt of red energy that had been breaking the glass from the inside shoots out past the Seraphex illusion.

"Mighty king! My incredible lover!" the Sera-fake says. "You have been trapped here for so very long! I had to work very hard to find where that sorcerer hid you, and to find the right way to break you out from his vault."

I notice that even in her artificial form, the Sera-fake is still carefully saying only true statements. Since this is partly drawn from channeling her energy in order to fool Rex's enhanced demon king senses, the full demonic code of honesty must still apply.

Rex advances on her, his massive steps echoing through the large room. He does appear to be favoring one side, and the dagger stabbed in his back is smoking and sizzling.

"Seraphex," the demon king says. His voice is silky smooth, too perfect and resonant, almost musical, especially when compared to the Demon Duke Volcanose, whose voice sounded like rocks and sandpaper by comparison. Now that he's out of the smoke of the prismatic prison, I can see his eyes, clear and bright blue.

"Rex, King of all Demons Who Still Exist," Seraphex answers, her voice dreamy and breathier than usual.

As Rex advances, Parth quietly begins moving, stealthily inching across the sea of broken glass to the fallen body of the ancient Chinese sorcerer.

Using the zoom feature on the scope of the Javelin, I take a glance at Liao Ling and see that she's still breathing. Feeling foolish, I immediately return to focusing on the giant demon. I can't let myself get distracted. The missile, which I've set up carefully for this purpose, is easily able to get a lock on his heat signature.

Luckily, at the edge of the screen I can still see Parth creeping forward, about to reach Liao Ling.

"Oh, my love, I see right through you," the giant demon says, and my breath catches in my chest as I think he's figured us out. "You think that you can come and break me out over a thousand years too late, when I was about to get out on my own? You think that will somehow make me forget your vile betrayal?"

He's buying it. I'm suddenly very thankful for metaphor being a thing, even if it makes it confusing to know exactly what a demon is saying.

"My sweet dark lord," Seraphex answers, "you have never been far from my thoughts. I can explain my actions and my many mistakes if you will give me a few moments of your time."

"We are demons," Rex says, advancing another step toward her. "There's no need for stories and excuses." His regal voice sounds angry, but I can see a tension in his body, a certain animal tensing in his shoulders.

Oh, hell. He's horny.

And I don't mean all the spikes and the big honkers on his head. He's seeing his ex, and he's getting all hot.

I can see Sera-fake's body giving subtle cues as well—I've got to hand it to him. This is gross, but Zambrano is weaving this illusion with skill and subtlety. The guy is a maestro.

"I can simply ask you, to force you to prove your fidelity to your king. Do you desire me again?" Rex demands.

Beyond the aroused demon king, I can see that Parth has picked up Liao Ling and is creeping toward the stairs.

The demon king advances another step, his body almost vibrating with barely-contained passion. I'm sure some folks might find it erotic, but for me it's truly horrifying. "Do you crave me?" he asks. "Do you want to crash together as two blazing stars, laying waste to all around us with our passion?"

He stands in front of her. And a long moment passes as Parth gets closer to the stairs, the small sorcerer's limp body in his arms.

I glanced to confirm that the system still says "TRACK" to indicate a lock on the demon below, whose heat signature has only grown more intense. Gross.

There's a long moment where he stares at her with a smile that's some uncomfortable mix of adoring and predatory. But his eyes narrow, and he leans forward, appearing to sniff the air. Then his eyes go wide, and angry smoke erupts from his nostrils.

"WHAT HAVE YOU DONE?" Rex roars, and his tail swings as his left hand lashes out at Sera-fake's throat. With a whoosh, the illusion disappears in a swirl of light and shadow, and the duck and the man who are crouched against the wall suddenly appear, miniscule by comparison to the massive horned figure.

Rex spins, having fully come back to his senses from his lust-addled mind.

"Now, Bryce!" Zambrano yells, but my finger is already pressing the "FIRE" button. With a roar and a whoosh, the missile exits the launcher and screams across the open air.

I have spent the past two weeks having nightmares of Rex dodging the Javelin, moving at superhuman speed and avoiding it, ruining our plan. But instead, he sees it, bares his teeth, and leaps into the air, spiky arms outstretched and ready to do battle with the missile.

"*Containify!*" Zambrano shouts, making a compressing motion with his hands and casting another new spell, this one designed to keep the explosion of the Javelin from killing us with its shock wave and shrapnel. I told him that the incantation was silly, but he insisted that it needed to be something long enough to be unique for magic to key in on and short enough to say quickly.

Demon and Javelin collide in midair, and the spiky beast disappears in an explosion, leaving an afterimage burned on my retinas. Zambrano's *containify* spell creates a blue sphere around it, but it doesn't fully contain the explosion's shock wave, it just dampens the effect enough that instead of being torn apart, my body is merely tossed back against the wall. I'm sure I'll have some nasty bruises if I survive this, but at least I'm alive.

Zambrano's spell saved us from dying immediately, but the explosion has largely burned out the oxygen in the room, and the first breath I take is both scorching hot and feels like it's missing a key ingredient.

Looking down, I see that Seraphex is flying up toward me while Parth is charging up the stairs with the body of Liao Ling over his shoulder, Zambrano close behind.

I drop the spent Javelin launcher, tossing it down off the staircase and turn to sprint up the stairs. As I get higher, the air starts to be more breathable. As I reach the point where the stairs exit this room, I glance back down at the scene below.

In the center of the shattered glass, Rex the demon king lies with a giant hole ripped in his chest. When we hit Volcanose with a missile, he was down for quite a long time. But I can see that Rex's body is already starting to reassemble itself, the hole rapidly closing. It's not a smooth flowing liquid like the villain in *Terminator 2* employs, it's more like a seething mass of sharp polygons scraping against one another as they grind back into place.

While his broken body is knitting itself back together and his mouth is smashed open, his eyes, blazing bright blue gems, stare straight into mine. The rage behind them strikes at me, somehow gripping and chilling my insides. The blade in his back is gone, but as he stands up, I can see that there's still a dark black hole where it struck him. It doesn't look to be healing as quickly as the purely kinetic damage of the Javelin.

I turn and run up the stairs, still choking on heat and smoke, with the afterimage of those piercing blue eyes still boring into me as I flee.

# CHAPTER 13

Running away. Top speed. Breathing ragged. Pulse pounding. Terrifying monstrosity chasing behind us.

Yeah, that again. It's been a nice break not having to do this for the past few months, but running from monsters does appear to be a core function of being Zambrano's intern.

God damn it. But here we go!

"This feels AMAZING!" Parth shouts, moving quickly as he runs along beside me despite carrying an entire human. "I haven't felt this alive since I wrecked my motorcycle two years ago! And I am so strong!"

"Be careful," Zambrano cautions, running along behind us as well. "That druid magic is not super stable. If you overexert yourself, it could get carried away and go into overdrive."

"Magic can get spooked?" I ask, trying to maintain a high speed as the others are backed up behind me.

"It's wild magic," Zambrano explains. "It's not well trained and carefully crafted like my spells. If you over-excite it, it can get . . . like a dog that gets too enthusiastic."

"The zoomies, I believe the modern generation calls it," Seraphex says, landing on my shoulder. I guess I should be flattered that she chose me, but it's just a little bit more weight on my shoulder.

"Magic can get the *zoomies?*" I ask.

"The scientific term is frenetic random activity periods," Seraphex adds. "Or FRAPs for short."

"Druid magic can have that effect, yes," Zambrano says. "My arcane endeavors are usually much more very well behaved."

"I don't care, this feels awesome," Parth says, and I have to accelerate just because he's crowding behind me with Liao Ling. I'm nervous that he's going to run into a wall with her or something, but I definitely don't have the strength to take her.

"Okay, we can slow down," Zambrano says. "We're close."

We come to a near halt on the stairs, and he steps past me to start slowly advancing up, doing his trap detection spell. Another dozen steps up, and he calls a full halt.

"Okay, as soon as we step beyond this point, we'll trigger the trap and go into the pocket universe. Now we just have to wait and be ready to move at a moment's notice."

"We should make it look like we stopped for a reason," Seraphex instructs.

"Let's take a look at Liao Ling, we need to do that anyway," Zambrano says, directing Parth to carefully set her down on the steps. "I know one fairly quick healing spell, maybe I can get it done."

"It's very unlikely you can get it fully complete in time," Seraphex admonishes.

"Oh, I can get it done," Zambrano says, starting to mutter and rehearse spellcasting motions.

I help Parth maneuver Liao Ling against the wall, paying special attention to make sure he doesn't bump her head in his enthusiasm. His druidic energy charm is making him a little bit punchy. Though I've never actually met him in person, so maybe he's just like this? Or it could also be the absolute mortal peril that we're in right now. Pretty understandable, either way.

Zambrano kneels next to the ancient sorcerer, though other than her traditional Chinese outfit of a dark indigo robe, black vest, and loose-fitting pants, she doesn't look ancient at all. She looks like she could be in her thirties. Her hair is pure white, the same as Zambrano's. Though I guess Zambrano is also very old, and we would have no way of knowing because he's done so much magical plastic surgery on himself.

"She doesn't seem to be in immediate danger," Zambrano says. "But she's still unconscious. Bryce, keep watch while I try to help with her injuries."

While Zambrano mutters and moves his hands to cast healing spells, I turn and go a few steps down the stairs and peer into the hazy darkness. There's a lot of dust swirling in the air, probably kicked up by the missile explosion, so it's hard to see clearly.

"Why do both Zambrano and Liao Ling have white hair?" I whisper to Seraphex, who's keeping watch with me. "Does magic drain the color of hair or something?"

"No, it certainly does not. Early on, sorcerers figured out how to use arcane energy to modify their own bodies and restore and reverse the aging process," Seraphex explains. "They focused mostly on the key elements that kept them alive and vigorous, and in Liao Ling's time they hadn't figured out how to get hair follicles to keep producing melanin as they got older. Those early generations of long-lived sorcerers had white hair and otherwise looked fairly young. Later on, they figured it out, but the fashion had been established, and so many sorcerers kept the signature look."

"Oh, okay," I say. "Sort of like how in the first *Star Wars* movie Obi-Wan Kenobi was wearing a brown robe to blend into the desert when he was hiding his identity, but that look got associated with the Jedi, and so in later movies they decided that was just how all Jedi looked. Even though he was originally meant to be wearing it undercover. The same thing as that?" I ask.

"I'm not able to lie to you," she says, without elaborating further. "And as your friend, I have no desire to unnecessarily hurt your feelings with criticism."

"Um, saying that kind of spoils the effect, you know? Now I know you think I'm wrong."

"Noted," Seraphex says primly, though she doesn't seem particularly chagrined. "But your metaphor does not strike me as particularly precise, apt, or appropriate," Seraphex says. "But it's not important, so I support you emotionally even if I can't actually agree with you."

I was hoping that this playful/hurtful banter would continue forever, but there's something moving in the smoke below.

"He's coming," I say. "Can he see us, Sera?"

"With demonic vision, he can already see every pimple on your face," Seraphex says with the usual unnecessarily hurtful detail, but there's a note of nervousness in her voice. "Let's go."

"Just one second," Zambrano says, saying a few more words and then grunting with effort as he initiates the spell and an orange glow lights up the area. "I'm so close, this healing spell is a delicate process."

"We need to go," I say, "he's coming at us, very fast."

Zambrano doesn't seem to understand that, while some healing magic for Liao Ling would be nice, it won't help her if Rex catches up and flattens all of us. He's single-mindedly focused on the spell, ignoring what's happening in the real world. Is this a sign of the sorcerer madness that overcame all his friends?

"We can do that later," I urge him. "Please."

"I don't want to start this over," Zambrano complains. "It's almost done!"

I glance at Parth, who is looking around with an air that clearly comes across to me as "I wonder if there's anything around here I could use as a weapon." As if there's anything that he could do against an ancient giant demon. But you have to admire his courage. Even if it's unrealistic, foolhardy, and likely to get him killed.

And then Parth throws his hands out, making two circles with his thumbs and forefingers, and shouts "*Bala-kṣepa*" as he pushes them forward. Damn it, he's actually gotten to learn some magic. I am suddenly crazy jealous as two green balls of energy shoot from his hands.

The balls of energy shoot down the stairs and explode and dissipate on the demon's chest, doing no damage and not slowing him at all. But still, it's magic!

"Almost there," Zambrano mutters, and I turn to look at him, panic building in my chest. Below, I can see the giant shape of Rex, barely fitting in the stairwell, charging forward.

"Your intern is right," Seraphex says urgently. "We have to go. You don't have time to finish the spell. The sorcerer will live."

"So close," Zambrano says as the orange glow gets brighter. "I don't want to have to set this spell up a second time, it's very tricky."

"Zambrano! Now!" I shout. The demon is coming faster and raises one of his massive, clawed hands, which has a red light emanating from it. I don't like that. Demons with huge muscles are bad enough, but ones that can shoot projectiles? That seems unfair.

"Okay, done!" Zambrano announces and leaps up, the body of the unconscious sorcerer in his arms.

We all run up the stairs just as there's a loud *crack*. I instinctively look back and see a similar red bolt that Rex used to break out of the slow-time cases. Inside there it took fifteen hundred years to pass through all the cases, but here under the regime of normal time, it moves far quicker—about as fast as a hawk swooping down at us.

As the bolt approaches, I can see that it's aimed straight for Liao Ling, whose body is slung over Zambrano's shoulder.

I'm on the wrong side of the stairs, too far away to do anything. But Parth is closer to them. He moves with incredible speed, boosted by the druidic charm, and I'm honestly not sure whether he was trying to push her out of the way or block the bolt. But in the end, all he's able to do is get in the way of the bolt, like a Secret Service agent trying to protect the president. The bolt slams into his left shoulder, he shrieks in pain, and the force of the blow propels him into Zambrano and Liao Ling, sending all three of them up the stairs in a pile.

My own momentum carries me up several more stairs, and then, suddenly, the smoke and particles in the air are gone, and the stairwell is quiet except for Parth, whose breath is coming in ragged, shocked gasps as he grips his wounded shoulder.

"We've passed into the pocket universe," Seraphex calls out, having managed to stay balanced on my shoulder. "Teleportrait!"

"Everyone grab me!" Zambrano shouts. Liao Ling's body is on top of him, and he's awkwardly digging the painting out of the hidden pocket in his suit jacket with one hand while using the other to push her body up enough so that he can pull it out. It looks like it's slightly bent and cracked, but he straightens it out and motions to me.

Parth looks up at me with bleary, confused eyes, so I grab his arm and pull him toward Zambrano. I put my hand on Zambrano's neck and lean my head over to make sure it's making direct physical contact with Seraphex.

As Zambrano stares at the portrait, there's a sudden roar as the gigantic demon king appears just a couple stairs below us.

"I want to go to there!" Zambrano shouts as the demon king's massive claws jab toward us. My hands tighten their grip on Parth and Zambrano, knuckles white as Seraphex screams at the demon king, a wordless cry of fury. One of the claws swings toward my chest, jagged and gleaming in the dull light. I suck in my breath as I brace for them to sink into me.

And then the demon disappears, the blue stone is gone, and we're dropped onto the glowing red stone of the maze, the second pocket universe.

Parth whimpers, clutching his shoulder, his face scrunched up in pain. But he takes a deep breath, levers himself up, and stands.

"Okay," he says, his voice thin but firm. "Where to now? Are we safe?"

I glare at Zambrano. This wouldn't have happened if he had just *listened to me*. Parth didn't have to be hit by that demonic spell. But instead of following the plan and moving as soon as we saw Rex, the stubborn sorcerer just had to finish his spell. All so he wouldn't have to do it again. Arrogant prick.

"My ex-husband doesn't have the ability to use teleportraits, or any other teleportation for that matter," Seraphex explains. "He'll be trapped in that pocket universe for some time. It's hard to say exactly how long."

"Years?" I ask hopefully.

"Days, a week at the most," Seraphex says sadly. "We've bought ourselves time but not that much."

"Pocket universes are very sensitive since they're so small," Zambrano says. "The spell that I altered to use the teleportraits between the two of them has probably connected them, and the underlying similarity of their math makes them already naturally close. When he forces the blue pocket universe to collapse, it will probably explode into this one. The force of which will probably blow this one up as well."

"So just on the off chance he can blow that thing up faster than we expect, we really don't want to be here any longer than we need to be," I say.

"That's correct," Seraphex agrees. "We should follow the way out of the maze again as quickly as possible. We probably have time, but there's no need to risk it."

"Let's go, then," Parth says. He has been standing very still while we talk, uncharacteristically quiet and reserved, but he has a look of grim determination on his face.

I grit my teeth, wanting to explode at the idiot dark sorcerer who got my friend hurt, but instead I walk along next to him as we navigate the maze. Zambrano leads the way this second time, breezily recounting the unimportant little details of his first escape and how he held off the pocket beast long enough for his allies to rescue him from the outside.

"How are you doing?" I ask quietly as we walk. Parth's breathing is shallow, but he is still able to move fairly quickly, holding his left arm in place with his right. The injury isn't bleeding, instead it looks almost black, like it's been cauterized by the heat of the red bolt that struck him.

"I'm fine," he says, though the tight knitting of his brows says otherwise. "It's just my left arm, you know. I'm a righty. So I can still fight. You know, shoot a gun, wield a sword, throw a spear, play a round of craps, flip the bird at a demon, whatever we need for the next challenge."

"You do need your left arm, you know," I say.

"Yeah, I mean, I do use my left hand to jerk off," he answers. "But I could probably afford to do that a little less anyway, you know? Motivate me to get better at asking girls out, or something."

"Mr. Parth, you are, curiously, both a brave and a disgusting creature, aren't you?" Seraphex notes from my shoulder. "Are those two elements of your personality related in some way?"

"Probably," Parth answers, walking forward with a pained grin fixed on his face.

"How bad is it?" I whisper to Seraphex, letting Parth get ahead and pretending I'm watching behind us for danger so that I can talk quietly with the demon duck on my shoulder.

"If left untreated, he'll die," she says.

"But we can treat it, right? Zambrano has something back at the warehouse?"

"Wounds from demon magic tend to fester and destroy the mortal body," Seraphex answers. "But there are cures, yes."

"Okay, we'll figure it out," I say, as much to myself as to her.

I'm half expecting the hulking demon king to come roaring after us, or another pocket beast to appear, or some other new danger to be lurking in this pocket universe, but we make it back out of it without incident.

When we get to the exit, both Parth and I are painfully forced through the hole in the bricks with the "camel through the eye of the needle" spell that Zambrano still finds amusing, and at this point I am too annoyed to even think about. I tried to land more gracefully but still end up tripping and falling into a wall. I'm fine though, compared to Parth, who almost falls on his shoulder. Luckily, I'm ready for him and am able to catch him before he totally slams down and makes his injury even worse.

Zambrano comes through carrying Liao Ling, making it look easy.

You're really not supposed to move injured people, and you're definitely not supposed to use magic to compress them to the size of a brick and shove them through a portal between universes. But other than some wincing, he seems fine, and Liao Ling is no different than before. She's totally unconscious but breathing regularly. I get Parth sitting against a wall and lie Liao Ling down on the ground while Zambrano spends a few minutes closing off the pocket universe's exit.

"Okay, it's closed off as best I can without spending a week inventing new spells. That should at least slow him down and force him to break out of this pocket universe as well," Zambrano says. "This pocket universe is anchored to this spot in real space, so he'll end up bursting out through here after he escapes."

"We should make our exit from this place," Seraphex says, nervously eyeing the blank spot on the wall where the hole to the pocket universe used to be.

"These two both need medical treatment as soon as possible."

"Let's get going," I agree.

I help Parth back up, and Zambrano grabs Liao Ling, carrying her more gently now that we're no longer being actively pursued by a ten-foot-tall demon.

"What exactly makes two demons married?" I ask as we walk up the same glowing red steps that we used to get out of this place the first time.

"We don't go down to city hall, if that's what you mean," Seraphex says. "We don't recognize silly concepts like governmental approval. We simply make a commitment to each other. From prehistory, my husband and I were the two most powerful demons. It simply made sense for us to become lovers. No other could stand with us as equals.

Even a demon duke like our friend Volcanose would wilt if he tried to couple with one of us."

"Gross," I say.

"So you were each other's only real choices? That doesn't sound like a great basis for a relationship," Parth comments.

"It . . . was never a healthy relationship, no," Seraphex says. "Cities burned to the ground when we fought. Or when we made love. For demons, marriage is a commitment that you make with words. And our word is our bond."

"So once you say that you're married, you have to stick with it forever?" I ask.

"Oh, demons are not quite so foolish as that," the duck on my shoulder answers. "Demonic pacts always have conditions and options. We've been doing this for thousands of years. While many contracts are binding, marriage is a special one. You must fully honor the requirements of the bond while it is intact."

"But you can end it, clearly," I point out, glad to see the light up at the end of this stairwell. We're almost out.

"Yes. In order to end a demonic marriage, one party simply states in the presence and full cognition of the other that they intend to terminate the arrangement. There is then a required waiting period of one century during which you are bound not to enact any plots or otherwise act against each other. This prevents sudden and destructive betrayals. And then, the marriage is concluded."

"And when did you and the former Mr. Seraphex officially call it quits?" Parth asks through gritted teeth.

"Oh, about eighty years before he was trapped in the prismatic prism," Seraphex answers. "He was very displeased, but I couldn't stand the sight of him anymore. The chaos that created in the demonic world was a major part of why Merlin and Liao Ling were able to trick us. We never would have been pulled into their trap if it were not for our internal cold war, waiting for the cooldown period to end."

"And do the years in the slow-time case count as time passing?" I ask, feeling sure that I already know the answer but somehow still hoping.

"They most certainly do," Seraphex says, shifting nervously on my shoulder.

We reach the top of the staircase, emerging onto the tiny little island with the barren seascape all around us. Zambrano wastes no time in gathering us in physical contact and using a teleportrait to take us back to the warehouse.

He places Liao Ling on one of the large, overstuffed reading chairs, while I help Parth down to another one. Zambrano starts by examining the ancient Chinese sorcerer again, casting some additional small healing spells as he pulls back her eyelids to shine a light in her eyes to check for signs of brain injury.

Meanwhile, I take a look at Parth's shoulder, carefully pulling back the scorched shirt in order to examine the wound. It's blackened and charred, like a burger that got accidentally left on the grill too long, and smelling far worse. It's bleeding at the edges but only a small amount.

"Why do you demons have all these rules and codes? The inability to lie or change your mind after you make a promise?" Parth asks Seraphex, pointedly looking away from the spot where I'm poking and prodding him. The duck has landed on one of the reading tables and is lying down, watching the four humans with her head cocked to the side.

"It's because they're all absolutely bastards," Zambrano answers before Seraphex can say anything. "Without the rules, they would constantly betray and undermine one another, and never get anything done. With ironclad agreements and guaranteed true communication, even complete and total assholes can build a society. They still find ways to be nasty, as I'm sure you can imagine."

I look over at Seraphex. She stares back at me blankly.

"Is that true?" I ask her.

Zambrano comes over to Parth and elbows me out of the way.

"More or less," she says. "It's certainly true that without the demonic code, there would be no way to form alliances and make progress. There's enough backstabbing in the demonic world as it is. But as for that being the 'reason' for the demonic code, I couldn't tell you."

"Where do demons come from?" Parth asks. "Like, originally. They clearly aren't part of Earth's evolutionary tree. Unless they're related to my great-aunt."

"I don't know," Seraphex says, barely even considering the question. "How are our patients?"

"You don't know?" I ask. "Just that simple?"

"I haven't put any thought into the question," Seraphex asks. "I was asking about the wounds that these two have. How are they doing?"

I open my mouth, confused at her response.

"They don't think about where they came from," Zambrano says. "Mental block of some sort. They can't explain where the demonic code came from either. Don't bother."

He looks at Parth's wounds and shakes his head. Parth, for his part, has leaned back and is breathing shallowly. I'm not sure if he's unconscious or just conserving his energy.

"How bad is it?" I ask.

"Beyond my ability to fix," he says. "This demonic bolt infests human flesh, worse than necrotizing fasciitis or a staph infection. And antibiotics certainly won't help."

"And Liao Ling?" I ask.

"She's in a coma of some sort," Zambrano says. "I'm not sure how to bring her out of it."

"You can't help *either* of them?" I shout. "What good are you? Parth wouldn't even be in this mess if you'd just *listened* to me. Instead, you had to finish your spell, just because you didn't want to start it all over again. And now he's going to die!"

Zambrano glares at me. "I got us out of there, didn't I?" he shoots back. "Lured the demon king into a pocket universe, closed the door behind him, teleported us away. What did you do? Pull the trigger of a missile that only slowed him down for a few minutes? Is that your big talent, having opposable thumbs? Being undetected by magic only goes so far."

"I just . . . All you needed to do was listen to me when I said we had to leave, and Parth would be fine," I say, glad to finally be able to voice my anger. "You easily could have waited until we were back here. But you just wanted to finish the healing spell you had started, even if it put us all in danger."

The sorcerer growls, but doesn't say anything more, taking another minute to examine each of the two patients.

"I was never good at this medical magic," Zambrano complains, finally looking down at Liao Ling, whose breathing is sounding raspy and stuttering, like she's having a nightmare. "At least not on other people's weird and gross bodies. The best I could do was to stabilize her."

"Weird and gross?" Parth says without opening his eyes or moving his head. "That's one of the most powerful sorcerers of all time that you're talking about. Watch yourself."

"There's no need to start sucking up to her before she's even conscious again. This coma is very deep—she certainly can't hear you. And I don't know how to purge the demonic infestation from your body. We're going to need someone with more expertise than I have in these matters."

"Who's that?" Parth asks.

"Merlin College Medical?" I suggest.

"Or maybe one of the Chinese schools?" Parth suggests. "I read a paper about some really impressive things they're doing in Shanghai. Oh, one of the guys in my dorm at school is in the arcane biology department at the Indian Institute of Magic. That could be worth a shot?"

"No, we don't need the help of a bunch of stuffy self-important academics and research doctors," Zambrano says. "Though that might be more tolerable than the self-righteous pricks that we will need to go to."

"Must we? Really?" Seraphex complains.

"We have to save them. And we need to do it quickly so that we can figure out what sort of disasters and conspiracies Rex is going to create, and stop them."

"Yes, fine," Zambrano says, with an eye roll and a groan of disgust. "We have to ask the damn druids for help."

# CHAPTER 14

"You hold the fort," Zambrano says with a nod at me as he walks to the wall. "I'll go get ready to deal with these assholes. They're going to want an offering of some sort. Enchanted dirt or stale water or whatever. It's fine. I know a guy in Lagos who sells this sort of thing and will know what they want this season. Gonna cost me an arm and a leg—she drives a hard bargain, and she'll know I'm in a rush."

He's complaining like always, but at least he's not wasting any time in trying to help our injured companions. I still want to punch his stupid handsome face, but once again that takes a back seat to saving the lives of my best friend and Earth's only hope against the demon king. But still, I just really want to plant my first in his face. Just once, why can't I do something that's just for *me*?

"Don't let them die," he says as he pulls a teleportrait from the Africa section of the wall.

"How exactly do you expect me to do that?" I ask. "I'm not a doctor!"

Zambrano shrugs as he examines the teleportrait and adjusts his suit, dusting it off and straightening his tie. "How the hell should I know? Neither am I! Keep them comfortable, neither is about to die."

"Can I take them to a doctor?" I ask. "What if Liao Ling wakes up?! And half of this is your fault," I add, gesturing at Parth, "because you're an obstinate idiot who needed to finish his stupid spell. I'm not qualified to be in charge of other people!"

"Bryce Alexander, you are hereby promoted from my intern to my executive assistant," he says, running his hands through his hair. "Now you're fully qualified to . . . assist with this mess on my behalf," he says with a dismissive wave of his hand. "Stall them for a while, I think that's the main thing executive assistants do at big companies, right?"

"They need a doctor, not me! And there better not be another freaking hat," I complain, but by the time I finish, he's already disappeared.

"Congratulations on your new position," Seraphex says from her place on the table. "I'm sure you have a bright future in the exciting field of administrative support."

"Watch out, or I'll have you start making an appointment on his online calendar every time you want to waltz in and say something snarky," I shoot back.

Not knowing what else to do, I run to the closest pharmacy and buy out their first aid section. I'm able to clean up and dress both of their wounds as best I can. I also give Parth a bunch of over-the-counter painkillers when he wakes up, groaning and groggy. I promise you that I would *never* give him more than the FDA recommendations in the dosing instructions on the bottle, and anyone who says they saw me shoving a handful of pills down his throat with a big glass of water is absolutely lying. The birch butlers are fussing around, cleaning up all the blood and trash from bandages, but I've come to trust in their abilities. It's not like I'm a doctor.

Luckily, with the cauterization, a lot of Parth's nerves were burned away, so while he's in a significant amount of pain, it doesn't seem to be totally unbearable. He drifts in and out of consciousness while Liao Ling remains out cold.

"How did we do?" Parth asks, eyes half open during one of his more lucid periods. "Did we make it out? Does the world appreciate my noble sacrifice?"

"We got out," I say, patting him on his uninjured shoulder. "We trapped the demon king, and we rescued the extremely dangerous damsel. But you're not going to make a noble sacrifice, we're going to get you to a druid who can fix you up."

"Hell yeah," he says as he slumps back onto the chair and closes his eyes again. "Get me some of that druid juice, bro."

"You got it, buddy," I say with a chuckle, but his clammy skin and the look on his waxy face have me very worried.

A few minutes later, Zambrano finally appears with a gust of wind and a quiet whooshing sound. He's frowning and holding a pair of heavy gold gauntlets with intricate twisting designs inscribed on them.

"What's that?" I ask.

"They're ancient gauntlets that hide the wearer from demons and demonic magic," Zambrano says, grimacing.

"Oh! That sounds super useful. Did you get something that the druids will want?"

"This is it," he says. "They've been trying to barter for it all week, apparently—they must have some way of detecting that there's a big demonic presence, or maybe they had some sort of surveillance on Merlin's Vault. But druids are a bunch of hippies who don't tend to traffic in worldly goods or participate in capitalism and acquire wealth, so they don't have the resources like I do. I think they'll be happy with the offer. We're on borrowed time with Rex out of the prismatic prison, so we need to try something."

"Oh, so we don't get to keep them," I say. "But they'll barter with us?"

"It's less of a barter situation," Seraphex interjects, "and more of an 'I'm so sorry for my past behavior, here's a trinket for your forgiveness' sort of arrangement."

"Everyone has their price," Zambrano says with a shrug. "Hopefully. I just hate to give up something so valuable just on the off chance we can get some healing. It would have been cheaper if it was just her and not your foolhardy friend."

"Who is hurt because of your stubbornness!" I exclaim.

Zambrano just makes a sour face and motions me to grab Parth while he picks up Liao Ling once more.

*He's helping*, I think as I wake Parth up and help him to his feet. *Don't punch him in the face, he's helping, and we need his help. Also, he could melt you into a puddle of goo with a flick of his toe, probably. And we need him if we're going to have any chance to stop Rex's machinations now that the demon king is out.*

Parth is much slower than he was during our escape, leaning heavily on me as we make our way to Zambrano.

"Have fun, boys," Seraphex says, hopping off the table and walking toward the stairs with a gait that I've come to recognize as her "I'm going to get some food now" walk.

"You're not coming?" I ask.

"I don't like hippies," she says over her shoulder as she starts hopping up the stairs.

"The druids are angry enough with me as it is," Zambrano says. "Bringing a demon along, in any physical form, will not be a help."

"Makes sense," I agree as Zambrano grabs my neck and stares at a teleportrait with a painting of what looks like a restaurant on it. "I want to go to there."

With a whoosh, we're in what feels like the back dining room of a restaurant. An older, balding man with wispy hair looks up from one of the tables, not the least bit surprised by our arrival.

"Grand to see you, ya divil," he says, his Irish lilt thick and slightly hard for me to understand. "Your motor's outside, ready when you are. If ye find trouble out there, don't be draggin' it back here."

The room is empty other than the man, tables, and a well-stocked bar. Beyond one door, I can hear the bustle of an active kitchen, and beyond the other, I catch a glimpse of another bar through a door with a small circular window.

"Good to see you too, Dermot," Zambrano says. "I'll do my best as always. I'd stay for a fish and chips, but we're in a rush."

"Ah, it's always life and death with you, innit? Yer a right drama queen, so y'are!" Dermot says as we head for the door. As we exit, I glance behind and see, perched on top of the bar, what looks at a glance like the little stick figure of a birch butler. Is this man a wizard, I wonder, with the same servants as Zambrano?

Unfortunately, Zambrano doesn't have a teleportrait particularly close to the druids, so we're treated to a several-hour drive through the Irish countryside in an SUV that Zambrano has hired. The driver, luckily, doesn't ask any questions. The landscape is lovely, but every moment is nerve-racking as Parth is huddled in the seat next to me, alternating feverish sleep and staring listlessly out the window.

Finally, the SUV climbs up a long hill, reaching a rambling old country house. It's perched on a bluff facing the ocean, and the sun is setting out over the water. We get out of the car, with Zambrano awkwardly carrying both Liao Ling and the gauntlets, while I let Parth lean on my shoulder and help him walk up the long path to the house. With the injured in tow, it takes us about five minutes to make our way up the hill.

As we climb up the steps to the old house, the door swings open and a woman with red hair wipes her hands on an apron ushers us in. Her hair is wild and unkempt, and her clothes remind me of those "traditional rural life" Instagram influencers, though more stained and lived in. Or what I imagine Martha Stewart used to look like, back when she was in her thirties and before she went to jail and started hanging out with Snoop Dogg.

"Welcome, welcome," she says with a much lighter Irish accent than the man in the restaurant as she ushers us in through the entryway to the living room. "Pardon the mess, I didn't know when you would arrive, and I like to watch my shows while I make dumplings."

The "mess" in question is a perfectly spotless room and one large tray of mostly wrapped-up dumplings sitting on the coffee table in front of the TV. I guess there's a tiny spill of flour on the coffee table.

"Zambrano," she says with a frosty nod at the sorcerer. "It's been quite a few years."

"Ah, yes, indeed," Zambrano says awkwardly. "It's good to see you again."

"Please, let me help with your injured," she says, assisting us in getting both Liao Ling and Parth lying on couches in the living room. "And who is your young friend?" she adds as we help them down.

"Oh, that's Bryce Alexander. He's freshly promoted!" Zambrano says. "He's no longer an intern, and now holds the title of . . . associate? Analyst? Actuary? What did I say?"

"You said 'assistant,'" I say, "but those other ones sounds cooler, so we can swap if you'd like."

"No, no," Zambrano answers, "Assistant it is."

"Oh, you poor dearie," the woman says. "We all need to make a living."

"Are you a druid?" I blurt out.

"Yes, young man. My name is Deirdre Moran, and I'm a practitioner of the untamed magicks. I have been trained in the old druidic traditions, in which we respect the autonomy of magic and accept its wild nature rather than attempting to force it into human ideas of precision."

I can tell Zambrano wants to pick a fight with her, but he holds it in and offers her the gauntlets.

"I've brought you a gift," Zambrano says. "Please accept it as a token of my . . ." He pauses for a moment. "I'm sorry, okay? I shouldn't have melted your castle. That was rude of me."

The woman shrugs. "I accept your gift, and your apology. My father said that that old castle was drafty and had so very many steps. With only a few of us left, we would have had to leave it anyway, eventually. And these gauntlets are indeed a fine gift. They will be very useful in the fight ahead."

"Can you tell the future?" I ask, eyes wide.

"Yes," Zambrano says, "are you going to feed us with ill omens and dark portents, and cryptic prophecies that always come true because they're so vague that you can always interpret them as fact?"

The woman smiles, eyes sparkling. "Oh no, no, those days are long behind us. Since assuming the responsibilities of being the new arch druid, I've done away with that. I always felt that prophecies were a crutch. And on close inspection, they didn't really make sense. If we could see the future and would only give cryptic misleading clues, was it really believable that that was the best way to guide events to a good outcome?"

"Hold on, you just made those prophecies up?" Zambrano says with a glare.

"Oh, yes. The elders believed that if you prophesied a noble hero, it would encourage enough folk to try that one would succeed. But lately, our world's 'heroes' haven't been exactly commoners who we could later forge a few documents and claim were long-lost nobility once they fulfilled our prophecies. They've been more . . ." She gestures at Zambrano.

"We did save the world though," Zambrano points out.

"Sometimes you saved it, sometimes you endangered it," Deirdre says. "But yes, I wouldn't be meeting with you if I didn't think you could help in our current situation. Come, let's see to these two."

She takes a minute to examine Parth's injured shoulder, which becomes immobilized as the demonic magic takes hold, and Liao Ling, who remains unconscious.

"These two are in bad shape," she says, brow wrinkling with concern. "But I think we can help them."

"Thank you," I say, breathing a sigh of relief.

"We'll need to use the old remedies," she says. "Please bring them this way."

We gather them up and make our way through the house and out through the back door. Farther up toward the bluff, there's a small ring of trees, and in the center of it a large circular white tent. Looking back at the house, I see the faces of two small children on the second floor, pressed against the window glass and staring at us.

Inside the tent, there's a fire burning, and the air is thick with the smell of burning herbs, which are hung in little clay pots around the edges of the tent.

An older man who had been tending the fire gives Deirdre a tight smile, helps us get the two patients onto cots nearby, and then exits through the main flap.

"Will you be able to use your magic to heal them?" I can't help myself from asking. "If it's untamed and wild, how do you know it will work?"

"I will explain so that you are comfortable with the process," Deirdre says patiently. "And as the other young man is incapacitated and you are his close friend, you will be making healing decisions for him. Does that seem fair, reasonable, and just?"

"Um, yes," I say. "That's actually very thoughtful." Maybe these druids aren't as bad as Zambrano and Seraphex make them out to be.

"There are multiple types of magic," the druid begins. "The most well-known is invoked magic."

"You mean real magic," Zambrano interrupts. "Actual magic that can be controlled and directed."

"Invoked magic," the druid continues, as if she were not interrupted, "allows the creation of specific spells, training the force of magic to follow specific commands and dictates. These spells can then be invoked by performing the necessary gestures and sounds, or with ingredients. Unique, recognizable patterns are important."

"Yeah, the useful kind that doesn't have unintended consequences," Zambrano says.

"A common type is untamed magick, or wild magic, or druidic magic as others call it. This is where we activate magic through gifts and point it in the direction of what we need it to do. We trust it to do what is best, not what we expect. We respect the natural order and put our trust in balance and the wisdom of magic."

"You trust it to act randomly," Zambrano says.

"The third type of magic," Deirdre continues, running her hand through her wild red hair, "is demonic magic. Demons do not seem to call upon magic themselves, but rather their abilities appear to me as magic that is already in process. It is continuously expressed, not invoked or encouraged into existence."

"So in other words, demonic magic is weird and evil, invoked magic is useful and predictable, and wild magic is unpredictable and useless," Zambrano says, his volume growing along with his vitriol.

"We will be using the magic of the druids to heal your friends. I must tell you that success is likely but not guaranteed. But I believe it is their best chance at survival. I also should tell you that there may be unintended effects, either good or bad, and they may take time to manifest. Our powers are unpredictable, and magic can at times be a playful trickster."

"Unlike real magic," Zambrano says, "which actually does what I tell it to. And doesn't randomly cause terrible outcomes that ruin everything."

The druid turns to the sorcerer and regards him calmly with her hazy green eyes. "I am sorry," she says. "I am sorry that my ancestors were not able to save the sorcerer Alix LaFontaine when you brought her to us."

"Your magic is useless," the sorcerer growls. "It barely does anything of value. That's why its last few practitioners are hidden around the world in little hovels like this. It's pathetic. *You should have been able to save her.*"

Deirdre nods slowly. "I wish we could have. But recall, it was you who mortally wounded her."

"I had to!" Zambrano roars. "I HAD NO CHOICE. I would have let her kill me if she needed to. If it made her stop, return to herself, I would have let her throw me to the demons if it made her happy. But she would have killed all of us, all of the Circle, and all of humanity if she had been allowed to continue." He slams his fist into the ground, stands, and storms out of the tent, throwing the flap aside and leaving it hanging open after he departs.

"You really wound him up," I say after Zambrano is gone.

Deirdre shrugs. "I can't predict the future through magic, but I can predict it the normal human way—which is to say, I was fairly certain that if he stayed in here, he would cause some sort of trouble. Now I can work in peace. Perhaps you could go calm him down but also keep him away for a few hours? This will not be a quick process."

"Sure," I say. "And . . . thanks. Thanks for trying, at least."

The druid smiles gently at me as she picks up a bowl of water and begins stirring it with first a silver rod, then a gold one, then one made of bone.

"It's my pleasure. And you will certainly need this ancient sorcerer if you're going to defeat the demon king and save the world."

"Are you *sure* you can't predict the future?"

She smiles. "Certainly, I can predict that you and these two sorcerers will defeat the demon and save us all."

"You can predict that?"

"I might as well—if you fail, we'll all die and no one will be around to tell me I was wrong, will they?"

# CHAPTER 15

I catch up to Zambrano out on the bluffs, and god damn if he isn't looking like a brooding hero with his white hair whipping in the ocean breeze, his hands stuffed in his suit pockets, and his gaze fixed out on the horizon.

"Shouldn't someone be watching the druids to make sure they don't pull any funny business?" he asks.

"I think we have to trust them at this point, one way or the other," I say. "Leave her alone to work her magic. I saw a couple more of them headed into the tent with more supplies. I think they're doing everything they can."

"Yeah," Zambrano says with a nod.

For a couple long minutes we just stand there, looking out onto the choppy sea. The sun has set, but it's still in that early evening magic hour even as the first few stars start to appear.

"What was she like?" I ask. "Alix LaFontaine?" I've heard that when someone is grieving, they don't want to avoid the subject but to be given a chance to talk about it to "process" it. Though I'm not sure how much that applies with someone who died over a hundred years ago.

Zambrano takes a deep breath.

"She was the most brilliant sorcerer that I'd ever met. She was already well established in the French courts when I met her, just a young idiot wizard trying to make a name for myself. I was instantly taken with her, but she was always with some duke or prince or what have you. But she taught me spellcraft, and she even tried to teach me humility. That part never really took. I remember the first spell we created together, one to heat and shape stone the way a blacksmith forges from metal. We used it to reshape the gargoyles on many cathedrals into the vilest little perverts, it was ludicrous. The archbishop of Notre Dame was *not* pleased, let me tell you. We kept the stonemasons well employed that year though.

"Alix was almost a hundred years older than I was, but after a few decades around each other, those things stop mattering to sorcerers. And eventually I ascended to the level of sorcerer and traveled the world learning from many others. When I returned, things had changed, and she saw me in a new light. She cheated on and broke up with a French duke to be with me. The whole incident actually sparked some nonsense called the War of the Three Henrys, but that's another story. After that, we were together on and off for centuries. We'd be together for a decade or two, then break up for another, then come crashing back together."

Zambrano pauses for a long moment, likely caught up in those memories.

"It all came apart at last when Seraphex was able to somehow project her power across the solar system, all the way from Mars, to come to this planet. We never figured out how she returned to Earth, but when Sera appeared in rural Texas, the Sorcerers' Circle geared up to fight her. Alix had always been clever in her spellcraft and an expert in demonology. She learned everything she could about demonic magic and invented spells that would help us trap and transform Seraphex. The duck shape in particular was my idea. It started out as a joke between us one morning, but it made sense in the end as the best fit. We would have transformed her into a brick if we could have, but there's only so far we could take that transmogrification and keep it permanently stable."

I listen silently, staring out at the sea along with the sorcerer, who suddenly looks much older and more harrowed than usual.

"Alix had always been fascinated by demons and demonic magic. As the druid mentioned, it's different from ours, like a power that is continuously in action, rather than called upon. But she learned so much about it and used her own magic to control and modify it. After we defeated Seraphex, the madness started to set in. She believed that, with their queen out of the way, she could open a portal to Mars and bring the demonic hordes here. She thought she could control them, having absorbed some of Seraphex's power in the battle. She had learned all that could be learned here on Earth and thirsted for more knowledge. I already told you what happened next."

"Yeah," I say gently. "You had to trick her into thinking you were on her side, going to help her open the portal, to get close enough to defeat her."

"I took the life right out of her. Drained it straight from the heart," he says, his voice breaking. "But some demonic magic was still in her body, keeping it alive. So I brought her to a castle that was not far from here. I swallowed my pride and asked the druids for help. They tried, in a tent just like that one, working on her day and night for almost a week. In the end, they were able to drain the demonic magic out of her. But she was gone. Her body failed, and that was that."

"I'm sorry," I say, putting my hand on his shoulder. For once, he doesn't shove me away.

"I saw it happen," the sorcerer says, his voice catching in his throat. "I saw her last breath shudder out of her body. As I drew my powers up, the druids fled. I started casting, and I didn't stop casting. I used that same spell we created together all those years ago. In my rage I tore that castle down, brick by brick. Instead of shaping it, I just melted it until it was just a puddle in the rocks it was built on."

A long minute passes as Zambrano ruminates and I digest this.

"I guess we're lucky that all it took to get back in their good graces was giving them those gauntlets," I say finally. "Very forgiving of them."

"Yeah, well, that and it's been a hundred years, and everyone who was there when I turned their castle into slag is long dead. Druids don't extend their lives the way that sorcerers do. Something about the natural order. Dumb crunchy snowflakes. Having to get old and die is so dumb!"

I want to argue with him on behalf of the noble druids, but I have to admit I agree. I'm not really a big fan of dying, and getting old seems like it would suck. If I could use some sorcery to prevent all that? You're damn right I'd do it. If it meant slowly losing my sanity and possibly becoming a terrible villain? Okay, maybe it's not necessarily that easy an answer.

We stand there for a long moment. Then a question pops into my head, and I can't help but let it out. "What was my birth mother like?" I ask. "Zuzanna, the great sorcerer of Poland? As a person? Back in the good old days, before she started to lose it."

Zambrano smiles. "She was a character. Pretty much every sorcerer is, I think. 'Big personality' comes with the territory. Not sure if our eccentric nature leads us to the magic, or the magic warps us. Probably a bit of both. But she was a wild one. She was a mentalist, able to create spells to affect moods, create unparalleled illusions, uncover hidden memories, and much more. That's how she was able to lock her own magical essence away. She understood the human mind in a way that no other sorcerer ever had before her. Whatever is wrong with Liao Ling? Your mother would have fixed it by now. She loved healing people from magical ailments."

"So she used her powers for good?"

"Oh, yes, when she wasn't using them for fun, at least," Zambrano said. "She was one of those people who connected with everyone and made everyone around her feel good. That's why Caravello shared the knowledge of how to work the arcane conduit with Zuzanna and no one else. I thought that secret died with her, but I guess it doesn't matter now since we threw one end of the arcane conduit into the sun," he notes with a shrug. "Zuzanna was a real spark plug. She helped the rest of us unlock our potential. She loved joy, surprise, adventure, made the most inappropriate jokes . . ."

"I don't want to hear about when you dated her," I snap.

"Oh, well there was that. But it went beyond the pleasures of the flesh," he says, setting my stomach churning. "But seriously, she was a healer and a crafty fighter when it came to that. She caught Seraphex in a web of mental tricks, somehow implanted some false memories that tripped up her demonic nature. She figured out that if you can convince a demon that they agreed to something, they're suddenly magically bound to it, at least until they figure out the ruse. But at that point, the rest of the Circle was all over the demon. She was a good person, Bryce. A great arcane researcher, a solid ally, and a good friend. And . . ." His voice trails off, but suddenly he's grinning even though there are tears in his eyes. "She might still be out there, huh? Old, sure, but it's possible. Alix is gone, but Zuzanna may still live."

"I think I'd like to meet her," I say, suddenly shaking off some of the shell of conflicted feelings I've had about her. "I think I might be ready for that."

"Just make sure she knows you're her son, or she'll probably hit on you," Zambrano says. "You're not much to look at, but she always had a soft spot for confused skinny boys."

I punch him in the arm, but he just grins at me and puts a hand on my shoulder. We stand there for several long moments until Zambrano clears his throat and turns to walk back toward the tent.

"Enough of that, let's go see if these druids have accidentally killed either your friend or Earth's only hope against the forces of darkness," he says, and I hurry to follow him.

# CHAPTER 16

The druids have not, thankfully, accidentally killed either of their patients. They haven't, as a matter of fact, done much at all yet. We spend the next two days waiting, anxiously checking our phones for any sign of Rex bursting back into our reality with vengeance on his brain. I ask if we can spend the night in the big house to be near Parth in case anything happens, but the druids have not entirely learned to trust Zambrano. We are curtly informed that the risk of us burning the place down in the middle of the night and killing the druids and their children is too high.

Which is fair.

So we get two rooms in a little bed-and-breakfast a couple miles down the coast, make them promise to call us if anything happens, and return each morning. The evening of the second full day there, Zambrano is working on a new teleportrait so that we can come and go from here as needed, and I'm wandering along the bluff again, when one of the druids comes out and shouts for us. We follow them back, and I'm greeted by Parth grinning like a maniac as he steps out of the tent.

He looks gaunt as hell and is walking unsteadily, but he's able to very gently wrap his arms around me in a careful hug.

"How are you feeling?" I ask.

"Oh, like a train ran over me and then backed up to make sure it had finished the job," he says. "But my shoulder and arm feel good, and the nice lady told me that the demonic presence is drained out. They told me that I lost so much weight because the druid magic drains my own energy for healing."

"Good you're recovering, at least," I say.

"I'll need a little recovery time, but I'll be ready for the next adventure," he says. "Just need to learn some more powerful spells first, right? My force bolt didn't do shit against that big-ass demon."

"You got hurt pretty badly," I say. "Do you see how dangerous this sort of thing can be? Are you sure you want to keep helping us?"

"Uh, what?" Parth asks. "You're going to try to keep me from this? You know what this whole ordeal means, right?"

"No, what does it mean?"

"I survived a battle against the most powerful and scary demon ever! I AM INVINCIBLE!"

"Riiight," I say as I put my head in my hands. But I can't help but laugh. I'm just glad he's okay and back to his usual self.

"Unless you need me right now though," Parth adds, "I definitely need some time to recover. The druids told me that if I try to run or fight for the next few weeks, the healing magic will be overwhelmed and I'll collapse."

"Probably good for you to get back though, right?"

"No, it sucks. I have to go back to school!" Parth complains, but even the effort of speaking loudly seems to exhaust him.

"Don't you have exams coming up? That might be worth taking care of," I suggest.

"Ugh, I guess so. I am behind," he admits. "If I can't fight, I should get back and study. Do you think Zambrano can take me? I don't think I'm in good shape for a flight around the world."

"Oh, yeah, sure," I say. "I'm sure I can convince Zambrano to teleport you back as soon as he's done with the new teleportrait to Ireland."

I'm pretty sure Zambrano took extra time with this teleportrait for the druid's coastal retreat because it's extra-large and he spent most of two days on it. It's a gorgeous seascape, and I can't help but admire his skill. When I ask him to take Parth to India, he rolls his eyes and complains, but he does it without too much fuss. I'd like to think he feels a bit responsible for Parth getting hurt in the first place. But if he does, he doesn't say anything.

That night we're able to spend back at the warehouse, where we fill Seraphex in on our progress and have to listen to her complain about how there's "absolutely nothing interesting happening" with us gone. Which is comforting, because I think if she was plotting some terrible betrayal, it would at least qualify as something interesting.

When we return to Ireland the next day, we're ushered into the tent in the middle of the circle of what I've learned are ancient oak trees, so tall that they form a loose canopy above the tent.

Inside, Deirdre calls us over to the cot where Liao Ling is lying. The ancient sorcerer has a silver coin placed on her forehead just above and between her eyes.

"I believe that I've healed most of her injuries," the druid says. "There was demonic infestation, similar to your friend, as well as a more traditional concussion and various blunt force trauma and laceration injuries. The untamed arcane energy doesn't like demonic energy, so it wasn't hard to encourage it to push out the energy. Then it was just a matter of healing charms and some conventional medicine."

I notice that in addition to sprigs of herbs, basins of water, and gold and silver implements, there are also conventional medical supplies like bandages, antibiotic ointment, and what looks like a bottle of some sort of painkillers. I guess the druids are fairly practical.

"I've kept her asleep to let her heal, but I believe we're ready to wake her up. I wanted to have you here in case anything goes awry."

"You mean in case she starts shooting fireballs or arcane bolts or something, eh?" Zambrano says.

"Something like that," Deirdre says with a smile. She removes the silver coin from Liao Ling's forehead, incanting something in what sounds like an old Irish dialect. And then as she finishes she puts two fingers to Liao Ling's head and speaks in English. "Forces of nature, thank you for sharing your strength with us," she intones. "At your leave, we invite you to depart." And then she turns back to us. "This may take a few moments. I think the untamed magicks had fun beating up on the dark forces and casting them out."

I want to ask a million follow-up questions about how her type of magic works and how it relates to Zambrano's more traditional and scientific style, but this clearly isn't the time, as Liao Ling begins to stir.

She groans, and moans, and opens her eyes.

And then she gives us all a wide grin.

She says several sentences in Chinese, bobbing her head cheerfully, but I don't understand at all.

I look expectantly at Zambrano, but he just shrugs. "Hey, I don't speak every single language, you know. Certainly not Middle Chinese from the sixth century."

She speaks more but quickly realizes that we can't communicate with her. She tries a few different languages, and Zambrano is able to get across a couple rudimentary concepts using the scraps of words that they share.

He's able to convey that the demon king is not here but also not defeated, and at that Liao Ling frowns.

Finally, she shakes her head in frustration. Deirdre and I back up in alarm as she starts incanting some sort of spell, but Zambrano just smiles and nods, holding up a hand for us to remain calm. Finally, Liao Ling falls back onto the cot, staring up at the ceiling with a curious expression, taking everything in the tent in as if it were brand-new to her.

"She's regressed her brain to have some qualities of infancy," Zambrano explains. "This way she'll learn the language very quickly. But she'll be a confused sponge and not really able to plan or express much. I don't *think* she'll need diapers, but I'm not familiar with her particular version of the spell."

Over the next couple days we're relieved to find that she does not, thankfully, require diapers. But she does require constant ordering of food, taking in each different cuisine with relish. Beyond the basics like "hello" and "bathroom," she gets to "pizza," "curry," and "hamburger" with surprising quickness. And with her brain overclocked like crazy, she just keeps eating nonstop. She gains back some body weight from the wasting effects of the healing and picks up English with shocking speed. The druids at first teach her like a child, but before long they just sit her in front of the TV while she watches Netflix shows at double speed, absorbing both the language and the modern world at a terrifying pace. Zambrano and I stop in a couple times a day, watching as she goes from helpless to fully communicative over the course of about seventy-two hours.

"You know," I tell Zambrano as we're walking to the house from the teleportrait's arrival spot on the third day, "seeing how easily she learned to speak English with magic makes it a lot less impressive how many languages you know."

The sorcerer shrugs. "Isn't speaking languages just an extremely basic skill set that any intelligent person should have on hand? I never asked you to be impressed or said it was impressive."

"Oh. Huh. I guess that's true." Damn, he got me on that one.

"Greetings, friends," Deirdre says as we walk up onto the porch. "Come on in."

"How is she?" I ask.

"I think the language-learning spell has mostly worn off," the druid says. "Her knowledge and personality have reasserted themselves, and she's back to who she once was. Though she does have a very strong command of English."

"Where is she?" Zambrano asks.

"Upstairs on the third floor, playing with the children," Deirdre says. "Come on up, loves, I'll show you to her."

As we mount the stairs, I start to get nervous. Liao Ling must have been raised in an incredibly traditional and restrictive society with totally different social norms and expectations from ours. And how do I even greet her? Is there some sort of bow or verbal greeting? And it doesn't escape my mind that she's a sorcerer and can deal with any affront with overwhelming magic that not even Zambrano may be able to counter.

We climb up to the second story, and the druid sweeps into the room, grabbing the two kids and hustling them out of the room. She's warmed up to us over the past few days, but apparently still is worried that we might corrupt the kids.

Liao Ling is sitting on the floor, continuing to play with the Lego sets strewn all over the room that look left over from the eighties or nineties. She's wearing jeans and a T-shirt that are a couple sizes too big.

Zambrano clears his throat, and the Chinese sorcerer glances over her shoulder, then carefully puts her Lego pirate ship on the floor and jumps to her feet.

"What's up, bitches?" she says with a big grin. "You asshats need my help to stop a demon apocalypse?"

"Excuse me?" Zambrano says.

"I'm sorry," Deirdre says, returning to the room and closing the door to the kids' bedroom. "She got on the internet last night while she was still in sponge-brain mode and absorbed some 'language.' Her English is impressive though, isn't it?"

"Does she use that sort of language in front of the kids?" I can't help but ask.

"Oh, we're not worried about that sort of thing," Deirdre says. "We believe in speaking to children like adults. We teach them that it's not the language that's the problem, it's the meaning and ultimately actions behind the language. For instance, some people can be very well spoken and say the prettiest things, tell you they've changed from who they used to be, take you out a few times, and then take you on a nice date to Seoul for Korean barbecue and just . . . get distracted and leave you there," she says with a sidelong glance at Zambrano.

"That was so many years ago," Zambrano says dismissively, "when I was young, impulsive, and foolish."

"It was twenty years ago," Deirdre says, "and you were already centuries old. I was *at* your five hundredth birthday party!"

"Oh, right," Zambrano says. "It was quite the spectacular night though, wasn't it? With the arcane fireshow and all that?"

"Yes, the lights were pretty," Deirdre says with an eye roll, though I don't get the sense that she's still that angry after all these years, just needling the sorcerer for her amusement.

"Thank you. I worked hard on them," Zambrano responds, ignoring her sarcasm.

"Focus, people!" I say. Partly because the fate of the world hangs in the balance, but mostly because I don't need to hear more about the idiot sorcerer's love life.

"Yes, you need my help, right?" Liao Ling says. "Or did you break me out of the prismatic prism because you thought I would be cool to hang out with and didn't notice the giant demon looming inside? Whoops!"

"The prismatic prison was about to shatter no matter what," Zambrano says haughtily. "Our *hope* was that you, great and famous sorcerer that you are, would be able to help us figure out how to trap or otherwise defeat him. And save all of humanity, as I have so many times in the past."

"Oh, yeah, the druids told me about that. You let the rest of the sorcerers die off, huh? Killed some of them yourself too? I mean, I got frustrated with the other spellcrafters, sure, especially that Merlin bastard. I can't believe I trusted him."

"I did what I had to do," Zambrano answers. "I have always acted in the best interests of this world. And I only killed a handful of sorcerers. Mostly, they've simply become less and less common over the years. Magic is harder to learn these days, apparently."

"Merlin intentionally trapped me in the prismatic prison, you know," Liao Ling continues, ignoring Zambrano's statement. "I stabbed the demon king in the back with the Caesar Special, and when I tried to use my spell to soar to safety, Merlin had a counter ready to go. Another of his little traps."

"We suspected as much," Zambrano says. "He was abominably clever with those traps, wasn't he?"

"Oh, don't you go admiring him like all the rest of them," Liao Ling spits. "We were at war for the fate of humanity, and he betrayed me for petty jealousy. He was never the hero he pretended to be. Are you any better?"

"I've long since given up on trying to convince anyone that I'm some sort of hero," Zambrano notes. "The common people are idiots."

"Maybe they're not so dumb after all," Liao Ling says with a shrug. "You certainly don't have hero vibes."

The two are starting to look at each other suspiciously, and I'm not stupid enough to get in the middle of this little clash of egos. Especially given the knowledge that sorcerers tend to go mad over time. Zambrano is already emotionally unstable—how long before he goes fully unhinged?

"How would you like us to address you?" I ask politely, trying to get things back on track. I know that most Asian names have the first name at the end, but I'm not sure how that translates from ancient times to modern ones.

"My full name is Liao Ling," she says with a shrug. "That's all anyone used to call me, though sometimes there were some swear words added in the middle. I certainly don't need any titles. In my experience, people who throw fancy titles around are usually trying to take advantage of you one way or another."

"Great, thanks," I say. "And how are you adjusting to life in our time?"

"It's freakin' *great*," Liao Ling says. "I worked so hard to become a sorcerer to escape all the bullshit of my home. Back then, women couldn't own property or run businesses or inherit anything. I found this T-shirt in the bottom of Deirdre's drawer—I would have been fined just for wearing it, just because it doesn't cover my arms. Though once I was powerful enough, there often wasn't much they could do about it." She rubs her thumb and forefingers together, and I step back in alarm as glowing red sparks fly from her hand. "I'm going to need some new clothes though. I hate your modern fashions almost as much as I hated the ones back in my time. These," she says, gesturing to both her own clothes and ours, "are so boring. I'm going to need to get them custom made."

"Well, I can certainly help with that," Zambrano says, brightening up. "I have a good shop in Italy, and I know several custom fabricators on Oxford Street in London, and there's a great new place in Hong Kong that I've been wanting to try out . . ."

"That sounds great," I say, "but maybe we should focus on the task at hand? Rex is going to break out of the pocket universe at any moment. It's up to us to save the world. Now that Parth is okay, all that matters is stopping the demon king no matter what it takes."

"Oh, right," Zambrano says. "There is all that. We should get back to the warehouse to start planning. I hate to admit it, but we'll need Seraphex's expertise on this."

"The demon queen is here on Earth? And she's helping you?" Liao Ling asks, taken aback. "I thought you were something of a great hero. I watched a documentary about how you defeated the Leviathan. There wasn't footage of your battle with it. But I saw the newsreels of the damage that mythic monster did to Japan earlier. And you're allied with Seraphex, the god damn demon queen?"

"Don't worry, she's been transmogrified into a duck," Zambrano says, practically beaming with pride. "She's on our side now. Mostly."

"I got her to promise to be friends with us," I say, unable to help bragging a bit myself.

"He did do that," Zambrano says, nodding in appreciation. "His recent promotion is well earned, I'd say."

"Fascinating, but still terribly disappointing," Liao Ling says. "That is an interesting development—I don't believe a demon has ever made that sort of pact before, at least not in my time—but she's still a demon. How can you ever work with her?"

Deirdre looks back and forth between the two sorcerers. "You know, druid lore says that demons were allowed to enter our world by sorcerers making deals with dark forces to try to gain power for themselves. Is more of that really going to help?"

"That's nonsense! Total balderdash," Zambrano declares. And then he looks over at Liao Ling. "Right?"

She shrugs. "I have no idea. Even in my time, demons had always been around. As much of a prideful little bitch that he was, even Merlin can't be held responsible for that."

Deirdre sighs. "In any event, I think that I've done all that I can to help you. Or all I can stomach, at least. Good luck."

We make our way out of the house and collect a few things that we'd left around while waiting here for the past few days. As we're standing outside, Zambrano is explaining to Liao Ling how the teleportraits work, and Deirdre bustles out of the house, holding something under her arm.

"Bryce," she says, "one more thing. Being assistant to one sorcerer is bad enough. With two around, it's hard for me to imagine your life expectancy is particularly long. Take this. you're going to need it more than we will."

The druid shoves the gauntlets into my hands, and I take them, feeling their hefty weight and the chill of the cool gold metal on my skin.

"Thank you," I say, looking at the gleam of the sunlight on its twisting designs. "These will probably extend my life expectancy by, oh, several minutes at least."

"Bryce, you know you don't have to do this, right?" Deirdre says. "You don't need to risk your life for him."

"I kind of do," I say. "For the same reason that you have to do healing for him even though he's a jerk to you. The fate of the world hangs in the balance. If me risking my life improves the chance of beating Rex by even a few percent . . . It sucks, but that math makes sense."

"That's very altruistic of you," she says, squeezing my shoulder with maternal affection.

I shrug. "Besides, without this, what am I? Some non-magical dud working on the assistant manager track at a Samba Smoothies. I guess there's a little ego in there along with the altruism."

"I certainly won't betray your secret to anyone," Deirdre says with a smile.

We both laugh, and she gives me a hug. It feels weird and unexpected to deal with someone who's actually nice.

As she returns into the house, Zambrano and Liao Ling are deep in conversation about the finger points of the magical pattern recognition that makes teleportraits successfully guide teleportation across the world.

Once Deirdre is gone, Zambrano turns to me and gives a wink.

"Nice work!" he says. "You played the part of a nice guy who only really cares about helping his friend and saving the world really well. Totally took her in! Killer acting."

"It . . . You think I was acting?" I sputter. I put the gauntlets into my backpack, admiring the shine of them but being very annoyed at how much space they take up. Thankfully, we're using the miracle of teleportraits to get where we're going, because there's no chance that I'd get these metal monstrosities through airport security.

Zambrano shrugs and puts his hand on my neck as he focuses intently on the teleportrait in his hand. Liao Ling grabs my upper arm, Zambrano says the magic words, and the Irish coast disappears.

# CHAPTER 17

The warehouse appears around us, and Liao Ling immediately drops my arm and steps forward to examine the many artifacts and magical items around the lab.

"Hey!" Zambrano says as she starts poking and prodding. "That is a priceless relic! And that test subject is very fragile!"

"You have the Sword of Wayland" she says, exclaiming as she sees the glass sword in a display case and runs over to it. "I thought that was lost after that knucklehead Walter died."

"You knew them?" Zambrano asks. "It was around the same time you were alive, I believe."

"Wayland was a friend of mine, in fact," Liao Ling says. "Brilliant artificer. Never quite reached the level of sorcerer, but he created incredible artifacts. I traveled from China to Scandinavia to recruit Wayland's help in forging the arcane conduit so we could banish the demonic scum from Earth. He forged the physical conduit that Merlin enchanted and powered with volcanic energy. And that bastard Merlin never gave me the actual spell that activated the conduit. Greedy, distrustful bastard."

"It's okay," Zambrano says, "Caravello and Zuzanna never trusted me with that spell either."

"Wayland certainly shouldn't have trusted Walter," Liao Ling notes.

"Who were they?" I ask. "Wayland and Walter?"

"Heroes of ancient Germanic myth," Zambrano says. "Not many details are known. But Wayland the Smith is supposed to have forged many great artifacts, including 'mimung,' also known as the Sword of Wayland, which was wielded by the great hero Walter of Aquitaine. Were you friends with him as well?"

"Ugh, no, he was an idiot," Liao Ling says with a disgusted shake of her head. "He stole the sword and some other artifacts from Wayland, and then when the Burgundians came after him, he used the sword to slaughter them. Cut right through their weapons and armor like they weren't even there. And then he spun that into some great victory and became king of Aquitaine. I really hate the hero-with-a-sword types. Always hogging the credit and doing nothing of real value. You really can't trust anyone who doesn't cast their own spells," she says. "No offense," she adds with a glance at me.

"None taken," I say. "Well, some offense taken, to be honest. But a manageable amount."

"Where did you find the sword?" Liao Ling asks. "We went looking for it when Walter died, but it was gone."

"It . . . well it just showed up," Zambrano says with a shrug. "A couple years ago. I haven't had it very long."

"A legendary magical sword . . . just showed up?" I say, shocked. "What, did someone just leave it on your doorstep?"

"Er, well . . . actually, that's not far off. Somehow it appeared right here on the inside of the door," he says, pointing to the doorway, the same one that I came in when I first entered the warehouse months ago. "And you know what, whoever dropped it there didn't actually trigger my magical defenses. The same as you— Wait, did *you* put it here?"

"Um, no," I say. "I'd never seen it before this summer."

"Is there another person out there with your embarrassing lack of magical sensitivity and ability to avoid detection? Do you perhaps have a long lost twin hiding somewhere?"

"Um, I don't think so," I say, "but who knows, I guess? I'm still stuck on the fact that a superpowered sword appeared on your doorstep and you didn't even question it?"

Zambrano shrugs. "I don't know, maybe one of the many people over the years who wronged me wanted to apologize? It was the week after my birthday, could have been a late birthday present. Don't look a gift horse in the mouth, as they say."

"Unless it's a large wooden one outside your city gates, right?" I point out.

While we've been talking, Liao Ling has been quietly casting detection spells on the sword. She nods in satisfaction. "It doesn't appear to have any sort of traps or tricks on it. And it's the real thing."

"Yes, it's perfectly safe," Zambrano says with a wave, as if he's already long since determined that the sword is not a threat.

"What does the sword do?" I ask.

"Oh, the usual," Zambrano says. "Unbreakable, cuts through most material, grants you strength and agility. But I don't know how to activate it, so it doesn't work. It won't let me use it."

"Its magic doesn't interact well with other forms of magic strength," Liao Ling says. "And you're dripping with performance-enhancing magic. I believe in modern slang that's called 'juicing'?"

"This isn't a sports league," Zambrano objects. "I need every edge that I can get. Plus, I cast the spells myself, that hardly feels like cheating to me."

"It feels like it to me," I mutter. "Unless you want to give me some of it."

"I'm not attuned to your body in that way," Zambrano says with a dismissive hand gesture. "And even if I could be, I really wouldn't want to. In any event, this new evidence would indicate that someone other than me could wield the sword?" Zambrano asks.

"Did you *try* it with anyone else?" I ask.

Zambrano shrugs. "No, not really. Didn't occur to me at the time. Who else would use it?"

"I don't know," I shoot back, "maybe someone who's constantly being put in danger for your schemes?"

"That is a fair point," Zambrano admits reluctantly.

"Will it help with Rex?" I ask. "Can I slice him up next time we meet him?"

"It won't cut through the flesh of royalty-level demons, unfortunately," Liao Ling states. "Believe me, we tried. Speaking of reprehensible demons, by the way, where's this demonic duck you've told me about?" she asks.

I glance up the stairs and see a small figure hopping down the steps. "She's actually coming down now," I say.

Seraphex hops down a few more steps and then sees Liao Ling and pauses on the staircase.

"There you are," Liao Ling says, her cheerful tone suddenly slipping into a much darker one. "You murderous bitch. You absolute monstrosity. Are you really her? Are you really Seraphex, demon stained with the blood of thousands? Murderer of so many of my comrades?"

"Those are not my preferred titles," Seraphex answers calmly. "But yes, I am Seraphex, queen of demons. And I remember you, Liao Ling. Sorcerer who exiled my people to a barren wasteland."

"That voice," the ancient sorcerer whispers. "It is you. I didn't really believe they had you here." Liao Ling raises her hands, and pulsing blue energy swirls around her. She yells several phrases in what I can only guess is Middle Chinese and thrusts out her left arm, holding her hand in a grasping motion. Seraphex is suddenly caught, raised up off the ground in a blue vortex of force.

"Destroyer!" Liao Ling calls out, and her right hand pushes forward, sending a bolt of bluish-white energy slamming into Seraphex. The duck squawks and shudders, her recently regrown feathers flying off her body and caught floating in the web of arcane energy around her.

"Sera!" I call out and instinctively step forward to grab Liao Ling. But before I can, Zambrano places his own hand on my shoulder, pulling me back.

"If you touch her, that spell will tear you apart," he mutters in my ear. "We can't stop this. Let it run its course, and maybe she'll calm down once she gets it out of her system."

"Killer!" Liao Ling calls out, pulling her right hand back and stabbing it forward again, sending another blast of the magical energy slamming into the trapped demon duck. "Beast!" she cries and sends another.

Zambrano holds me back, gripping both shoulders tight as Liao Ling sends lance after lance of energy into Seraphex until the duck is nothing but a featherless, charred wreck. Finally, breathing heavily, Liao Ling ends the spell, and Seraphex drops to the ground in a heap of plucked feathers and ash.

The sorcerer spins on her heel, glaring at us. "How can you possibly consort with such a monstrosity?" she demands. "She killed my brother. That was when I swore to defeat her and to put aside my rivalry with that asshole Merlin and make an alliance to save humanity. And you welcome her into your home? Feed her, protect her? Strategize with her? She will only betray you in the end. I will kill her."

"If human sorcery could kill me, Zambrano would have ended my life decades ago," Seraphex notes but doesn't move from her pile of feathers and seared duck flesh.

"I didn't know about your brother," Zambrano says lamely. "I hated her too. But she's proven useful. And she will help us stop Rex, who is a far greater threat."

"You should not share your home with such creatures," Liao Ling pronounces. "I certainly would not."

"I have been keeping this world safe for centuries!" Zambrano shoots back.

"Hey, we're all on the same side here," I interject, but Zambrano ignores me completely.

"How dare you question me!" he roars at Liao Ling. "You have been gone for the entire development of modern civilization. Why would I even need your help? Your knowledge is ancient, probably so far out of date that it's useless. Why would I even think that you could be helpful?"

"Whatever," Liao Ling says, shrugging and walking away. She strides over to the wall of teleportraits. "You are no friend of humanity, Zambrano. You host a demon in your home. You cannot bring yourself to trust me. You disgust me."

And then before any of us can do anything, she grabs a teleportrait, stares at it for a split second, and disappears with a whoosh.

"I didn't know she was able to do that," Zambrano says, surprise in his voice. "She must have figured it out from my explanation of the underlying magic."

"Well, she was quite rude, wasn't she?" Seraphex says, picking herself up and shaking the charred remains of feathers off. She is badly burned, both feathers and duck flesh, but she's standing up like she's not in any pain or has bodily impairment.

"You killed her brother!" I yell in frustration, flopping down on one of the chairs.

"It was a *very* long time ago," Seraphex says. "And he was trying to kill me at the time. He was a wizard, but not nearly as prodigious as his younger sister, Liao Ling."

"Maybe she's right," I say to Zambrano. "Maybe we shouldn't be consorting with a demon. She did try to betray us once."

"Once while you've been around," the sorcerer points out, sitting down in one of the chairs and rubbing his temples. "Plenty more times before that. I'm not sure why I've put up with her." He turns to the demon queen, who is standing on the warehouse stairs in the form of a duck, feathers scorched and burned. "Liao Ling isn't the only one who lost someone to you. Your energy corrupted and killed Alix. Probably hastened the unraveling of several of my other friends in the Sorcerers' Circle."

The duck looks at him. She opens her beak, but then closes it.

"YOU KILLED HER." Zambrano pulls up his own hand, summoning an angry red magic and then drops it down, shaking his head. "You killed her. And to keep an eye on you, I let you live here. And you never even apologized. Because you don't feel any goddamn guilt."

Seraphex opens and closes her beak several more times, but no sound comes out.

"Go ahead. Say what you want to say," he says, practically spitting the words at her. "The airy justification or bullshit witticism you have. However you want to mock me. *Say it.*"

Seraphex stands stone still, staring directly at the sorcerer. I've backed away, half expecting another explosion of magic energy and not sure that Zambrano will be able to control himself in his rage and limit the damage only to the demon. I vaguely notice my phone buzzing but reach down and silence it. Probably spam anyway.

"I'm sorry," she says in a much smaller voice than her usual regal tones.

"You've never said that before," Zambrano whispers. "Why would you say that now? After all this time? What would it do?"

"I never said it before," Seraphex explains, as if she's also figuring it out for herself, "because I didn't feel it. I couldn't feel it."

"What changed?" I ask, curious despite the combination of anger and fear fighting it out in my gut.

She turns to look at me. "My promise. When I agreed to be friends to both of you, I knew it would be terribly inconvenient, but I didn't think I had a choice. I didn't realize what friendship really was. In order to be your friend, I had to have empathy. I had to care about someone other than myself. I had to be able to feel bad for things I did to you. And let me assure you, it is the absolute worst. Do you humans just go around feeling . . . this . . . all the time? It's terrible! I've always been filled with hate, but it's never been directed at *myself*. What am I supposed to do with this?"

She shakes, ruffling her torched feathers, and turns and hops back up the stairs.

Zambrano has fallen silent and is just staring after her in a mix of sorrow and confusion. I'm right there with him—I don't know how to feel either.

"This is weird," I say. "With Seraphex in her amusing duck form making wise cracks, it's been easy to forget how much of a villain she really is. In Liao Ling's time, she killed, plotted, and destroyed on a massive scale. So much so that they had to exile her to another planet in order to put a stop to it. I've put that out of my mind."

Zambrano grunts in agreement. "I suppose I did too. For far longer."

"But now she's changed," I continue. "Something about the demonic code and the magic governing it has altered her identity, her ability to feel. In a philosophical sense, you could say she's a different person."

"It's the reverse of the old ship of Theseus thought experiment. If you replace each part at a separate time with new identical parts, we ask if it's the same ship," Zambrano muses. "But if you keep most of the same parts and replace the sails with a steam turbine, does that make it a new ship? It's all nonsense word games."

"But it makes a difference in how we treat her," I point out. "We have to kind of decide how we feel about it. To what extent do we hold her to account for her crimes?"

Zambrano shrugs. "Does it really matter? I'm pretty sure I need her help to stop Rex. I'm a pragmatist, Bryce. I'm not exactly known for standing on the finer points of ethical principles. I would happily ally with the old pure evil Seraphex if I had to, to stop Rex from coming to power on Earth. And any punishment we levy against an invincible demon probably won't have much effect on her, other than losing her help."

"Fair points," I admit. "So what now?"

"I really didn't think Liao Ling would just run off on us after all we did to help her. And she really was quite rude." The sorcerer stands up, his young-looking body moving with the weariness of a much older man. "We make nice with everyone and try to put together a plan to stop the demon king from laying waste to civilization."

"A plan to make a plan," I say. "I guess that's a start."

I glance down at my phone, which has now buzzed several times in a row. Someone's calling me. Who calls anyone these days? I pick it up and see several missed calls and a text message.

*Hey, Bryce, it's Mei Song,* the message says. *I think I'm outside your warehouse, the one in Queens, Vulkatherak had me arrange surveillance on it when I worked for him. Do you still live there?*

*Are you there now?*

*Can I come in?*

*We need to talk.*

Why is the Demon Duke Volcanose's former executive assistant outside our warehouse?

# CHAPTER 18

I explain the message to Zambrano. He is quite skeptical.

"You want me to let some demon-employed harlot into our private sanctuary? Our secret lair? Our sacred home?"

"It's a warehouse in Queens," I point out. "Not Wakanda or the Vatican or something."

"Okay, fair point. But I hope you're not letting her in here just because you have some depraved crush on someone who is probably our enemy."

"She helped us! And also, you're one to talk. Is there any historical magic user from the last five hundred years that you haven't had a fling with at some point?"

"I have no regrets," Zambrano says, "and make no apologies. I'm sorry, Bryce, I can't un-bang your mom, and I wouldn't if I could."

"You are so gross," I say. "I feel like you think about that a lot more than I do. Anyway, can we let this woman in so we can find out why she's tracked us down?"

"Sure," Zambrano says. "I'll deactivate the mystic defenses. I haven't done it in a while. Don't worry, she *probably* won't get incinerated when the gem guardians detect a sentient being passing in front of them."

"Ugh," I say with an eye roll. This is a dig at me, since with my magical potential locked away, I wasn't identified by the arcane defenses as a person and so I didn't get blasted by them. "Okay, forget it. I'll bring her in through the delivery door." We don't need anyone else getting hurt, as lovely as it was to spend a few days with the druids.

"That's better anyway," Zambrano says. "Let's not let her into the lab, she's probably spying for someone. Or maybe sabotage. Hmm, yes, let me put some safeguards on the lab. I'll meet you upstairs."

I text Mei the address to the delivery door and quietly let her in that way.

"Hi, Bryce," she says, furtively stepping past the door as I quickly close it behind her.

"Hi," I say. I'm really not sure what our relationship is now. We worked together to stop Volcanose the demon duke, but on the other hand, she worked for the bastard. Do we shake hands? Hug? Glare at each other like boxers at a weigh-in?

"Um, right this way," I say. In the end, we settle for just awkwardly walking down the hall.

"Zambrano is . . . not in a great mood," I warn her.

"Noted," she says with a shrug.

Do I have a crush on her like Zambrano says? Honestly, every time I've run into her I've been either desperately afraid for my life or for the world, or both. Unlike Parth, whose weird interest in Liao Ling didn't seem to be at all diminished by constant peril, that sort of thing makes it hard for me to focus on any sort of romantic interest. Plus, Zambrano does have a point about her choice of employers.

Zambrano meets us in the hallway, having closed the door to the downstairs lab and currently in the act of putting some sort of protective spells on the door.

We end up sitting around the small table in the kitchen, Zambrano staring at her skeptically.

"Well?" he says, leaning back in his chair.

"It's nice to finally meet you," Mei says. "I've always admired your work, and I've never had the pleasure of meeting a dark sorcerer before."

"Wait, are you just here looking for a job?" Zambrano demands. "You think working for a demon duke qualifies you to work for a so-called dark sorcerer? Which is nonsense, by the way—there's no such thing, and if there were I wouldn't be one because I am a responsible and upstanding citizen who is misunderstood because the peasants out there are jealous that I'm so much better than them."

"You'll have to excuse him," I say, "he's . . . well I'm not sure what. But he's generally good guy-ish if you don't look too closely at the details."

"In any event," Zambrano plows on, ignoring me, "I already have an assistant. And my internship program is not open to applicants. The last applicant that I accepted had a bad attitude and a pattern of willful disrespect. And broke *so many* company phones."

I want to object. But his characterization is, I have to admit, factually correct.

"Oh, no, I'm not looking for a job," Mei answers, either ignoring or not understanding the sorcerer's attempt at humor. "I have employment already. I work for a well-regarded collector of artifacts, art, and antiquities in Turkey. He's recently had some major property damage at his estate, so I am getting paid a lot of overtime."

"Hold on, you work for Slickwad?" I say, hardly able to believe it. I mean, wow, Mei really does know how to pick them.

"Slickwad?" She asks.

"He means Slickwardinaeous, famed collector of magical items and other oddities," Zambrano explains. "I heard that he had some sort of mishap at his residence, some sort of artifact gone awry?"

"Yes, something that he brought back from the Pacific Ocean," she says. "Wait, did you . . . ?"

Zambrano grins, this opportunity to show off improving his mood. "I don't know what you're talking about. I haven't been in Turkey since that friendly visit to Istanbul about a month ago. But I'm glad to hear that he's enjoying his new acquisitions."

"Wow, you two really are trouble," she says. "Do you know how many different companies I've had to contract with to repair the damage? Carpenters, plumbers, electricians, artificers, security firms, arcane security firms, so many government officials to bribe . . ."

"I mean, you do work for an absolutely disgusting demon," I interject. "Though at least this one isn't trying to open a literal portal to hell. So that's nice."

Mei shrugs. "What can I say? The cost of living is cheap over there, and the health care is great. As an executive assistant, I have a maid, a cook, and live in a building with private security. I wanted to work in the organic vegan food vertical, but the only other job offer I got was from a cosmetics company. Do you know what kind of cruel testing they do on animals?"

"That's enough, you two," Zambrano says. "We're not here to talk about the job market. Why did you come to interrupt the perfectly lovely afternoon that we have had so far, Ms. Song?"

"It wasn't for the award-winning hospitality, that's for sure," she says.

"Do you, um, want a glass of water?" I offer. I glance over at the cabinets, which are largely bare. "A Pop-Tart? A Go-GURT? Wait, I guess neither of those is vegan."

"No, they are not," Mei says. "Look, let's skip the unpleasantries and get down to business. My employer has been selling off some of his collection to pay for all the repairs and recovery efforts for key elements that ran off during the unfortunate destructive event. I've been managing deliveries and negotiations for some of the less valuable ones, and I've been hearing things. The demons were spooked when the demon duke shot himself into space, but this is on another level."

"What's the chatter?" Zambrano asks, suddenly serious.

"At first I thought the duke was coming back," Mei says, "but that's not it. Demons that have been hiding and quietly indulging their hungers are suddenly arming themselves, settling old grudges, paying off debts, that sort of thing. Like they're all about to be drafted for a war, or something. One of them said, offhand, 'I need to get this settled. The king is coming back.' I don't think she was talking about LeBron James."

"No, she wasn't," a voice says from the doorway. We turn over to see Seraphex standing there. Her plumage has once again mostly regrown, and she's only looking a bit overcooked, like a burger left on the grill a few minutes too long. "He's come back. I felt it, just a few minutes ago. He's out of the pocket universe and in this world."

"Who is?" Mei asks.

"Why should we tell you?" I ask. "So you can run and try to get an even higher paying job with the newest big bad on the planet?"

"No," Mei says quietly. "I don't want a job from you. I'm scared. Like, I don't mind working for clients who have complicated moral backgrounds. But this feels . . . apocalypse-y."

"Zambrano, maybe we should step outside" I say, "talk this over? Mei did help us last time, so I'm inclined to trust her. But we should figure out how much we want to share."

But he just gives me a weird look as if he doesn't understand what we would have to talk about. Instead he turns to Mei and shakes his head.

"You work for someone who is very upset at me. I'm sure he sent you to spy on me, or to try to get revenge of some sort. And you don't seem to know anything useful. Or have anything to offer. Do you have any tools that you can offer to help defeat an immensely powerful and ancient demon?"

"Well, no, not immediately," Mei starts, "but—"

"Useless," Zambrano says, and then, *"Blue bubble bouncer, bubble bounce this bothersome bore."* He snaps first with his right hand, then his left, then his right again.

A small blue bubble forms and glides over toward Mei. She jumps backward, but it expands and envelopes Mei, picking her up off the floor. Caught in a heap at the base of the bubble, she yells and pounds against its blue walls, but we can't hear her through the magical barrier.

Zambrano points to the door, which opens at a gesture, and the bubble carries Mei off. It looks like a giant soap bubble, but her pounding fists on it don't do anything to it. It floats off into the hallway, and I stand to follow it. It drifts right through the door to the street outside, which has also popped open. The bubble carrying Mei passes through the twisted space-time to deliver her outside the warehouse a few blocks away. Once it's about fifteen feet outside the door, the bubble evaporates, Mei is dropped unceremoniously on the pavement, and the door swings shut and locks.

Annoyed, I turn and stomp back to the kitchen.

"Pretty cool spell, don't you think?" Zambrano says. "That one I made myself, you know. I crafted the bubble to be soundproof so I wouldn't have to listen to someone's bitching while they're being bounced. Not smellproof though, which I found out one unfortunate time."

"Are you going to alienate every possible ally that we could have here? The druids don't trust you, Liao Ling thinks you're a monster, and now Mei won't share information with us in the future."

"Do we really need them?" Zambrano asks. "If they don't want to work with me, why should I work with them? It's not my fault if they can't get me or what I'm about. If that means the world ends, that's on them, not on me."

"You really would sacrifice the world for the sake of your ego, wouldn't you?" I say.

"I've saved the world several times over!" Zambrano objects. "And what does my ego get for that? Endless hate and suspicion from every government on Earth!"

"Bryce has a point," Seraphex chides him. "We do need help to defeat my former husband."

"Ugh, fine," Zambrano says. "If you want to go crawling to Liao Ling begging for her help, that's okay by me. I'll even teleportrait you there. Is that enough? Are you happy? Am I a hero now?"

I take a slow, deep breath. First, he gets my friend hurt. Then he pushes away all our potential helpers. Last time I got this pissed off at Zambrano, I threw a fit and ran off. But Rex is back in our universe. We don't have time for drama like that. One way or another, I need to keep going.

"Okay," I finally say. "If that's how you want it to be. Take me to where she is. I'll talk to her. But it would be a lot better, Zambrano, if you were able to talk to her with me. *Nicely.* She just woke up in a brand-new world completely changed from her time. Magic has helped her adjust quickly, but that only goes so far."

"She wanted to go," Zambrano says with a shrug. "She made her choice."

"You should stick together," Seraphex says. "It may be dangerous out there. They could be waiting."

"Who's they?" I ask, pausing to look back at the demon duck.

"Mei Song is right," Seraphex says. "Now that my former husband is back, he will be quickly seizing control of the worldwide demonic network in a way that Vulkatherak never could."

"So what's he going to do?" I ask, dreading the answer.

"He's back on the playing board. He is very powerful, but not infinitely so. First, he will be gathering information. Understanding this new world that he finds himself in. Modern governments have weapons that can hurt him in ways that he never knew before. Waging massive direct warfare was never his way. He will seek to destabilize the world, to create some sort of disaster that will create mass chaos and have governments at one another's throats. And he'll look to quietly eliminate anyone who could stop him. Given that sorcerers imprisoned him for fifteen hundred years, and there are currently two sorcerers alive . . . I'm sure you can do the math there."

Zambrano scowls at Seraphex. And then at me. And then back at Seraphex. And then back at me.

"Ugh. Fine. I'll go with you, we can try to come up with some sort of accommodation with her. But I'm not apologizing."

"She's just woken up fifteen hundred years past her time, with everything she knows gone and a completely strange new world that she barely understands. Maybe we can have some patience with her?"

Zambrano shrugs. "Sure, I'll try to be nice, I guess. But she better do the same," he says like the big dumb baby that he is.

I shake my head. "Okay, I guess I'll take it. How do we find her? Can we follow where she went?"

"Unfortunately, I don't have duplicates of most of the teleportraits," Zambrano says. "They have to be repainted every year or so, so there's no point to it." He walks over to the wall where there's now an empty space. "It looks like she took . . . Santa Cruz, California. I'm not even sure why I have that. I must have been dating someone from there. Probably some floozy."

"Some floozy?" I ask. "And you don't remember who, even though it's less than a year ago?"

"Yes, I believe I remember. She was, like, the chief scientist at the Santa Cruz Institute for Particle Physics. I met her at some charity event. Like I said, some floozy."

I just roll my eyes. "So we need to go to, what, San Francisco? Los Angeles? San Diego?"

"You don't know the first thing about West Coast geography, do you?" Zambrano asks, amusement at my expense seeming to ease his bad mood slightly.

"No, I do not."

"I have one for Oakland," Zambrano says. "San Francisco is closer but I don't have one for it. Who actually wants to go there these days?"

So we take a few minutes to gather our things and take a teleportrait to Oakland. After a couple hours in a car, we head to the spot where Liao Ling would have arrived. While we drive, Zambrano is writing in a notebook, muttering to himself and making complicated spellcasting gestures. Luckily, none of them seem to cast any actual spells as far as I can tell. The spot where she would have appeared is a little nook off the main paths in a park by the beach, where a person appearing and disappearing wouldn't be too likely to be noticed.

"It's been a few hours. She could be anywhere by now," I note.

"That's what I've been working on for the past couple hours," Zambrano says. "She may have more raw power, but the art and science of magic have advanced quite a lot since her time. I have ways of masking my presence that are more or less automatic and second nature. But she just went through an intense magical transformation, which should still have trace effects of active magic. Her magic is different in crucial ways as well, so I'm hoping to use a traditional lodestone arcane technique to find her."

It all sounds very interesting and impressive and technical.

Unfortunately, it doesn't work at all.

I stand around for half an hour while Zambrano tries to use some sort of metallic rock to point in her direction. But it never indicates consistently in any one direction. I pull out the demon-hiding gauntlets that the druids gave me and put them on, taking this chance to test them out. It gives me a vaguely tingly feeling, like just a little bit of electricity is dancing around my fingers and palms. As the effect builds up, something happens to the light around me as well, and I start to see everything around me in shades of desaturated blue. I can still see myself just fine, and I show up in selfies I take of myself. It's like a real-life Instagram filter. But hopefully like this, demons won't be able to see me.

I text with Parth for a minute to update him on what's happening and hear the latest on his exams. He's recovering well and starting to feel stronger, which is a relief. Though I get the sense that he hasn't been working too hard on his exams, he seems to be doing all right. I explain the current situation and how helpless Zambrano seems to be in finding Liao Ling. I can see the sorcerer's frustration building as it's not working.

*He's getting more and more upset,* I type. *I'm starting to worry he's going to blow a fuse and go ballistic or something.*

*Gotta figure out how to reel him back,* Parth answers. *Maybe you could do something to help find her?*

*I don't know the first thing about this sort of spell,* I answer. *Do you?*

*Nope,* Parth answers. *What about social media? Could you check there?*

So I try that, opening up various apps and filtering down to posts from our local area. And let me tell you, I would *not* recommend doing that unless you absolutely have to. It is absolute drivel, grossness, and idiocy of all varieties. There's a reason all the social media apps default to a curated feed of the so-called best from around the world. It may be mostly junk, but it's at least slop that has some reason to be interesting.

But my suspicion is that Parth is right, and whatever Liao Ling is up to, it will stand out from the standard local social media nonsense and I'll be able to track it down. And I am proven correct.

Twenty minutes later, the social media posts have led us to the boardwalk. We arrive at a laser tag joint, with a big sign outside that says LARRY'S LASERS, full of arcade games and sci-fi laser tag gear. They even have a section of classic enchanted games like Wizard Poker, with the cards that have magical figures that rise up out of them and battle each other. It's pretty empty because a laser tag game is in progress.

Zambrano spots it first, pointing up at the scoreboard.

At the top, with about three times as many kills as anyone else is "LingShot."

# CHAPTER 19

Welcome to Larry's Lasers!" A middle-aged guy wearing a bright yellow shirt says. "Do you want to get in on the next game? We've got a couple slots available when this game ends."

"Nice place you've got here," Zambrano says, looking around at the arcade. It's a pretty impressive business, with a mix of classic and modern arcade games, a food vendor, and what looks like a cool setup for the arena.

"Thanks! It's kind of my baby," the guy says, nodding in appreciation. "I'm laser-focused on making sure everyone who comes in has a blast and leaves beaming with delight."

"Are you . . . Larry?" I ask. No employee could possibly be paid enough to drop those puns with every customer who walks in off the boardwalk.

He points at his bright yellow shirt. It says "Larry" on it in bold block letters. Not sure how I missed that.

"Yup! This is all mine," Larry says. "Larry's Lasers, home of the fastest guns in the west—and also in the universe."

"In the universe?" Zambrano asks with a frown.

"They're lasers—they shoot at light speed," Larry says with a chuckle, apparently thrilled that Zambrano walked into his verbal trap. "You have to admit that's the fastest speed in the universe, unless you think you're smarter than a certain Mr. Albert Einstein."

The egotistical sorcerer opens his mouth to answer, but I jump in first.

"We have the very greatest respect for the established laws of physics," I say. "We're just here to meet our friend."

"No problem!" Larry says. "Just let me know if you need anything. We've got our famous cheese fries and our own pizza oven if you want a slice."

"Should we go in and grab her?" Zambrano asks once Larry has walked off.

"We're trying to be nice, remember?"

"I've never had a very good memory," he shoots back, but we wait the three minutes that it takes for the game to end. There are cameras that show the action inside, and I can see why some of the kids here were taking videos. She's all over the place, leaping and somersaulting, virtually unhittable and cutting down the opponents easily.

"Oh, hey there, lads," Liao Ling says as she comes out the arena, high-fiving her teammates, who have ridden her coattails to a landslide victory. "Want to try your luck? Think you can dodge the LingShot? Looks like there are open slots. Maybe you'll be some real competition for us?" The opposing team looks some mixture of confused, embarrassed, and curious, but they do seem to be hanging up their gear and heading for the exits. "No active spellcasting though, that's not fair."

"Your magically enhanced speed, strength, and reflexes are perfectly fine though?" Zambrano questions.

"She didn't live through the whole performance-enhancing steroid era, remember?" I say, elbowing Zambrano in the ribs.

"Or any of the other eras, pretty much," Liao Ling says cheerfully. "I watched some history videos on YouTube earlier though. Did you know that many figures throughout history were actually reptilian shapeshifters from outer space?"

"Oh, no, that's not real history," I say.

"It was in a video from a place called 'The History Channel,'" Liao Ling points out. "Why would they put something in there if it wasn't actually history? That doesn't make any sense."

"Well . . . I guess there are a lot of things in modern times that don't make sense," I say. "Um, it's *not* true, right?" I say, glancing over at Zambrano. I'm sure those dumb late-night conspiracy videos are fake. But then again, one of my friends is a demon turned into a duck.

"I don't know," Zambrano says with a playful shrug. "They would have been in the shape of humans. How would anyone tell the difference?"

I look back and forth between the two of them and quickly realize that there's no way I'm going to figure out how to explain or manage this situation. Better to just plow forward.

"Look, Liao Ling," I start. "I'm sorry about the Seraphex situation. I get that she's your enemy. She's done some really horrible things. I think she might have changed a little bit since you knew her, but she's still a demon. And she's still accountable for what she's done. And she's helped us in the past. Other than trying to backstab and trick me into helping her get her powers back at the last minute. I'm not doing a very good job at making this case, am I?"

"No, not really," Liao Ling says, though she's smiling slightly. "Remember that for you, the terrible things that terrible demon inflicted on humanity was fifteen hundred years ago. For me, it just happened." Any hint of a smile disappears, and she looks down at the ancient carpet of the arcade. Around us, the *beeps* and *boops* of video games blare, and the next round of kids is grabbing their laser tag gear to head into the arena. "She killed my brother four years ago, from my perspective. I sacrificed everything to bring revenge to Seraphex and all of her kind."

"I'm sorry, that's really hard," is all I can think to say.

Liao Ling suddenly snaps back up to look at us. "Have you had cheese fries before?" she asks, chipper and enthusiastic again. "They are *so* good here. What incredible cuisine this place has! Has this land of California always had such culinary masterpieces? I never visited it in my time—if I could have taken delicacies like these to the emperors, princes, and dukes in China, maybe they wouldn't have hated me and completely erased me from history!"

"I don't know that now is a good time to get a snack," I say. "There may be demons looking for us."

"No," Zambrano says with a wistful sort of air to his speech. "Let's get the cheese fries. We've had a long week. I think we all deserve the cheese fries."

"I know I do," Liao Ling says.

I shrug and follow along. They are clearly set on this. At the food counter, I order three separate baskets of cheese fries. There's no way that having to share a group helping of cheese fries between these two is going to aid with this diplomatic mission. Larry pulls out a fresh pizza, slapping it down on the counter with one of those giant metal spatulas, and Liao Ling demands that we also try that. Zambrano is paying for all of it, so I just let it happen. You never turn down free pizza.

"Come for the cheesy jokes, stay for the cheesy fries!" Larry says as he hands me a tray full of fries. I hope this guy is making money off this place, because as far as I can see he's the only person on duty here, and he's working his ass off.

We end up sitting at a slightly sticky table in front of a row of claw machines, chowing down on the fries and pizza. For the first couple minutes, it's pretty quiet, the silence made only somewhat more comfortable by the fact that we're all stuffing our faces. I've realized that I haven't actually eaten anything in quite a while. The threat of extinction or enslavement for your whole species can really spoil your appetite.

"Okay," Zambrano says when his pizza is gone and his cardboard tray is down to just little scraps of fries and a pool of cheese. "I know you don't like Seraphex. I get it. She also killed someone close to me. I know that my relationship with her is . . . unusual."

"You can say that again," I mutter, but quiet enough that neither of them pay attention.

"But she's made a promise to be our friend and help us defeat Rex," Zambrano continues. "Without her, our chances are a lot worse."

"Can we kill her afterward?" Liao Ling asks, using one of her final fries to scoop up a truly massive amount of cheese. Two minutes ago it would have looked delicious, but now that I'm full, seeing the yellow goop dripping down makes me feel sick.

"Unfortunately," Zambrano says, "I literally have no idea how to do that. Trapping her in a restrictive form was the best solution we could come up with. So we can't do that . . . unless you have some forgotten magic that can kill a high-level demon."

"If so, maybe we could use it on Rex?" I add hopefully.

"Nah," Liao Ling says with a shrug. "I was hoping you might have something, with you modern sorcerers having fifteen hundred years to research. No? That sucks. Look, I just don't want to associate myself with someone who would keep a murderous demon as a friend, and . . ."

She pauses, glancing around.

"That's rude," she says, her voice suddenly a whisper.

"What is? I ask.

"Something is showing up to interrupt this lovely meal," she says. "Something demonic. Not our friend Rex though. A lower order demon or demons."

Zambrano stands, pulling off his suit jacket and neatly folding it over the back of his chair.

"What a relief, all this talking about our feelings was killing me. Finally, something we can blast to hell."

There's a distant *whomp-whomp* sound, and the air I breathe in suddenly has a sharp, electric taste to it, like after a thunderstorm. All the flashing lights and sounds in the arcade suddenly go dead along with the overhead lights. The only illumination is the late evening sun coming through the front windows.

"What's that? Do we really want to hang around here? This could be a trap."

"Oh, it definitely is a trap," Liao Ling says, flexing her fingers. "I can't sense exactly where, but there's at least one demon approaching. This is going to be fun."

"We should get out of here," I suggest. "Even if we can beat the demon, there are civilians here," I say, pointing to the crowd of kids piling out of the laser tag arena, whining about how the power outage cut their game short and loudly pressuring Larry to give them a refund—which, to his credit, he's agreeing to. "Too much chance for collateral damage."

Zambrano shakes his head. "That sound, and the smell of ozone in the air—they've blown up an AMP."

"What's that?" Liao Ling and I ask at the same time.

"It's an arcane magical pulse," Zambrano says, as if I'm supposed to already know that.

"Okay, but what does it do?" I ask.

"It scrambles magic in the area, bending the rules of reality ever so slightly for a little bit," Zambrano says. "It's not enough to stop us from using spells here, but it puts a disruption field around us that disconnects us from the outside world. No arcane communications, and no teleportation." He pulls out the small teleportrait that he always keeps in his jacket, staring at it for a few seconds. "Can't make any connections to the outside world, the math doesn't match up."

"Ah!" Liao Ling says. "No escape route means we have no choice but to blast our way out."

"That's right," Zambrano says. "Regardless of the collateral damage."

"Maybe we try to minimize the collateral damage, actually?" I say, gesturing to the kids. "We could use non-magical escape routes, maybe?"

"The kids will be fine," Zambrano says, pushing his sleeves back and stretching his hands.

"Can you just go outside?" I say. "Run somewhere? Draw them away, so this battle happens elsewhere. Or just use some other spell to escape—we don't need to fight here in the middle of the boardwalk!"

"I'm not running away from a couple low-level demons," Zambrano growls. "Let them come to us."

It's clear to me that he isn't even considering my ideas. Before I can make another try to convince him, Zambrano and Liao Ling are scoping out the spots to take cover behind the driving games, so I realize it's up to me to get the kids to safety.

I go over to the entrance to the arena where Larry is busy handing the players coupons for free games when the power turns back on.

"Hey, folks," I start. "Someone very dangerous is coming here. I'm sorry, but this is not going to be a safe place to be. We need to get you all out of here."

"Why should we listen to you?" one of the kids asks.

"Yeah, it's just a power outage," another one says. "We'll wait until the power comes back on so we can play again.

"Zambrano, little help here?" I say.

With a grin, he raises his hand, and it explodes in a small but bright orange flame. "They can stay and watch if they want, fine by me."

"Wait, is that . . . It's the dark sorcerer!" one of the kids blurts out.

"Just a normal sorcerer," Zambrano says. "Good-guy sorcerer, sometimes. Light sorcerer, perhaps? Incredibly charming and handsome sorcerer—absolutely."

"Whatever he is," I say urgently, "he's about to be in a fight, and it's going to be very dangerous."

Larry turns pale and glances around at his arcade, chock-full of expensive machines that have gone from cheerfully beeping and flashing to ominously dark and silent. Then he takes a deep breath and nods. "Okay, you're right, we need to get these kids out of here," the owner says. "There's a back exit, I'll show you."

He opens the door marked staff only and sends the kids through the kitchen, where a door leads into a back alley. They complain, but he isn't having it, and within twenty seconds they're all gone.

"You should go too," I say. "It's not going to be safe in here."

"Okay, yeah, I guess so," Larry says, but then pauses and points at one of the video monitors that shows the inside of the laser tag arena. The security cameras are all still on, the system must be on some sort of battery backup.

"Oh, shit," I say. There's one kid still in there, hiding behind a low wall in her home base with her laser gun held at the ready. She must not have realized that the power is out because the guns are battery powered and still operate.

"I'll go get her," Larry says with a grim expression.

"Is there another exit in there?" I ask.

Larry shakes his head, pointing to the entrance and exit that both come into this room.

"Okay, go grab her," I say. "If you hear things out here, I'd just hide in there."

Larry sprints into the arcade, and I can see him on the cameras, leaping over obstacles as he runs to grab the girl despite his out-of-shape-looking middle-aged body.

I snap away from the monitors as I hear a crashing sound in the front of the room. I don't think the glass door was locked, but it's being smashed in anyway. A large figure stands there, a silhouette backlit by the sun, a massive-looking humanoid creature with muscles and a ragged texture at the edges. Then the wall next to the figure in the doorway suddenly crumbles, smashed by a powerful force and, not to be outdone, an even larger figure steps into the breach.

The instant one of them starts talking, I know exactly who it is.

"Oi, Tunker, look what we have here, luv. Not one little human sorcerer, but two."

"Oh, and the froggy man is here, too," Tunker replies. The nickname would make me smile if I weren't afraid for my life, knowing that the rockhide demons likely still aren't over the time that I used an Amazonian azure frog to knock them unconscious.

Tunker is the slightly smaller of the two, but she's still a massive figure made of rock that could probably crush me with a single finger. Realizing my mistake, I jump behind the big race car games, pull the gauntlets out of my backpack, and shove them on. I fumble for a second, cursing myself for not putting them on earlier, but I was distracted by all those stupid kids.

"That's it?" Zambrano says, squinting up at the two figures. "All he sent was two rockhide demons? Against not one but two of the greatest sorcerers of all time?"

As my vision goes to bluish-gray filter mode, I step out from behind the game to see Bronk stepping forward. His grinning face becomes clearer as he steps into the floor of the arcade, and I'm praying that these things actually work. At least initially, the demons don't seem to look over at me at all.

"We got us a new guvnor 'round 'ere," he says. "New boss guy, new rules."

"'sright, Daddy's back in town," Tunker says, flashing a grin of what look like some sort of diamond teeth. "And he gave us some new pep in our step."

Bronk looks over at her with a crestfallen expression of confusion and disappointment. "Wait, I thought I was the daddy round 'here? T'other night, you said—"

Tunker just rolls her eyes. "I says a lot o' things in the heat o' the moment, ye daft lunk."

Bronk stares at her angrily for a moment and then turns to face the two sorcerers, clearly intent on making them pay for his erstwhile lover's rudeness.

"Eye of Jupiter!" Zambrano calls out as he conducts an intricate motion with his hands and then pushes them forward, making it look like he's throwing an invisible ball at Bronk.

Debris from the broken wall around Bronk flies backward, pushed by the sudden field of gravity. It's the same spell that Zambrano used to trap me under a huge weight when I first snuck into his warehouse months ago. Bronk pauses for a moment, steadying himself in the gravity. And then he steps forward, slower than before but inexorable.

"Rex has supercharged them," Liao Ling says, shooting a spell of her own at Tunker, who steps forward despite a shower of tiny meteorites crashing into her.

"A demon king can do that?" Zambrano says, casting out a set of blue tendrils of energy that tangle at the two rockhide demons' legs. The rock figures pause for a moment but then start to thrash and shake the blue energy off.

"It's his main thing," Liao Ling shouts. "That's how he kept control over the other demons and gained so much power, by being able to make others stronger. I can counteract it, but I'm going to need a minute. Buy some time for me?"

"With pleasure," Zambrano says, stepping into a defensive posture and beginning the gestures of another combat spell. Meanwhile, Liao Ling retreats and starts muttering incantations and gesturing with her hands as if she's doing pottery in thin air. And glowing light and steam are both coming out of the space in between her hands.

That's the moment when I realize that I have no idea what I'm supposed to do in a situation like this. I don't actually have the strength to harm either of these monstrosities. No special abilities, no Javelin rocket launcher, and I sure as hell can't cast spells. I guess . . . maybe I'm not actually needed? Should I just get out of here? I hate the idea of running away like a coward. But on the other hand, I think as I dodge the claw from one of the claw machines that's been shattered by a spell that missed, running away could be a really good idea. I could just not be here, the place where all the ridiculous danger is happening. Which is what I told Zambrano we should be doing anyway!

"Bryce," Liao Ling says quietly, stepping farther back and next to me. "I'm going to need your help to deliver this."

God damn it. Well, there goes that plan.

# CHAPTER 20

Okay, what do I do?" I ask, moving to stand next to Liao Ling. Looking down at her hands, I see what looks like a small dagger made of light. She's sweating and straining, but the dagger is growing more solid with every passing second.

Meanwhile, Zambrano is slowly retreating, throwing spell after spell at the rockhide demons, and using some sort of telekinesis to toss arcade machines at them. Debris is flying everywhere as he taunts them, leaping back at each attempt they make to charge him.

"This translates as a Caesar Special," Liao Ling announces proudly. "The pure magic version, much less powerful than what I used on Rex. You need to stab this in their back, right between the shoulder blades. It will sap out the extra energy that Rex gave them."

"Um, okay," I agree. She hands me the dagger made of light, and it feels weightless in my gauntleted hand. "Will they be able to see it coming?" I'm not sure how these gauntlets work yet. Unlike the Javelin missile, the ancient gold gauntlets didn't come with any sort of instruction manual or video.

"Anything that you're wearing or holding will be hidden," Liao Ling assures me. "The enchantment of that is very thorough. Magic is pretty smart like that. Now go take out the first demon."

She starts working on another Caesar Special, and I creep forward, trying to assess the situation. Which is hard because the air is basically filled with glowing magic and pieces of arcade games mixed with occasional slices of pizza and french fries.

I step forward but immediately jump back as two balls from an exploding pinball game fly past my face.

I look all over the arcade for anything to help. The laser tag gear isn't going to be of any assistance. The arcade games I can hide behind, but I can't move them. I glance into the little food court area, and I see the giant pizza spatula lying on the ground. It's stupid and dangerous, but I may be able to use it.

So a minute later, I'm creeping up through the arcade, which has become a war zone, holding the dagger made from light in one hand, and a giant metal pizza spatula in the other, wielding it like a Roman legionnaire in a shield wall. As I advance, shrapnel of all sorts bounces off it. I hope the demons don't see the debris ricocheting randomly, but with Zambrano leaping around shooting spells at them like a maniac, they don't seem to notice.

The problem is going to be getting close enough to actually shank these bastards. I circle around, dodging glass from an arcade game, stuffed animals from the claw machines, and quite a few straight-up chunks of wall and floor. Finally, I get an opening. Bronk has turned to Liao Ling and is starting to advance toward her, despite sparks flying from his joints that seem to be slowing his movements. I've never seen this spell before, but I guess it's some sort of magically induced electro-arthritis? I'm not sure what it is, but who cares? I can sense that this is my moment.

I sprint forward, charging for his backside. I close quickly and raise the dagger to strike, but at the last minute, he stumbles, falling to one knee as a shower of sparks fly out of his right knee. He flings one of his hands up, and it hits the pizza spatula, sending it flying and knocking me off my feet.

Which is lucky, because he seems to notice that something is off, due to an object appearing in the air out of nowhere. He swipes at the air in front of him, right above me. I look up from the ground, watching in the blue and gray filtered light as he punches the air for a moment.

I hold my breath and lie perfectly still, hoping against hope that these gauntlets really work and that I won't be given away by something like a weird pattern in the dust on the ground.

But finally Bronk turns back toward Liao Ling. I leap up, jumping into the air and planting the dagger squarely between his rocky shoulder blades.

The rockhide demon freezes and howls in pain.

Zambrano, seeing this, charges him, hands clenching as he yells, *"Profitez de la sensation des articulations anciennes d'Alix."*

The sparks coming from his joints intensify, as if the spell restricting them has been redoubled. For a moment the joints explode in sparks, and then his whole body grinds to a halt. Without the demon king's extra power, the spells become too much for him. Slightly over-balanced, he falls forward, crashing to the floor like a statue.

"Bronk! You idiot!" Tunker yells.

Throwing off one of the blue vines of energy, she charges Zambrano, who is leaning over, hands on his knees and breathing heavily. I see in what feels like slow motion as she approaches the sorcerer, who glances up, eyes wide. I want to intervene, but without another dagger, I'm helpless.

But Zambrano snarls at her, stepping back as she advances.

"Nine-ton hammer!" he cries, swinging one arm at her with a black and purple glowing hammer appearing in his hand as his arm draws forward.

Tunker is only a few paces from him, so the hammer doesn't have far to travel, and it smashes into her chest. The force of it hits with a louder punch than the previous spells and sends the rockhide demon, despite her massive weight, sailing through the air. She crashes through the wall, flying into the laser tag arena, and it sounds like she takes out another wall in there as well.

Zambrano drops to the ground, slumping against a *Pac-Man* machine with a glassy look in his eyes. My best guess is that he was saving that one last big spell for something just like that. I run over to him.

"Are you okay?" I ask, kneeling next to him.

"Yeah, I'm fine," he says. "Just . . . winded. Give me a second."

"It's ready," Liao Ling says, stepping up to us and handing me a second dagger made from light. "Let's get in there and finish this."

Leaving Zambrano behind, the ancient Chinese sorcerer and I follow Tunker through the demon-sized hole in the wall. Unfortunately, the cartoons are wrong, the demon's body smashing through didn't make a hole shaped like her, just a ragged gap.

We get into the arena, and my eyes take a moment to adjust to the lower light, just some red emergency lights that I guess have come on automatically now that the power is out. We see that Tunker appears to have hit another interior wall and partially collapsed it, but she's not lying in the wreckage.

We hear voices off to the left and advance cautiously. Turning a corner, we see what I've been dreading. Tunker is standing over the girl with a grimace-like smile on her face. Larry is sprawled off to the side, nursing a bloodied nose and holding his left shoulder like it's been hurt.

"Dunno what you done to Bronk," she says. "But it ain't happening to me. Try anyfing, and this girl gets crushed. I'm gonna pick 'er up and walk out of 'ere right as rain."

The girl is lying on the ground with the big rock demon's fist poised over her.

Liao Ling bares her teeth at the demon.

"I'm not letting you take her," the sorcerer growls. "I've been here before, with worse creatures than you. I know demons. And I know *you*, Tunkerasmodine. You may not remember, but we have met before. I demolished you at Mount Baekdu in the Korean mountains, and I'll gladly do it again. Step away from the girl."

"If you let me scarper outta 'ere in one piece, I won't do the girl in," Tunker says. "You 'ave me demon's word on that."

"You won't kill her? But someone else can, right? Or you'll just maim her? Or strand her in a dangerous foreign country? No, you will step away from the girl, or I'll disassemble you and spread your pieces across the Earth." She draws her hands back, whispering a few words in Chinese, and orange energy gathers, swirling and sparkling around her fists. "No, this is the future. In the old days, we could only spread your essence around over this planet, and you would rebuild over the course of decades. What happens when your essence ends up scattered across the Gobi desert or the asteroid belt?"

Damn. Liao Ling does *not* screw around. Behind us, Zambrano has stepped into the room, though he's still breathing heavily.

Tunker shrinks slightly but isn't easily cowed. "I've been stuck on this rock full of 'umans without me own lot for fifteen 'undred years, 'cept for that short bit when Seraphex 'ad her wee little portal open. Since then, I've even been forced to shack up with that numpty Bronk."

"She's buying time for you," Zambrano whispers, casually stepping up right by my back and speaking right into my ear. "Sneak up there and stab the demon."

The demon and the ancient sorcerer stare at each other as I advance, trying to move stealthily. This is much harder in a static situation, without a battle raging around me to create distraction. I can hear the impacts of every step that I take, no matter how carefully I move.

Larry stands, slightly unsteadily but stronger by the second. "It's okay," he says. "Demon, take me instead. Just let the girl go, and I'll go with you. No child gets kidnapped from my arcade. I have a customer service guarantee, you know. They're supposed to leave beaming with delight, not being dragged by a monster."

Larry looks at me, but I keep advancing, holding a finger over my mouth to try to communicate to him that he shouldn't mention me. He raises a confused eyebrow but looks away.

"A nipper's a much better bargaining chip," Tunker says. "Why would I want some old codger when these daft 'umans value the life of a young'un so much more?"

The three of them keep negotiating, all the while the little girl is frozen on the ground, paralyzed by fear. I finally get behind Tunker and get closer. I raise the dagger, and finally Larry seems to understand. He starts edging toward the demon and the little girl, glancing down at the girl and holding his hands up.

"Please, take me instead," he says. "I'll make a much better hostage. I won't try to get away, or yell and scream. Just let the girl go."

I glance at Tunker's fist, which is still close to the girl. But her arm is fairly extended, and I don't *think* if she suddenly starts spasming that it'll immediately hit the girl. More likely it will pull back from her. And Larry looks close enough to grab her. Tunker doesn't seem to see him as a threat. I don't like it, but it's a chance we're going to have to take before the argument between Liao Ling and Tunker starts to move to a more kinetic phase. Which feels increasingly likely as they trade barbs.

So I take a slow, deep breath and then swing my arm forward, stabbing the dagger of light into the space between the rockhide demon's shoulder blades.

Tunker spasms just like Bronk did, and just as I'd hoped, pulls her arm back. Larry leaps in, gritting his teeth in pain as he scoops the girl up and pulls her away.

As soon as the girl is clear, Liao Ling lets her orange magic spell go, unleashing a gushing torrent of energy at Tunker. The demon howls and steps back. I can see her structural integrity fading under the onslaught. But, screaming in rage, she lashes out with one fist. It misses the girl but collides with Larry, who is flung across the room by the force of the blow. His body clatters against the wall with a sickening crack.

The orange blast intensifies, and I see Zambrano flinging out his hands and adding a spell of his own, some sort of red darts that also strike the demon, slicing at her rocky body.

Broken and slashed apart, the rockhide demon finally collapses to the ground in a heap. And not a metaphorical one, but her actual pieces are cut apart, stone limbs spread across the arena floor.

As soon as she's down, I sprint across the room, running to kneel beside Larry.

He looks up at me, eyes swimming in pain.

"I can't move," he croaks. "And I can't feel my legs. Are they still attached? And is the kid okay?"

"The kid is fine," I say. Larry's face is white, drained of all blood. "And your legs are still attached. We just need to get you to someone who can help. You're going to be okay," I add, though I have no idea if it's true or not. "Can you do anything?" I say, looking to both Zambrano and Liao Ling.

They both come up to Larry and take turns casting various healing spells. Larry does seem to calm down, the immediate pain subsiding. But he doesn't move out of the awkward position on the floor he's stuck in. I'm afraid to move him for fear of making it worse.

"Can you move at all?" I ask him. I pull the gauntlets off and stuff them in my backpack.

He raises one of his arms. "These, yes," he says. "My legs . . . no."

"What now?" I ask. "Call 911? Can the druids help? What do we *do*?"

"Druids are for magical ailments and mental states," Zambrano says grimly. "They don't do acute trauma like this. We've done what we can without magic. Something is really messed up in his nerves or spinal column or something. I was never the one with the medical magic, that was always Olujimi. I can only really do the good stuff on myself. Larry needs a hospital, doctors, all that. I can cast some basic healing spells that will keep him alive until then."

He starts casting a spell, and I pull out my phone, which miraculously has survived this battle.

I'd say it's a good luck phone, but looking down at Larry, unable to move his legs, it doesn't feel so lucky.

# CHAPTER 21

So there I am, with the two most powerful sorcerers in the world, calling 911. But even as I'm dialing, I can hear sirens of all sorts outside. Stepping to glance outside the arena, I see that at the doors above, police are cautiously entering, weapons drawn.

"In here!" I call out. "We need the paramedics! It's not dangerous, just get the EMTs! Someone is hurt!"

I run out, continuing to ask for help. Within a minute, the EMTs are rushing in with a stretcher, and I direct them to where Larry is lying with his body a twisted wreck but a blissed-out look from whatever pain management spells the sorcerers cast on him. Another EMT and one of the cops usher the girl away, putting a blanket around her shoulders and shooting suspicious glances at me.

Looking around at the arena as the medical team carefully transfers Larry onto a stretcher to take him to the ambulance, I realize that Zambrano and Liao Ling have disappeared. Typical. I get it though. The authorities aren't exactly friendly. To them. Plus, now that emergency services are crawling all over the place, there are also civilians starting to peek in at the edges, cell phones pulled out to record, because of course they are. Can't people just enjoy the aftermath of a mysterious magical battle and live in the moment without feeling the need to document everything? I have to hope they just think I'm another random civilian caught up in the disaster.

I stick with Larry as they package him up and take him to the ambulance, and I notice the cops staying close by as we do. They're giving an energy like they're waiting to pounce on me.

"How is he?" I ask the EMT after they've loaded him into the ambulance.

"We've immobilized his spine. Likely due to nerve damage of some sort," the woman says. "He doesn't appear in immediate life-threatening danger. I can't say more, the doctors at Dominican Hospital will have to do a proper diagnosis."

"Can I go with him?" I ask.

"Are you family?" The EMT asks.

"No," I say, shaking my head.

"Only one family member can go, sorry. You'll have to stop by at visiting hours once he's in recovery. They'll take care of him there," she says, giving me a pat on the shoulder and hopping into the ambulance.

As she does, I feel my phone in my pocket buzz and pull it out to see a text from Zambrano.

*Had to bail, don't get along well with authority figures. LL and I teleported back to the warehouse. Is Larry okay?*

At least he cares about Larry. But it's really starting to sink in how unnecessary this whole battle was.

None of this would have happened if Zambrano had just listened to me and run away. But no, he wanted to show off and fight the demons. Again, someone's hurt because of his stupid ego. Both of the sorcerers just wanted to get into a fight with no regard for the collateral damage. They wanted to show off their magic, consequences.

Two of the cops step up to me. "We're going to have to ask you to stay here while we call this in," one says. "Pretty sure they're going to have some questions for you."

They guide me to a nearby bench, where I sit, watching tourists, cops, firefighters, and a few more EMTs running around. The cops have established a perimeter around the building and are pushing back anyone who tries to enter.

My phone starts buzzing, and for a second I want to ignore it. Why should Zambrano get updates on somebody who got hurt because of his stubborn refusal to listen or use caution? But I pull it out anyway.

It says "MSA Brooklyn Office" as the caller. No secret message apps or codes or anything.

"Hello?" I say.

"Bryce!" It's Agent Crane, which makes me breathe a small sigh of relief. "What the hell happened out there?"

"We were just at the arcade," I start. "And the two demons must have caught up to us somehow."

"You were just casually chilling at a laser tag place in Santa Cruz?" She demands. "Really? With some new Asian wizard who really likes to play laser tag?"

"Um. Actually, yes. That's . . . pretty much what happened? She was playing laser tag, we came to talk to her, and then two supercharged demons attacked us."

"I'm going to be checking every single security tape, tourist video, everything," she says. "If you're lying to me . . ."

"I'm not," I say.

"The media and the MSA higher-ups are going to pin this all on Zambrano. You have to know that. It's like violence between drug gangs. They're going to blame both sides. They don't care. And now we have to send a demonic containment unit there to deal with those demon bodies and make sure they don't reconstitute themselves. Everyone in the country is going to be demanding special demonic protection. People are going to be freaking out."

"Yeah," I say, sighing.

"Look, I'll try to help. You're really lucky that guy or that kid didn't die, or we would have a *much* bigger problem on our hands. I'm going to have the cops let you go, but I swear to god, if it looks like you and that dark sorcerer asshole caused this on purpose . . ."

"I get it," I answer. "Look, can you at least explain to your higher-ups that we're trying to help? That there's a new player, and he's really bad? Zambrano is . . . He's not exactly a good guy. He's selfish and annoying as hell. But he at least sometimes listens to me. I tried to get him to escape, but he wanted to stay and fight. But he's on our side. He wants to protect humanity. Because if nothing else, he's still one of us."

"You'd better get him to listen to you more," Agent Crane demands. "We can't have any more magical battles on US soil. Chicago, Yellowstone, now Santa Cruz—my ability to protect you is wearing incredibly thin. Congress is almost certainly going to have my bosses in to testify *again*, and let me tell you, they really, really do not like that. Get your sorcerer under control."

"My sorcerer?" I ask. "Do you really think I have control over him?"

"Figure it out," she says. "Get him to listen to you."

"Okay," I agree. "I'll try."

The phone beeps as the call ends, and I stick it back in my pocket. The cops hang around talking on their radios for about a minute.

As I'm standing there, I get a text message. I'm expecting it to be Zambrano, maybe apologizing for bailing on me, but instead it's Mei Song.

*Another classic Zambrano boondoggle, huh?* Mei writes. *It's all over the news. Your boss is an idiot. You're just lucky no one is dead. And it looks like no one has identified you, all the footage people are sharing are of the demons outside.*

That's good. At least I won't have to explain all this to my parents. Yet.

*Yeah, he messed this one up,* I admit.

At least my phone survived this encounter, I think, as I watch her type.

*Let me know if you need help,* she answers. *If the old idiot can stomach it. Or without telling him.*

*I don't want to keep secrets,* I answer. *That's the sort of BS he always pulls. Let me work on him, okay?*

*Sure,* Mei replies.

I'm pondering if there's anything more I need to say, when one of the cops walks up to me.

"You're free to go, I guess," he says. He looks like he wants to say something else, but it's clear he's just kind of baffled at the order he got. He shrugs, and the cops walk back to the building to join their buddies who are taping it off and putting up barriers around the broken holes.

I walk away, trying to avoid the cameras of tourists who seem intent on documenting as much as they can from outside the police lines. I send Zambrano a terse couple of text messages, and he agrees to pick me up at the place that Liao Ling originally teleportraited in, since she returned that teleportrait to him. So I have a long walk back along the water.

I try to use the time to calm down and collect my thoughts, but it doesn't help much. Zambrano just keeps ignoring my suggestions, instead listening to his own ego and narcissism. He may not be as far gone as some of the other sorcerers, but he's certainly showing signs of losing it.

And I keep telling myself that this is about saving the world. And yes, I'm willing to risk my life if it gives billions of people a small increase in their chance of survival. And yes, it's about that.

But I also want to save Zambrano. Pull him back from the grip of the sorcery even if it's only temporary. But I can't do that if he won't listen to me.

Finally I get to the spot where we arrived and text Zambrano to let him know I'm ready. He takes a few minutes to do who knows what, then teleportraits in from the warehouse. Seraphex had perched on his foot, and hops off, eyeing me with what actually looks like concern.

"Hey, Bryce," Zambrano says, then stops. He can see the rage still on my face.

"You're an idiot," I say. "You just keep ignoring me, pushing me away, and then making terrible decisions. You're a—"

"A what?" he roars, cutting me off. "You've seen the works of genius that I've created! No one else can do the things that I can!"

"A brilliant idiot," I finish. "You're incredibly clever, powerful, and knowledgeable. And you frequently get offtrack, short-sighted, or panicked. You almost gave up and ran away from the demon duke. You let Parth get hurt because you needed to finish a spell just because you didn't want to have to start it over later. And you couldn't stomach the idea of running away from the rockhides, and now Larry is in the hospital and may never walk again. He's lucky to be alive, along with that kid as well."

Zambrano opens his mouth. Then closes it. Then furiously raises a finger, starts to say something, and stops.

"Am I an idiot?" he demands, turning to Seraphex. "In the way that this non-magical fireball-bait is suggesting?"

The demon duck shakes her head, clucking in amusement. "Yes."

Finally, he leans back against the wall, and heaves a sigh. "I used to be so practical," he says. "I was always the strategist, the pragmatic one when others got caught up in fanciful ideas. But I'm losing it, aren't I? Slowly, but surely."

"You . . . don't always speak or act in the most logical manner, is all I'm suggesting," I say, trying to be slightly nicer about it.

"And so you think *I* need *you*? Me, the brilliant sorcerer who has vanquished so many foes? The inheritor and perfecter of the grand tradition of modern magic? I need you?"

I shrug. "I don't know. Do you?" I can't force him to see my point, but I have to put the question to him.

He fumes, glaring at me. He balls up one of his fists in anger, and for a moment I worry that he's going to blast me with a spell. But he just shakes the first at me.

"Well . . . yes!" he shouts. "But you're—you're not supposed to point it out! It makes me feel bad!"

I laugh, and he glares at me.

"You two do make . . . quite a team," Seraphex interjects. "It would be nice to say that I've always believed in you, but I have to be honest, so I'll just say that sometimes longshot bets pan out."

Zambrano sits for a long minute, silently brooding, somewhere between fuming and calculating. "So what, if I don't listen to your silly little opinions, you'll run off? You'll just bail on me if you feel like I'm not paying attention to every idea that you suggest?"

I take a deep breath, thinking that over. What *will* I do? What do I actually care about here? Why am I doing any of this any-way? It's not because hanging out with Zambrano is some great experience. He's my friend, in some sense, but it's certainly a toxic relationship. I wouldn't tolerate this from anyone else, but . . .

I keep telling myself that it's just some calculation about helping to save the world. But despite myself, I also care about Zambrano. I want to, anyway.

"Look," I say. "I may not be as stupidly fearless as Parth, but I'm not running away. As long as there's a danger to the whole world and you're the only one who can stop it . . . I'll be here. If we get killed trying to stop Rex, so be it. But if you want me to be here as your friend, if you want my respect, if you want to have the best chance at winning—things have to change."

"Okay, I know you're not wrong," he says with a sigh. "Not totally. The flashes of anger, the ego, overconfidence in my own abilities . . . I've seen all that before. The sorcery slowly changes your brain. Sanity slips away with such intense and prolonged magic use. It's still fairly minor, luckily, but we both know what it is. So I admit it: I have a problem. What are you asking for? Really?"

"You've been through a lot," I admit. "You've sacrificed a lot. To save dumb peasant humans like me, and my family, and my friends. And it's changed your brain. Clouded your judgment and your emotions. What I'm asking for, is to use me. To trust me. To plan with me. To default to believing me if I tell you something. Obviously, I'll be wrong sometimes too, but I need you to open up and let us plan this together. You know, if Seraphex can agree to change and be friends with us . . . maybe you can do the same."

"I am friends with you, now," Seraphex adds. "Before, I noticed the signs. They build very slowly over the years. I . . . was counting on it. It was a weakness, one that was growing over time. I hoped eventually you would become fully unstable, and in that state, you might release me back to my full demonic form. But I don't want that for you, not anymore. I don't want you to lose control to the magic."

He glares back and forth at the two of us, anger flashing in his eyes. "Magic doesn't control me. I control magic! I'm the greatest spellcrafter, the only one standing between the Earth and utter destruction. I don't need you, you need me! You and all your pitiful mortal . . . Ugh, listen to me," he finishes lamely. He drops his head into his hands. "I'm an old, narcissistic, antisocial asshole. And I may not even be the most powerful human alive anymore! It was pretty cool for a couple decades when that was the case. Okay, Bryce, unmagical prodigy boy. I'll do my best. I can't see clearly, so I'll plan things out with you. I'll outsource my judgment to you as much as I can."

"Okay. Yeah, that would be good," I say, though I'm still pissed. All my anger about his obstinate, egotistical ways has boiled over, but I need to stay focused. By any reasonable measure our relationship is messed up. But we have an incredibly dangerous demon to stop. And, well . . . a lot of this has been pretty cool. Does some part of me enjoy feeling like I'm involved in something incredibly important? Well, yeah, sure. And why shouldn't I?

"So, what next?" Zambrano asks, bringing me back to the task at hand. "Since what I've been doing doesn't seem to have been working."

"Damn, you called my bluff," I say, leaning back in the chair and trying to gather my thoughts. "I guess now I have to have something to say, huh?"

"You wanted this," Zambrano says with a dry chuckle. "Let's give it a shot."

I take a long moment, thinking through the options.

"It seems to me, step one is to assemble our team. We need to get Seraphex and Liao Ling on some sort of speaking terms. We've got to figure out a strategy to take down Rex. We should also apologize to Mei. She wants to help us, and she has access to contacts and resources that we don't."

"Call her on the phone, I can pretend to be Zambrano." Seraphex stands, ruffling her feathers self-importantly. "I am a big dumb idiot of a sorcerer who made a big old boo-boo. Forgive me pleeeease?" she says in a perfect imitation of Zambrano's voice. I always forget that she can do that.

"Ugh, please no. Are there any problems we can take on first that can be solved by a fireball?" Zambrano complains. "You know, just to get some momentum before we do the hard stuff?"

The door at the top of the stairs opens, and Liao Ling walks out, scowling at both of us. She clomps down the stairs, taking a bite out of a Pop-Tart that she appears to have helped herself to. She also looks freshly showered, and she's gotten herself some new modern clothes. She must have run out to one of the local stores while I was trudging across Santa Cruz. They are brightly colored—a pair of blue pants, green sneakers, a red headband, and a crop top that is blindingly yellow—and look like they were bought at one of those cheap fast fashion dollar stores that are spotted all over the less affluent neighborhoods of Brooklyn and Queens.

"You lads had a really nice heart-to-heart," she says. "I hope you've worked out all your little feelings."

"You were listening to that?" I protest.

Liao Ling looks at me like I'm an idiot. "Yes, I was. Do you take me for a fool?"

"You know, we used to have rules against that sort of eavesdropping in the Sorcerers' Circle," Zambrano says.

"Your little Circle thing didn't exist in my time," Liao Ling says, helping herself to a seat on one of the big chairs. "And if it had, they wouldn't have let me join it. Too much of an 'unpredictable and volatile liability with the potential to start improvising and wreck our carefully prepared strategy at any moment' as Merlin so eloquently put it one time. Anyway, I'm ready to help you with your plan now."

"That's . . . nice to hear," I say, already regretting this course of action. But two unreliable and dangerous sorcerers is probably better than one?

"I'll even talk to your pet demon, but she has to promise not to betray me. That's reasonable enough, isn't it, you foul creature? We are supposed to be on the same side here, after all," Liao Ling says.

Seraphex stands on the lab bench. She eyes the three of us, ruffling her feathers and drawing up to her full height, though a duck's full height isn't very impressive. "In the matter of defeating my former husband, the demon king, I will act as your ally and take no actions to your disadvantage until he is defeated, as long as you honor the same alliance toward me."

"Is that good enough?" I ask, looking to Zambrano and Liao Ling to see if they feel like the promise is strong enough.

"It is the ancient form of agreement," Seraphex says haughtily, "that my kind have used to forge alliances for all our history."

"In that case, foul beast," Liao Ling says, "I accept. Pointing out that you're a disgusting demon doesn't violate our alliance, does it?"

Seraphex sits down with a satisfied air. "No self-respecting demon would make an agreement that precludes taunts, insults, and mockery."

"This is no game, hell spawn," Liao Ling says. "I hate you."

"Don't worry, angry little sorcerer," Seraphex says, "the feeling is . . ." She pauses for a long moment, then turns and stares at me. "Hmm, it's not mutual. I don't hate her. Why can't I hate her? I want to hate her."

I shrug. "I like her. I guess it wouldn't be a good friend sort of thing to do, to hate your friend's friends."

Seraphex pouts. "This is terrible. Friendship feels terrible. I can't believe I agreed to this."

"Too late now," I say with a shrug. "So . . . now that all our interpersonal issues are fully resolved and won't cause any future problems whatsoever—how do we defeat Rex?"

# CHAPTER 22

As we start to strategize, everyone is reasonably polite to one another, which is a relief and kind of surprising. But I guess Zambrano, Liao Ling, and Seraphex are, in the end, total nerds. They get off on technical nonsense, so much so that often I have to pull them back from getting deep into theoretical discussions of ideas that wouldn't be useful even if they did work.

"Given some time and materials," Liao Ling offers, "I can create the fully powered version of the Caesar Special, the weapon that we used on the rockhide demons at the laser tag place. The basic spell is simple enough, but I need something powerful to bind it to in order to make it effective against such a mighty foe. It won't stop Rex, but it will slow him down and weaken his defenses. I'll need to get some ingredients and use the focus of a druidic stone circle. Are there any of those still standing?"

"You mean like Stonehenge?" I ask and show her a picture of it on my phone.

"Yes, the Giants' Dance!" Liao Ling says. "That's what they called it in my time. That should work. I'll need the help of the druids to activate it, but I think Deirdre Moran will be willing to step in."

"You think Deirdre Moran is going to help you activate the druids' most sacred power source? A little healing, sure, but you think they'll open Stonehenge to you?" Zambrano objects. "Druids hate sorcerers."

"Druids hate sorcerers who ask for their help and then destroy their castles in a fit of anger," Liao Ling notes. "They are rather fond of sorcerers who rid the world of powerful demons for fifteen hundred years. We got along well once I was able to explain my history and fill in some gaps in theirs. The druids of my time actually were quite friendly with me as well—probably because by comparison to Merlin I was pleasant to them."

"Suck-up," Zambrano says sourly.

"Mei might be able to help with the artifacts from Slickwad's collection," I say, pulling out my phone to text her. "If we can convince her to get over how rude we were when she visited."

"Just tell her your boss is an asshole, she's probably used to that," Zambrano says with a shrug. "That's how assistants usually get things done, right?"

"Huh. That actually might work," I say. "So overall this is a good first step. What will we do if we have the fully powered version of the Caesar Special?"

"We'll still need to throw a huge amount of pain Rex's way to actually weaken him," Liao Ling says, ignoring Zambrano's petulance. "Even Merlin and I didn't have enough firepower between the two of us to do more than temporarily hold him in place in order to toss him into the prismatic prison, which we'd been building for years."

"Damn it," I say with a sigh. "And I'm guessing you'll need me to do my magical demon invisibility thing?"

"See," Zambrano says, with a grin, "you do have value!" It's basically the same sort of insults he's been throwing at me for months, but this time he pairs it with a friendly pat on the back. Call it progress?

"How about the Sword of Wayland?" I ask, gesturing to the glass sword in the case across the room. "If he's weakened by the Caesar Special, could that hurt him?"

"It might hurt him," Liao Ling says, "and would probably do some damage against a lesser demon. But it can't pierce his demonic armor."

"Hmm. Could modern weapons help with getting enough firepower to hurt him?" I suggest.

"It's possible," Seraphex says. "A combination of magic and your military technology might be able to weaken him. It would need to be very powerful. The Javelin missile temporarily stunned him, but it only lasted for a matter of seconds."

"So what do we do with him after we get him under control?" I ask. "What's the end solution here?"

We throw out a whole bunch of ideas, but a lot of them just don't go anywhere. We talk ourselves in circles trying to figure out how to create a box similar to the prismatic prison to hold Rex. It turns out the facilities to make slow-time cases at that size and effectiveness don't currently exist, and the time it would take to build up that full supply chain would give Rex space to conquer the world several times over.

"Liao Ling," I ask, "you mentioned spreading the remains of the rockhide demons across the planet or the asteroid belt. Would that work for Rex, if we could beat him in battle somehow?"

Seraphex screws up her face. "Demons can reassemble themselves if defeated. If we scattered his remains across the asteroid belt, he'd put himself back together in a decade or two."

"What about outside of the solar system? Or out on Pluto or something?" I ask.

"Might buy us another few years. But once he's reassembled, he would be able to use magic to accelerate himself. Even slow acceleration adds up quickly to high speed."

"That's one of the reasons we had to trap him in the prismatic prison rather than send him to Mars with the rest of the demons," Liao Ling adds. "We figured that if Merlin was able to travel to Mars, Rex would probably figure out a way to do it as well."

"And you weren't worried that I would be able to do that?" Seraphex pouts.

Liao Ling shrugs. "It took you over a thousand years to find your way back, so I guess we were right. Hope you enjoyed your extended stay in literal hell."

"Let's stay on track," I say, cutting Seraphex off before she can retort.

"Would the sun harm him?" Zambrano asks. "He has somewhat of a fire element basis, so he's normally not very bothered by flames, but . . ."

"To be honest," Seraphex says, "I'm not totally sure what effect the sun would have on him. But I doubt it would be good."

"It wouldn't, like, supercharge him?" I ask. "Just checking."

Seraphex sighs. "It might actually do something like that. It is a potent power source. He might be able to channel it and grow stronger. Demons can harness the power of volcanoes and such. It might overwhelm and destroy him—there's no way to know. But it also might make him a godlike entity. Or it could unbalance the sun's fusion, cause massive solar flares, bathe the planet in radiation."

My phone buzzes, and I glance down, hoping that it's Mei texting me back, but it's just a couple messages from Parth. I'll give him a call later—he's still too weak to join us in the field, but I want to run these ideas by him.

"Fascinating," Zambrano says. "It would be a very interesting experiment to try to find out—"

"Please," I say, cutting him off, "let's not accidentally create a demon god of unthinkable power or make the sun explode, okay? That's way too risky for, like, Earth's future."

"I would be unharmed by solar changes, but indeed it would affect me negatively to see my"—Seraphex almost chokes on the word—"*friends* be harmed."

"Okay, fair," Zambrano says, nodding in agreement. "No recklessly endangering the entire course of our universe by creating demon gods. Noted for future reference."

"You really do need me around, don't you?" I ask. "Is there some sort of pocket universe we could try? One with different time passing, or different rules of physics that would take away his powers?"

"The fact of the matter," Seraphex says, "is that anywhere that we trap my former husband, he will have time to plan and plot and trick us. So we could trap him somewhere, but just because we can't think of a way out doesn't mean that he won't. That's why the prismatic prison was so effective. It didn't give him time to think, plan, or use his powers.

"And with pocket universes," Zambrano adds, "we don't have the way to slow time down or change the rules enough. His power is just too great. There's no desert island we can strand him on, here or out in the nearby galaxy, that we can guarantee he won't find a way to escape."

We explore a few other ideas, but none of them amount to more than a temporary solution.

"We could keep him here on Earth," Zambrano says in frustration, "and keep having to defeat him every time he reforms. Or send him across the solar system, but then we'll have no idea when or how he'll return."

I feel my phone vibrate a couple times, but it's just more messages from Parth. We tend to text bomb each other when we're doing research.

"Maybe we just figure out which way holds him for a little while and try to build a new prismatic prison?" I ask. "Start creating the tools and supplies needed to do it, then get him on the second round."

"That is not sufficient," Seraphex says, an edge of desperation in her voice. "We need a solution that can hold long term. Beating him in battle once is an unlikely prospect. We will only get one chance at it. If he wins and gains dominion over this world, you all will die in excruciating fashion. But that will be a mercy compared to the unending torment that he will unleash on me."

"There's a nice consolation prize, then," Liao Ling says with a nonchalant shrug.

"Hey, we're all on the same team here," I remind everyone. "We'll figure something out," I add, though I can feel the frustration in the room about to boil over. "Maybe we should take a break for a few minutes."

My phone starts buzzing insistently, so I pull it out. This time it's Agent Crane. There are a bunch of texts from both her and Parth, and also some news alerts that I set up to monitor mentions of Zambrano.

"Uh-oh," I say with a sudden sinking feeling. I step a few feet away from the others, but I figure I can't really take this in private without it seeming very suspicious. "What's going on?" I say as I answer the call.

"I can't talk long," Agent Crane says, her voice tight and controlled. "I've been iced out of pretty much every channel. I think they're only keeping me on because I have a relationship with you. But the top brass here at the MSA think I've been compromised and tricked into trusting you. They're almost certainly monitoring this call, but that can't be helped."

"Why? What happened?" I ask, heart thumping.

"You and Zambrano were sighted by global surveillance systems in the western Pacific multiple times. And then an hour ago, the Leviathan has been sighted for the first time since it was trapped in 1929. It attacked the port at Midway and killed a number of civilians. They're tracking it on its way to Hawaii, and the military hasn't been able to stop it. The MSA and military top brass are convinced that Zambrano has finally lost it and released the Leviathan. Please tell me you were there trying to stop it from being released."

While she's been talking, I've been pulling up news stories on my phone. It's horrible. Mangled US Navy ships. A wrecked submarine. Absolute carnage and destruction at the port at Midway atoll.

"It's . . . well, honestly it's kind of a coincidence," I say "And complicated. But we didn't set it free. The demon king was going to get free and cause disasters regardless of what we did."

"That is not what I was hoping to hear," Agent Crane says dryly.

"I'm sorry. We're trying to help, I promise," I say.

"Bryce, the navy is scrambling to fight this goddamn ancient sea monster that's been let loose. They've already lost a couple ships. It's headed toward Hawaii. If the Leviathan makes it there and starts killing civilians, the MSA is going to run out of patience. They'll put out a global arrest order on both Zambrano and you. Dead or alive."

"Are you sure?" I ask. "They'll actually kill us?"

But the line has gone dead.

I look back at the two sorcerers and the demon duck.

"I'd imagine you all heard every word of that?" I say. "Magical enhanced sorcerer and demon hearing abilities?"

They all nod.

"This is the first step of my former husband's plan," Seraphex says. "Destabilize the world. Sow chaos. Maybe even get world governments to take out Zambrano so he doesn't have to. He doesn't like to fight face-to-face if he doesn't have to. Especially after being trapped for so long, and outplayed by us in the pocket universe, he'll be hoping that someone or something else will do his dirty work for him. Hence, the rockhide demons that he sent after you."

"He is also still weakened by the wound from the Caesar Special that we used to trap him in the first place," Liao Ling adds. "He'll need time to recover and want to keep us busy at the same time. He won't show himself until he believes he has nearly won."

"That's true," Seraphex says. "He will wait until he's regained his personal powers and has his allies in order before confronting us or the world governments directly."

"Well, releasing the Leviathan is his first play," I say, clenching a fist in frustration.

"I hate playing his game," Zambrano gripes. "I wish we had the tools to simply take him on directly."

"It's all about strategy. We have to keep ahead of him," Liao Ling suggests. "But make him think he's getting what he wants. Instead, we will use the opportunity strategically. You go and fight the Leviathan. While Rex's attention is focused on watching his plan play out, I'll go to the druids and get their help in summoning a weapon that we can use to weaken him."

"Okay, that makes sense to me," I say, and Zambrano nods his agreement.

Liao Ling wastes no time getting started, leaping to her feet, and I'm struck again by how bright her clashing clothes are. I don't say anything because I've long since learned that criticizing people's fashion choices is almost never useful or productive.

"In my time, you know," she says, noticing me looking at her new outfit, "I could have been executed for wearing yellow like this, it being the color of royalty and all. Well, they would have tried, anyway. This new phone I've got is cool," she says, holding up the smartphone that she must have also gotten while she was out shopping. "But being able to wear these colors fulfills my soul."

My phone buzzes, and I see that it's Mei. Shrugging, I put it on speaker.

"Hi, Mei," I say. "Look, I'm sorry about when you visited, and Zambrano is sorry too."

I glance over at Zambrano. He rolls his eyes but leans forward.

"I'm sorry," he says. "I think I just really wanted to use that spell again."

"Gross. Apology not accepted," Mei says. "But we can work together anyway, since the world is about to end and a sea monster is apparently going straight for Hawaii. I have family there. So I'll do whatever it takes. What do you need?"

"We need some artifacts; I'm guessing Slickwad may have them or have information on where to get them," I say. "I'm pretty sure you have some experience with that as well. Look, we're going to go try to deal with this Leviathan situation." I glance over at Liao Ling, who is watching me and looking at her own phone, trying to figure out exactly what I'm doing. She looks confused but is tapping at it gamely. Connecting the two of them together feels like a big risk for some reason, but I guess you've got to trust the people you're allied with.

"I'll connect you with her," I say. "She can fill you in on what she needs. And . . . she's not experienced with the modern world. She might need some help with her phone."

"Oh my god, Bryce Alexander, are you seriously dropping your tech support problems on me?" Mei says.

"You said you'd do whatever it takes," I point out. "Plus, she's very nice. I'm sure you'll hit it off."

"Okay, fine," Mei agrees.

"Am I nice? Maybe. Unless you cross me, obviously, then I'm an unholy terror," Liao Ling says. "To be honest, this rapid language learning spell has scrambled my personality. New future world, new future me, I guess."

"Okay, sure, I'll see what I can do," Mei says. "Give her my number, and we'll talk. If it'll help save the world."

"That's the goal," I say. "Thank you, Mei."

"Yeah," she answers, and the line goes dead.

"You two have so much in common!" Zambrano exclaims.

"Yeah, we both want to not have everyone we know die," I grumble.

I give Liao Ling a quick lesson in how to use her phone to call and text all of us. To her credit, she does pick it up very fast. It's cute, seeing a contacts list with only three names in it, like a teenager getting her first phone. I do notice that there are several social media apps already downloaded, which terrifies me, but I can't very well put parental controls on a fifteen-hundred-year-old sorcerer's device.

Impatiently, Liao Ling pulls the phone away from me, grabs the teleportrait to Ireland, and disappears in a whoosh of air.

Zambrano, Seraphex, and I sit there for a minute, catching our breath.

"You know," Zambrano says, "Back in 1929, it took the whole Sorcerers' Circle to trap the Leviathan. What exactly are the two of us going to do against this one?"

"Um, yeah," I say. "Well, things have changed, right? We've also got the US Navy on our side potentially. Are we sure they won't be able to take it down on their own?"

Zambrano shakes his head. "The Leviathan has almost unbreakable scales, and it can magically heal back from essentially any wound that does get through, magical or conventional. It's just got so much magical energy stored up over its incredibly long lifespan. Their missiles and bombs will mostly glance off it, and any damage done will be quickly healed. At this point it is invulnerable to most kinetic damage, and it stays underwater until it's ready to strike, so there's no way to get to it with a bomb or a missile or something. A truly massive bomb might do something, but I doubt they'll be willing to go that far, especially if it's close to US territory."

"That's not good. What about," I say, glancing around the room for help, "the Sword of Wayland?"

"You really want to use that thing, don't you?" Zambrano says, callously calling out the little part of me that absolutely does want to stab something with that badass glass sword. "Unfortunately, those scales are really tough. You wouldn't be able to cut through them to get to the insides. Though if we could get the sword lodged in its more vulnerable flesh, that would actually damage it over time. It would open a wound that it couldn't heal, causing its magic to strain against the damage and fail."

"Huh." I purse my lips. "Does it have a mouth? Eyes? Other vulnerable parts?"

"That is a classic trick," Zambrano says, nodding. I'm noticing that he's actually being fairly patient in explaining this and taking my ideas seriously. "The eyes have their own transparent scales, but . . . if you could get it all down the mouth, the digestive tract is also very tough. That thing is designed to eat damn near anything and digest it successfully. Just shooting something into its mouth or getting it to swallow a bomb won't work, otherwise we could just tell the navy to do that."

"Oh, damn," I say. "Well, it was a worth a shot." I ponder it for another minute. "What about the lungs? Does it have lungs?"

"The lungs?" Zambrano asks. "Yes, it does have lungs; its physiology is fairly similar to modern water snakes. But with the giant tentacles, as you know. So a few small differences. But it has the same digestive and breathing systems as snakes, just much larger and more durable."

"The mouth is the way to the digestive tract, which is shielded. But it's also the way to the lungs, right? Like, when you swallow something down the 'wrong tube' and it's really unpleasant."

"And," Zambrano says, starting to smile, "what if the thing you swallowed down the wrong tube was an ancient magical sword that can cut through almost anything? That would mess that bastard up quite nicely, I think."

I grin. Maybe this really can work, us collaborating on problem-solving.

"So," Zambrano continues, "We just need to throw you down its throat with the sword, and you take a quick turn into the trachea and puncture its lung."

"Wait, I have to go *inside* of it?" I ask. "I figured it would be more like leaping up and stabbing it in the neck or something."

"After you have punctured its lung," Zambrano continues, ignoring me, "the beast should weaken steadily, draining directly off its huge magical reserves to keep itself alive. After a few minutes, it will get weak enough that I can siphon its energy directly. This wasn't possible when the Circle was fighting it because we didn't have the sword."

"But we'll only be puncturing one lung since there's only one sword. Doesn't it have two lungs? Will taking out just one lung really help?"

"Snakes only have one useable lung," Zambrano says dismissively. "Do they teach you *anything* in those modern schools? Or is it all just talking about how math makes you *feel inside*?"

Okay, so in terms of working together as a well-oiled machine, we're not all the way there yet. But it's a start.

"Just don't miss when you're jumping into the windpipe," he adds, "because its stomach is full of exceedingly powerful acids."

"Sure," I agree.

"Also, once you've weakened it enough, you'll need to get out quickly. The arcane energies within it may become unstable as I try to drain them away."

"What exactly will happen?" I ask.

"I'm not certain," Zambrano answers. "I've never done this before."

"Nothing that's good for a frail human body, of that I can assure you," Seraphex says.

I roll my eyes. "Spectacular."

# CHAPTER 23

A few hours later we're back on the yacht that Zambrano says he won in a game of Wizard Poker. Luckily, he had it docked in Hawaii, and he had made a teleportrait for its galley, so we're able to go straight there. I reluctantly left behind the demon-hiding gauntlets because I desperately don't want to lose them, and Seraphex is convinced that Rex will continue hiding until he has regained his full power. I do, however, have the Sword of Wayland. I hold it in my right hand, and it feels incredibly light. We tested it on the concrete curb and a metal dumpster in an alley near the warehouse, and oh boy does it *work*. The trash company will probably not be thrilled that we poked a hole in their dumpster, but it's all for a good cause, right?

It's evening, and the sun is coming down toward the horizon, just starting to turn reddish. It would be a lovely night for a cruise on a luxury craft like this if we weren't plowing into a battle.

"What exactly *is* the Leviathan?" I ask as we stand on the prow of the ship, racing across the waves toward certain danger. I want to believe that we look like heroes with the saltwater breeze spraying our faces, but I'm not dumb enough to try to take a picture and ruin the fantasy. Seraphex has taken up a spot farther back on the deck, sitting in a sunny spot. "You said it's not a demon, so you told me not to bring the gauntlets. But what exactly is it?"

Zambrano shrugs. "A mythic monster is the technical term. The Circle's best guess is that it was enchanted thousands of years ago and just kept growing. Like the one gigantic old fish in a pond that somehow eludes fishermen for years. Just keeps on getting bigger every year. We believe that when it was a little sea snake, it was given some sort of enchantment by a magic user and has just steadily grown in power as it has eaten and stored energy from sea life ever since. Honestly, I think it's some wild druidic magic gone awry, but the druids have never been willing to admit to it."

"Oh, interesting. Are there more of them out there?"

"Not really," Zambrano says. "At least, not ones that are roaming free. The inexorable spread of humanity to every nook and cranny of the world was not really compatible with mythic monsters still being out there. It's kind of like me in a way. One of the last of its kind, unappreciated by the modern world that it finds itself in. Downtrodden by the bureaucrats, politicians, and journalists. An iconoclast, desperately struggling against an unfamiliar and unfair world that doesn't see it for what it truly is. Poor, misunderstood thing. I understand where it's coming from."

"What's it going to do when it gets to Hawaii?" I ask.

"Oh, it's going to wreck the port and kill everyone, for sure," he says. "In the early 1920s, it first ate a ship, killing everyone on board, and it took a liking to human flesh. It started seeking out ships and raiding harbors. It's an absolute killing machine with a taste for the bodies of *Homo sapiens*."

"And you think you're similar to that?" I ask with an eyebrow raised.

"Well, I was never into cannibalism *per se*. But let me have the romantic metaphor, okay?"

"Humans have always been so afraid to partake in consuming their own species," Seraphex says, waddling up to us primly. "I've always thought it was a particular sort of cowardice. You're all just made of meat in the end."

"At least we're meat with opposable thumbs that might be able to untie knots if it were, say, trussed up with rope and thrown overboard," Zambrano retorts, but with an affectionate smile.

That's when the captain starts waving, calling us up to the bridge. Leaving Seraphex behind, we jog up the stairs to where he's waving us in. When we get there, the radio is blaring.

"Civilian vessel, this is *USS Howard Taft*. Admiral Wilcox speaking, commander of US Pacific Fleet. You have entered a restricted maritime zone. This area is currently under special operations due to an unidentified supernatural threat. Identify yourself immediately and state your purpose. Be advised, failure to comply will result in interdiction. You are ordered to maintain your current position and stand by for further instructions. Over."

Zambrano takes the microphone from the captain, who seems relieved to have someone else to speak to the threatening voice.

"This is Zambrano, sorcerer of the Circle," Zambrano says, straightening up with pride. "I'm here to help you with your little water snake problem, Admiral."

"They tell me that you released this thing. Is that true?" the admiral demands.

"No, we didn't," Zambrano protests. "I was one of the people who trapped it in the first place! We're here to put it down once and for all."

The admiral sighs. "This is a restricted zone, Mr. Wizard. Please turn your craft around."

Zambrano reaches forward to open the channel and ream him out, but I grab his hand, shaking my head. He fumes.

"What were you going to say?" I ask.

"He gave me his fancy title, I gave him mine. And he ignored it. I was going to call him captain and threaten to blow up his little oceangoing tub of an aircraft carrier. Explain that he could have help against the Levithan, or he could have to deal with both a deadly giant sea snake *and* a pissed-off sorcerer on his hands."

"And . . . do you think that would be likely to help stop the Leviathan?" I ask.

"Well, no, not precisely," Zambrano admits.

He thinks about it for a second, then nods. He takes a deep breath, and then, calmer than before, he gestures toward the microphone.

"Shall I try to convince him?" he asks me.

"Nicely?" I ask. "Diplomatically?"

"Will 'mostly' be good enough? These military types always need to have a dick-measuring contest. Or pissing match. Whatever phallus-inspired metaphor you feel like applying. Though what the hell is a pissing match, after all? Like, who can urinate the most? The farthest? The yellowest? Disgusting."

I shrug. "Yeah, just try to make friends rather than enemies? Understand things from his perspective?"

"Hmm," Zambrano says. "Oh, fine, Bryce. For you. Let's give that a go."

He takes the microphone, thinks for a moment, and then presses the button to transmit.

"Admiral, I recognize that you have a job to do here. But I have a job to do as well. I'm sure if you consult with your colleagues at the MSA, you'll find that I was one of the sorcerers responsible for trapping this thing before you were born. Unless you want to break a half dozen international treaties and drop a nuke and hope this sea serpent is still there when it hits, we're going to be your best shot. Worst case, it eats us, and then your government has one less headache to deal with, right?"

There's a very long pause. The channel opens briefly, but no one speaks, and then it cuts off for another minute. I glance around for help, but the captain has disappeared at some point during the conversation.

"I don't trust you," the admiral says, "But we've been throwing ordinances of all types at it all day. Missiles, torpedoes, naval guns, and nothing penetrates that damn thing. It just keeps on its course for Hawaii. Two of my ships are disabled, and we're busy evacuating a third that is sinking. We've lost good sailors today. And it didn't just try to sink the ships—it ate them. It was specifically feeding off my people. If you want to take a swing at this thing, be my guest."

"Understood," Zambrano says, face growing more serious. "I'm sorry for your losses, Admiral. I remember what that was like, in the 1920s. We lost several crew members from the ship that the Sorcerers' Circle chartered. We'll do our best to take care of this thing for you, Admiral."

There's another pause, then a crackle of static, and the admiral's voice comes back on.

"Understood, sorcerer," he says. "And good hunting. Admiral Wilcox out."

Zambrano takes a look at the various screens, frowning.

"One more thing, Admiral," he says, pressing the radio button to talk again. "There's a small vessel that just departed on a heading opposite of ours. They'll probably need a rescue if you can spare a ship to pick them up."

I look at the screens that Zambrano is examining and see one that shows a rear-facing camera. Rapidly moving away from our yacht, there's a small speedboat containing what looks like the captain and the entire crew of the yacht.

"I guess they overheard the radio traffic and figured out that we weren't on a joyride here," Zambrano says. "Probably better that way, I'm sure I'll have my hands full just keeping you alive, let alone a bunch of sailors."

"Don't we need them to, like, drive the ship?" I say. Zambrano seems to know a good bit about this type of boat, but I'm realizing that I have absolutely no idea how to do anything on board a massive yacht like this. Not that I would have any better idea about a little boat. There wasn't a lot of boating happening in central New Jersey. Canoeing a couple times at summer camp doesn't quite cut it.

Zambrano shrugs. "Oh, I was planning to bring the Leviathan to us anyway. It's got a taste for human flesh, like I said. Like sharks, it can smell blood from a mile away. That's not quite far enough, as we don't know where it is, but we can augment the effect. Make the smell spread much farther and wider. The spell is also great fun for pranks too," he adds.

"Please, no need to demonstrate that," I say. "We can stick to using it for its intended purpose."

"Oh, Rodney Wint created it in boarding school to get back at a bully. Filled an entire dormitory at Harrow School with the smell of flatulence. That was how we found his talent for sorcery and recruited him for the Circle. But then we used a modified version of the same spell on the Leviathan."

"Okay, sounds good," I say. "What do we do?"

"Are you going to get all pissy if I ask to open one of your veins for a little bit of blood magic? It might recognize mine and stay away given what I did to it last time."

I sigh. "I mean, what's an assistant for if not to drain some of his blood out for his boss's spells? It's not going to imperil my immortal soul or anything, is it?"

Zambrano shrugs. "Probably not?"

"Oh, you humans and your silly preconceptions," Seraphex says, having hopped into the ship's bridge. "We demons enjoy blood, but blood isn't some core part of your identity. It's just fancy salt water that humans carry around because they never actually evolved to survive on land. They're basically ocean-dwelling creatures that lug their own little miniature oceans around wherever they go because they couldn't adapt to land. It's incredibly inefficient."

"That's actually poetic," I point out. "Anywhere we go, we take our oceanic origins with us, a warm reminder of where we began."

"That's a very human way to consider it," Seraphex says.

"Anyway, how do we do this? Do we need to get a knife to get some blood?"

"The first rule of blood-related magic," Zambrano says, leading us down to the deck, "is you don't cut your hand open, like they always do in shows and movies. Do you really want to have a big nasty cut on your hand that will take weeks to heal? So dumb. Second rule: don't use a knife! Why even have a cut at all?" He pulls out a small syringe. "It's not the nineteenth century, we have better ways of doing this."

The prick of the syringe is slightly painful, but a lot less painful than cutting my hand open would have been, so that's nice.

Zambrano takes the syringe and drains the bright red blood into what looks like a small copper saucepan from the ship's galley.

"We just mix it up in a copper vessel with some bird's eye chili peppers and a hint of motor oil, and we'll be good to go," he says.

"Motor oil?" I ask. "That's a spell ingredient?"

"Castrol SAE 30, to be specific," Zambrano says. "You have to make the ingredients of a spell a unique combination so that the magic can recognize the pattern. Rodney was kind of a car geek. We're lucky they still make the same stuff for antique cars and lawn mowers. I always keep a couple quarts on hand in case it ever goes out of production. You never know when you want to leave some university or government agency a stinky surprise. It really takes the edge off some of the abuse that I have to face, you know?"

The sorcerer performs a few magical motions above the copper saucepan, then with a shrug, twiddles his thumbs above the pan, then puts his mouth in the crook of his elbow and blows a loud fart noise.

"Look, Rodney was only fourteen years old when he created this spell. It's silly, but the underlying theoretical work is solid. Arcane trigger movements don't have to be serious and look cool."

Thick steam starts to rise out of the pan, and its bottom begins to glow red. Zambrano makes one final pinching motion and leans out over the guardrail and drains the blood out. It drops into the seawater below, spreading out in a tiny inky pattern and causing the ocean to release a small burst of steam as it spreads. Then Zambrano yelps as the heat of the pan reaches up the handle, and he flings the pan itself out into the ocean where it disappears under the waves.

Seraphex takes a few sniffs of the air, eyeing the water with interest.

"Does this smell have an effect on you?" I ask the demon duck.

"I'm not some base creature like the Levithan, made of pure instinct and bloodlust," Seraphex answers haughtily. "I have intellect, and I can tell that the enticing blood smell in the air is an illusion. So I shall ignore it."

"Okay, fair enough," I say. "Zambrano, how long do we have?"

"Well, if I had to estimate, maybe from zero to forty-five minutes. It takes time for the spell to spread the smell out, and while the Leviathan can swim fairly fast, it's still only about twenty-five miles an hour or so. And it might be quite far away."

"Zero?" I ask.

"For all we know, it's under the boat right now," Seraphex says, yawning and stretching her feathers out, not appearing worried at all.

"Could we throw the duck into its mouth?" I suggest. "That helped with Mr. Chompers in the pocket universe. And it was kind of satisfying."

"It's a big beast. I would be stuck in its belly for a long time, and do it no particular damage," Seraphex says, casually scanning the ocean.

I clench my right hand around the hilt of the Sword of Wayland. What have I gotten myself into here? But I have to remember, I'm doing this for all of humanity. Not just for everyone in Hawaii who's in danger, but to stop Rex's plan to bring hell on Earth.

I look over at Zambrano, who has knelt with both hands on the deck and is speaking quiet words in a language I don't recognize.

As he does, low thrumming vibrations spread out from his hands. Seraphex hops over to him, saying something with a mocking air, the specifics of which I can't quite hear above the sound of the wind, ocean, and the boat's motors.

I'm also doing this for my friends, as weird and annoying as they are.

"Old Polynesian boat-stabilizing spell," he says, noticing that I'm watching him. "It'll keep the thing from being able to capsize the boat. Learned it from some really amazing navigators. You know, they liked me back when . . ." His voice trails off as he remembers.

"Back when what?"

"Back when he wasn't a jerk to everyone," Seraphex adds. "When was that last? Was it in the seventeen hundreds?"

"You're asking that last bit as a question because you know it's not true," Zambrano says with a scowl. "Feels like it though. I can't help it if all my friends and lovers are dead and I'm slowly going insane. Are you ready, Bryce?"

I'm standing on the deck, holding a magic glass sword in my hand, but I sure as hell don't feel ready. Here we go anyway. We're as ready as we're going to be.

I grit my teeth and grip the sword, ready to take on a mythic monster. I can feel its strength and protection flowing through my body. I'm pissed that Zambrano never let me use this before, but I guess he didn't realize it would work for me. Let's go.

We've also got waterproof earpieces set up for easy communication. I've got mine magically stuck to my ear, the amber nexus strapped on in case I need to breathe underwater, and a headlamp on my head so I can see inside the Leviathan.

"You look good with the earpiece on, Sera," I say. The demon duck looks pretty funny with her radio earpiece magically affixed to her head. "It kind of looks like you're about to come onstage with a burst of fireworks to kick off the North American leg of your new album tour."

"I can make my voice sound like anything you like, so why not?" Sera jokes. "I could fill in for any pop star who gets sick or is too hungover to perform. But I've always wanted to play my original songs . . ."

"Sure, and we've seen how loud you can perform," Zambrano says, "so you wouldn't even need a PA system to blast what I'm sure would be just absolutely delightful music. What would you sing about? Subjugating the entire human race? Your tearful breakup with Rex, the demon king?"

"Okay, okay," I say. "Let's focus here."

We run over the plan one more time. It sucks, but I do get to use an awesome magical sword. Still, somehow I ended up with the roll of entering an ancient monster and trying to pierce and collapse its lungs from the inside. I really should have listened to my high school guidance counselor when he suggested I go into software engineering.

But I'm psyched and ready to rock.

And the ocean just sits there, empty. We're far enough out that there aren't any gulls or anything else. On the horizon, I can see a few ships of the Pacific Fleet.

It's not until twenty-seven minutes later when the Leviathan actually shows up.

# CHAPTER 24

Seraphex spots it first, her demonic eyes apparently able to see through quite a bit of water.

"Leviathan incoming!" she squawks as she jumps out of her relaxed position and leaps into the air, soaring up into the sky.

Zambrano and I scan the water, watching the empty waves in the area where the duck is flying.

"It's definitely here," Seraphex says, her voice coming through in my earpiece. "Fairly deep down but rising rapidly. It'll be at the yacht in a minute or two."

"I see movement down there," the sorcerer says, pointing off the bow, and I can hear his voice both through the earpiece and in real life.

And then it rears out of the water, a massive snake with a mohawk-like fin atop its head that continues down its back. It opens its mouth, and a long tongue lashes out. Which is terrifying, because I'm supposed to go in there.

And then the tentacles come out of the water alongside it, thrashing through the water as it advances toward our yacht, mouth opened hungrily and yellow eyes gleaming.

"We only get one shot at this," Zambrano says. "Let's do it."

I gulp. "Okay, let's go," I say.

"*Blue bubble bouncer, bubble bounce this bothersome bore,*" he says and snaps with his right hand, his left, and his right again. "Sorry, that's just the spell's trigger words. Nothing personal. It's just a coincidence that you're not very interesting as a person," he adds, completely unnecessarily, as the blue bubble forms and glides toward me.

A moment later I am picked up, glass sword and all, and floated out over the ocean. As Zambrano explained, the bubble blocks out all sound, so I'm not able to hear the Leviathan as it roars, charging through the waves at the yacht. But as I float out over the ocean, the Levithan changes course slightly and churns in my direction.

It's strange and unnatural to see this mythic monster bearing down on me with no sound, its tentacles rippling through the water, splashing eagerly as it gets closer. Its head ducks down into the water for a brief second, and then the entire body launches up out of the ocean. The wet scales gleam in the sunlight, and the tentacles undulate around me. And then I see a flash of yellow eyes and white teeth, and its jaws close around me, closing shut with a sloppy crunch.

The bouncer bubble holds me for a moment, then pops, depositing me into the mouth of the beast. As it makes incidental contact with the Leviathan's mouth, I notice that the Sword of Wayland, the incredibly sharp glass blade, has begun glowing with an orangish light, which supplements the headlamp that I'm wearing. I can feel its power thrumming through me. The glow of the sword lights up the entire mouth.

The interior of its mouth is dark and glistening, with the walls thick with mucus. This thing is huge, even bigger up close than it seemed from a distance. The mouth is at least thirty feet across, and it's ringed by teeth that are half my height.

I'm barely able to stand, as the mouth is waving back and forth gently, like the deck of a small boat. I'm guessing that the creature is back underwater now, as the movements feel smooth.

I get my feet under me and hold up the sword, just in time to see the creature's long and sinewy tongue coming right at me. I stumble back, slipping and falling on my butt as the creature's head moves. The tongue swings toward me, and almost without me willing it to, I slash at it with the glass sword.

The tongue pulls back, but I see the cut that I made knitting itself together, healing in real time before my eyes. Zambrano mentioned the Leviathan's healing powers, but it's another thing to actually see it in person. In a few seconds, there's only a light bit of scar tissue, and then there's no wound at all. The tongue does, however, cower away from me. It may have been able to heal, but it didn't enjoy getting cut.

"I'm in the mouth," I say quietly. "Advancing toward the windpipe. Had a run-in with the tongue but was able to keep it at bay."

"Great," Zambrano's voice comes in my ear. "It hasn't attacked me yet, but I'm ready for it."

"I can still see it," Seraphex adds, and I can hear the wind in the background of her voice as she's flying high above the scene to track the Leviathan.

I reach the back of its throat and see the slit that a bunch of photos of snake mouths show me would be the windpipe, the route down into the lungs. This might be the most challenging part of the infiltration—how to get down the windpipe without getting swallowed into the stomach.

As I advance, I can see that the esophagus, which leads to the stomach, is closed. The Leviathan seems to be breathing through its nostrils, but I still feel musty air coming through the windpipe as I get close.

The esophagus is just a thin slit along the back of the throat, with the windpipe open above it. I charge forward, sprinting for the opening.

Just then, the tongue swings back toward me again, and the esophagus starts to open. It must have felt me toward the back of the mouth, and some instinct made it figure it might as well try to swallow me and let its powerful stomach acids sort things out.

As the wet ground underneath me shifts and opens, I take a final few steps, desperately hoping to make the trachea. The windpipe is open, and I take a leap as the esophagus underneath me yawns into a chasm. Given extra strength by the sword, I fly through the air and look down. Below, for a split second I see straight down. The acidic stomach bubbles, and I can see a mix of bones and steel pieces of what looks like a ship of some sort.

I go through the windpipe opening with the sword first, and hang on to it tightly. I tumble down the tube, and the sword guides my hand to make sure I don't impale myself or chop off my feet. I come to a halt when I land on my back in a long chamber, with air rushing out, and then rushing back in. It expands and contracts, and I have to duck down every time it contracts. Along the walls there are tiny sacs, which make the lungs' interior look and feel like a giant sponge. Unlike the inside of the mouth, the walls here seem thinner.

"Okay, I'm in the lungs," I say, praying that our connection holds this deep inside the Leviathan. "Anywhere in particular?"

"Just cut a big hole in the side of it," Zambrano says, "then keep cutting as you climb back out. The lung should collapse and rob its strength."

I take a deep breath and then plunge the sword into the side wall, slashing through its spongelike texture. A massive gap appears, and the lungs suddenly begin to strain. Some air escapes out into the snake's body, and a small amount of blood leaks into the lungs. I stand back, biting my lip.

"The beast appears distressed," Seraphex reports in my ear, and I put my hand to the wall to steady myself as the snake thrashes. Luckily, at least the sponge material is easy to grip. I should be able to climb back out on it.

But I watch in horror as the large gash that I made in the Leviathan's lungs closes up, healing the same way that the tongue did.

"Um, it's healing," I whisper. "What do I do now?"

"Oh, that's not good," Zambrano's voice says in my earpiece.

"No, it is not. The Leviathan appears to be less upset," Seraphex adds. "It may have recovered. It's circling toward you on the yacht, Zambrano."

"What next?" I ask.

"Cut it to hell," Zambrano says. "See if you can overwhelm it."

Gathering myself, I grip the sword. And then I go nuts. I walk down the length of the lung, slashing cut after cut into the lung walls. I'm tossed around as the giant tentacle snake thrashes, but by the time I get to one end of the lung, the other end has already healed.

Breathing heavily, I curse and stab the lung, this time leaving the sword stuck up to the hilt in the lung wall. "It just keeps healing!" I shout.

"Sorry, Bryce," Zambrano says. "I didn't realize it had that level of power. I guess this is why we trapped it last time rather than killing it. Maybe you should get out of there, we'll teleportrait home and try to come up with another plan. Maybe lure it away from Hawaii to buy time."

"It's been headed there very steadily, with just a few detours," Seraphex says. "That's going to be hard to do without dropping loads of human bodies into the ocean to draw it away. I'm happy to help with that, if it's the plan."

"Okay, we're not doing that, obviously," I say. "but isn't there anything else we can do to it from in here?"

They're both silent for a moment, and I look at the sword, buried as it is to the hilt. Air and blood are flowing around it—and it's not healing.

"Um, guys," I say. "I think I might need to leave the sword here." I explain what's happening and remove my hand gingerly, looking to see what happens.

The creature begins thrashing, wriggling back and forth with displeasure. But the sword stays perfectly still, not moving or yielding, as the snake's lung becomes slightly smaller and more collapsed with each breath it draws.

"It's a good plan," Zambrano says. "The sword's magic should make it stay in the most damaging position. It's very powerful. But if you're leaving it there, you need to get out of there now."

I take a long moment to look at the sword. As soon as I take my hand off it, I feel the power and strength that it had been giving me drain away.

"Damn, I was hoping that sword would become, like, my thing, you know?" I say. I had visions of fame, of being a legendary hero. And the most basic accessory for a hero is a magic sword.

"Get out now if you're coming," Seraphex says. "The snake is looking very unhappy. I'd guess you have a few minutes, but the sooner the better."

I would like to stay and think this through, trying to calculate the odds of success and whether this risk is worth it or not, but there's no time for that now. We need to defeat this mythic monster before it can wreak havoc on Hawaii and proceed to destabilize the world and enable Rex's takeover.

I leave the sword behind, climbing hand over hand up the lung and back up the windpipe, reporting my progress, intermixed with a good bit of complaining, along the way.

"I'm not going to have the sword to protect me in its mouth," I say. "I'm going to have to dodge the tongue and teeth and avoid the esophagus. Any ideas on that?"

"Bad news on that, Bryce," Seraphex's voice says in my ear. "The Leviathan hasn't opened its mouth since you went in there. I believe it is attempting to ensure you stay trapped in there, maybe hoping it can swallow and digest you. It has very powerful jaws and doesn't like to lose its prey."

"Well that sucks!" I gripe. "The tongue probably would have gotten me anyway. Should I go back and get the sword? It's probably not too late. Or is there any other way out?" I'm still climbing up the spongy lungs, enjoying grabbing and ripping at the Leviathan's innards, though every injury immediately heals.

"Well, I can think of one way out, but it's through the acidic digestive tract," Zambrano says. "Not a plan that I think you are likely to enjoy, or survive."

"Yeah, I don't want to be liquified giant snake poop," I say.

"How about the nostrils?" Seraphex suggests. "The openings are far smaller than the mouth, but from here it looks like they're large enough for you to get through. All you need to do is climb up and keep going past the mouth all the way up and out the nasal cavity."

"Sure," I say as I start climbing. "Just crawl out the giant monster's nostrils. Easy-peasy."

# CHAPTER 25

Got it," I say, and I keep climbing. I pass the mouth, and before long I'm in the mythic monster's nose.

How am I certain?

The snot.

It's everywhere, and it's sticky as hell. I guess if the Leviathan's stomach acid can be strong enough to melt down parts of naval ships, its snot can be sticky enough to hold me. I try to crawl forward, but without the enchantment of the magic sword to give me strength, I'm only able to force my way forward a dozen feet.

For about two minutes, I'm forced just to hold my position as the snake moves wildly, with up and down switching places several times.

Finally the snake's head stabilizes, and the nostrils in front of me open, letting in fresh air and light. They're only about ten feet away, but the opening gets narrower and narrower, leading toward a hole that I can definitely fit through. Or at least, I could fit through, if it wasn't almost entirely filled with snot. Through the bit of the nostril that's open to the outside, I can see alternative views of the ocean and sky, with occasional sparks of magical energy and the sound of explosions of arcane energy.

"The Leviathan is weakening," Seraphex says, "but it's going to take some time. Bryce, you need to get out of there. The arcane energy is starting to go critical. You don't want to be inside of the Leviathan when that happens."

"I'm trying!" I say, attempting to wriggle forward. With every movement, my stomach turns as I get deeper into the sticky snot. The giant monster bobs its head back and forth, making it like a really unpleasant amusement park ride.

After several attempts, it's clear I'm not making much progress. I keep trying to inch forward, but the stuff is gripping me like glue, and it only gets thicker ahead.

"I don't think I'm strong enough to do this," I complain.

"I'm trying to help, but I can't risk getting too close to it; it's still too strong," Zambrano says. "My most damaging offensive spells damage and push it back, but it heals immediately and comes back for more. It is weakening, but slowly—and you don't want to be in there when the magic collapses. Can you try going back down through the mouth? Maybe I can figure out how to force its mouth open."

I try to back out, but that's even harder. This stuff feels like those glue traps they use for rodents, with every motion getting the mucus deeper into my clothes and hair. It's disgusting, but it's pulling at me, and every movement I make only gets me more stuck in this monster's boogers.

"Bryce, the Leviathan is circling the yacht and starting to show signs of desperation. It's an injured beast. Zambrano is going to have a very tough time getting to you. He just needs to hold out until it weakens and the magic collapses, but that's going to take time. You're going to need to get out of there on your own."

"How?" I ask, trying to pull my arm out of the sticky goop that I'm trapped in. "I can barely move!" I almost throw up but am barely able to choke it down. That would only make things so much worse.

"Make it do the work for you," Zambrano says. "It has a nose and snot. It must be able to sneeze, or something like it."

"I have to make it *sneeze?*" I shout.

"Do you have a better idea?" he shoots back, and I can hear a slight strain in his voice as he shouts a spell. I feel the impact of it on the Leviathan as it reels back.

"Well, no," I admit. "But how do I do that?"

"Irritate it!" Zambrano says. "And I won't even make a joke about how you're already an irritant—that would be too easy, and I have more respect for myself than that."

I try to move, squirming as much as I can and am able to get one arm free and poke and pound on the inside of the giant monster's nostril.

"I'm hitting it," I say, "but it's not working."

"Just getting poked doesn't make a nasal passage react that way. Vibrations could do it. You've got to tease it out."

"You want me to tease a giant snake with tentacles into sneezing?" I ask.

"What I want is to teleport home and take a bath, but that is the plan that I am suggesting," Zambrano says. "Give audio irritation a shot."

Not knowing what else to do, I turn to put my mouth next to the disgusting slimy wall of the nostril and scream as loud as I can.

"LET ME OUT!" I yell, but it does nothing.

"Not high-pitched like a scared teenager," Zambrano says, "Low pitches! Think bass! It needs to feel the vibrations."

Rolling my eyes, I take a deep breath and try to sing out in as low a tone as I can. I was never a particularly good singer, but I did sing the bass parts in a school musical I was in the chorus for one time. I know, I was a really cool guy in high school. I get close and try to give the nose my best low note.

To my surprise, I feel a slight shudder. The nostrils seem to tense slightly, sniffling up that way you do when you have a sneeze coming. I try again and get the same result. I try several more times, but it doesn't seem to build up into an actual sneeze.

"I think this might be possible, but I just don't have the volume. Do we have like a portable speaker or something down there?"

"I don't think so, and even if we did, I wouldn't be able to get it to you," Zambrano says. "But I can think of one idea."

"Oh, no," Seraphex protests.

"Yes, definitely there's one possibility to help you," the sorcerer continues. "Who can make any voice or sound, and very loudly?"

"You wouldn't dare ask that of me, a demon queen. I can see from up here how gross it is in there."

"You're his only hope," Zambrano points out.

I hear Seraphex let out an exasperated sigh.

"Very well, Bryce. Since you're my friend. I'll fly into a snotty monster nose," the demon duck yells. And then, ten seconds later: "INCOMING!"

The duck dive-bombs into the nose, landing in a splatter of snot. It gets all over my face, the one part of my body that I'd been able to avoid getting slimed so far.

"This is so gross. This is awful," Seraphex squeals as the snot coats her webbed feet and feathers. "Ugh, I hate this. I hate this so much." Not about to waste any time, she takes a deep breath, and a much deeper, more resonant voice blasts out of her at a massive volume. "I AM NOT ENJOYING THIS! I RESENT FRIENDSHIP!" The massive bass from her voice shakes the nasal cavity and jiggles the snot. "FRIENDSHIP IS MAKING ME FEEL HORRIBLE! FRIENDSHIP, IN MY FEELINGS AT THIS PARTICULAR MOMENT, SUCKS!"

The Levithan sniffs twice, and then my stomach turns as it reels back and sneezes. I see a shower of snot and the demon duck explode out the nose, and I'm blasted forward. For a moment, I can see the blue sky growing larger and closer, but then I'm slammed into a pile of snot at the top and right at the edge of the nose. Now I can see fully out through the nostril, taking in the sky, the ocean, and Zambrano on the ship below, blasting a spell up at the giant sea monster.

I try to pull free, but the force of the sneeze got me stuck in a deep clump of snot, really a solid booger, right at the top of the exit of the nose, halfway in and halfway out. Below, I see Seraphex tumbling and trying to shake the snot off her body.

*This is it*, I think as a giant tentacle swings my way, reaching up toward the nose. *Now I'm in the open, and it can kill me. And probably eat me, snot and all.*

But the tentacle isn't trying to murder me. It reaches back into the nose, pulling out a chunk of snot, and tosses it into the ocean. And then it swings back and wraps around me, pulling me and the booger I'm attached to out. For a moment the tentacle swings wide, and I soar across the ocean.

And then, like the disgusting booger picked from its nose that I am, the Leviathan flings me away.

# CHAPTER 26

I catapult across the sky in an arc and slam into the water, the force thankfully disconnecting me from the majority of the snot as I fly deep. For a long moment I'm trapped underwater, unable to gain my bearings. Luckily, I'm wearing an amber nexus, so I'm able to breathe as I sink down into the water, pulling pieces of monster snot off myself.

I swim up to the surface and splash out of the water, wiping water and snot off my face and trying to assess the situation. I put my hand to my ear, checking that the earpiece is still in place.

"Can you hear me?" I ask. "I'm okay, swimming in the water fairly far off. At least the Leviathan doesn't seem to be coming after me."

"I can hear you, yes," Seraphex says. "I'm just busy trying to peck this beast's eyes out. Nobody gets their snot on me and doesn't pay a price!"

"Unlike you," Zambrano's voice comes in my earpiece, "maybe the Leviathan doesn't pick its nose and eat it. And don't lie to me, I've seen you when you think I'm not looking."

This is completely, categorically false. But I don't bother to correct the sorcerer. He has more important things to worry about.

The Leviathan is slowly advancing on the yacht. I can see the small dot of Seraphex swooping in to try to distract it, but it's not paying the least bit of attention to her.

Zambrano is standing out on the prow of the boat, blasting out rays of blue magic. They are hitting the monster, and each time it's struck, it's driven back briefly.

"What's happening?" I ask.

"I'm holding off the Leviathan as its lung collapses," Zambrano growls. "Just a couple more minutes. If I can just exhaust it enough, I'll be able to drain its power out. Even the Circle couldn't do this, and I'm so close!" he crows.

Floating in the water, I watch as Zambrano stands on the deck of the yacht, blasting magic at the Leviathan. Every time it swings a tentacle at him or rears forward with its head, a blast of magic hits it, forcing it back and sending it reeling. Sometimes its attacks are clearly visible as it lunges above the water, and sometimes Zambrano sends his magic down into the water, and all I see is an explosion of boiling water as the impact happens in the depths.

But as a minute passes, I notice that the Leviathan is methodically circling the yacht, slowly but steadily moving closer. With every blast, it takes a moment to regroup and then advances again, the radius of its circle contracting.

"Sera, how's he doing?" I ask quietly.

"I'm *fine,*" Zambrano says with a grunt. "I've had these spells in my arsenal for a hundred years. They're specially designed to hold off this beast. Olujimi's finest work."

"He's struggling," Seraphex says matter-of-factly. "At this rate I believe that the Levithan will reach him before its lungs run out."

"Zambrano . . ." I start.

"*What?*"

"You need to ask for help," I say.

"Help? Who's going to help me? I just need to keep holding this thing back," he mutters.

"Admiral Wilcox," I say. "A good chunk of the US Pacific Fleet is lurking out there. They're probably watching. But if you don't ask for help now, they probably won't be able to get here in time.

"What can they do? With their little toy cannons?" Zambrano says, grunting as he casts another spell at the Leviathan as its tentacles surge out of the water.

"They can distract it. Keep it occupied long enough to waste its energy away," I say. "Do you have some big special spell saved, waiting for when the Leviathan gets too close and dodges your attacks?"

"Ugh, no," Zambrano says.

"And what happens then?"

"Well, probably I die," Zambrano says. "Maybe I'll be able to teleport away in time if I realize soon enough. And then I guess you die."

"So we need help," I reiterate.

"Okay, Bryce, very well. You're right. I agreed to hear you. You think we need help, we'll call in help."

He waits for the Leviathan to rear up again and sends it back with an especially strong blast of magic, then leaps with some sort of magical assist up to the bridge of the yacht.

I hear as he grabs the wireless radio handset and returns to the deck in time to send another blast at the Leviathan.

"Admiral Wilcox?" Zambrano says, his voice coming over my earpiece.

"This is Wilcox," the admiral's voice says. "We're watching this fight over our drone feed. Your magic is quite . . . impressive."

"I know," Zambrano says. "But about that—to be honest, I could use a hand. We've injured this thing and it's weakening, but I need to hold it off longer for it to collapse, and frankly I'm running out of juice. I need other combatants here to spread its focus. Can you help with that?"

"You're asking my sailors to risk their lives, sorcerer," the admiral says. "Are you sure?"

"I'm risking my own here as well, Admiral," Zambrano says. "If we can beat this thing now, I can drain it. Otherwise, it'll probably be at your main fleet in Honolulu in an hour or two, and it may overcome the little trick we've used to weaken it. We can't let up on it, we need to take it out now."

"Acknowledged," Wilcox says. "We have one destroyer and one submarine that can assist. Transmitting orders now."

It takes a few more minutes, and in that time, I can see Zambrano's spells getting weaker with each successive attack. The Leviathan also becomes more desperate, thrashing wildly but moving slower overall. On the horizon, I can see one of the ships getting increasingly larger, but it's still quite a ways off.

Finally one of its tentacles reaches up onto the deck of the boat, and Zambrano is narrowly able to dance out of the way.

"You may need to teleport out," I say, "before it's too late. I'll take my chances here, hopefully the Leviathan doesn't bother with me, and Sera can guide the navy to pick me up later."

"Not yet," Seraphex says. "Help is here!"

I hear it more than see it, but something off to my left disturbs the water with a loud thumping sound. After that, there's the high-pitched whine of a powerful motor flashing through the water. And then, where the giant sea monster has surfaced, a massive explosion goes off on its side, followed by a huge spray of water. It appears to only make a small dent in the Leviathan, which heals immediately just like the smaller wounds that the sword made.

Still, this affront does serve to distract the Leviathan, which turns away from Zambrano's yacht and dives down into the deep. The ocean is silent for a moment, and I think that I hear the sound of distant motors, but that might just be my imagination.

This lasts for about a minute, after which I see the Levithan surface at some distance. It roars into the sky, venting rage at its submarine prey having escaped.

It turns and plows across the water in a fury, headed straight for the yacht.

As it closes, Zambrano blasts it with another shower of magical energy, charged back up after having time to catch his breath, and it reels.

I've been distracted and haven't noticed how close the destroyer has come. Now it opens fire, a vast array of guns firing and missiles soaring from its many weapon emplacements. Some of the barrage misses, but the majority of it slams into the giant sea monster, pushing it back, even if not damaging it significantly.

Floating at sea level and treading water to keep my head up, it's hard for me to follow what happens next. There's a complicated dance as Zambrano, the destroyer, and the submarine take turns enraging the monster and then pulling back while the others take a turn. Luckily, desperate and flailing as it is, the Levithan falls for each of their gambits, always switching to focus on the latest assailant. Not knowing what else to do, I pull out my phone. Its screen is cracked and it's waterlogged, but it does still seem to be working. Despite the cracks, I'm able to turn on the camera, which works perfectly once I wipe the Levithan snot off it.

After several more minutes of attacks and misdirection, the beast seems to understand what's going on and turns away from pursuing its latest target, the destroyer, which is peeling away as it throws what is probably millions of taxpayer dollars' worth of ordinance at it. It ignores the fire and charges straight for the yacht. The yacht is unable to move, but Zambrano stands on the prow, flinging down magic as the monster advances.

This time it has given up on strategically retreating under fire, instead simply plowing though. Torpedoes strike its side, and rounds from the destroyer glance off its back, but it crashes through the waves, its tentacles writhing in fury.

It closes on Zambrano, who stands his ground, arms windmilling as he blasts the Leviathan with the same spell over and over. It looms out of the water, and I see a tiny shape fly in from above, its feathery wings bringing it just in front of the monster's nose.

Distantly, I hear Seraphex's voice, broadcast as loud as if it's on a concert speaker. "NO! BAD SNAKE! LEAVE MY FRIENDS ALONE!"

The snake sneezes, and the very last of the air blasts out of its lungs. It collapses back into the waves, writhing as it floats on them.

Zambrano holds up a single hand, shouting a phrase that sounds guttural, a series of grunts in some primal language that I don't recognize. His upraised right hand glows orange, and I see ethereal streams of power leaving the body of the Leviathan, and its body is shrinking.

And then the glowing becomes increasingly brighter, almost as bright as the sun. I only see bits of this, able to catch it as each swell of the ocean raises me up a few feet in the air.

"I can't control all of its power," Zambrano says. "The spell that had contained it is failing. The Leviathan is going to explode and release all its energy. I have to teleport out. Get underwater!"

I see Seraphex streaking away from the yacht, up into the sky.

"Dive, Bryce!" she says, and I immediately comply.

I dive under the water, swimming down as fast as I can. Luckily, with the amber nexus, I don't have to worry about holding my breath or the pressure. I do feel the earpiece slip out, the magic that stuck it in place finally giving way. Within just a few seconds I'm able to get down into the murkier depths, where the light from above filters through much more dimly.

I feel more than hear the explosion, a massive thundering blast. The cold water itself starts to warm, and I look above to see the light suddenly even dimmer as the uppermost layer of water steams off.

I'm thankful that I have the amber nexus, and I continue swimming for some time, staying deep in the chilly depths. Finally, from what I can see, the air and water above look calm. I slowly come up to the surface, first testing with a hand and then sticking my whole head above water.

The destroyer is mostly intact, though it has some blast damage along its prow. It doesn't look to be sinking, and I do see figures on the deck, assessing the damage. Hopefully they were able to take shelter before the blast. The Leviathan and the yacht are both gone, with a dark red stain on the water and a scattering of random floating debris where they used to be.

# CHAPTER 27

Once the destroyer recovers from the explosion, it sends a small boat to pick me up. The captain asks me a few questions, but it's clear that he knows this is all above his pay grade, so mostly they just dry me off and give me some fresh clothes, protein bars, and a water bottle, and they hustle me onto a helicopter to Honolulu.

On the helicopter ride I think I see a duck flying along with us, though we quickly outpace it. It could also have been a seagull or something, I've never been that good at bird identification.

Once I'm back within cell service range, I'm able to text Zambrano and confirm that he made it out safely. The marine guards accompanying me look at me suspiciously when I use the phone, but none of them seem to have been given orders to stop me, so they don't take it away. Or maybe they're just critical of a dumb kid with a cracked cell phone screen, who knows?

He's already back in Hawaii, having teleported to New York and then back to Honolulu, but they land me at the naval base at Pearl Harbor. Zambrano offers to smash in and break me out, but I tell him I'm fine. I end up waiting for a couple hours in a holding room of some sort, which is fine by me because I'm able to catch a little sleep on a couch.

I wake up with a start as the door opens and Agent Crane steps in.

She gives me a weak smile, sighs, and sits down at the table. She gestures to the other chair, but I stay stretched out on the couch.

"I was en route to Hawaii the moment the Leviathan was sighted," she says. "Sorry I missed the main excitement. The MSA hadn't totally given up on finding a use for me, even if it was just as extra cannon fodder against the monster."

"Do you believe that we're the good guys yet?" I ask.

"I believe that you believe that you're the good guys," she says with a wry smile. "That's all I'm allowed to believe, officially."

I shake my head and laugh. "Seriously?"

"The MSA's stance at the moment is that their persuasion and threats convinced Zambrano to be cooperative for once. Admiral Wilcox said some very positive things about you, but the Pentagon really doesn't like having someone else swoop in and save their behinds. Both the MSA and the military brass are trying to take credit for the great success today."

"So they're still being obstinate assholes, then?" I say. "Why is the government like this? Have they given you your job back yet?"

Agent Crane shrugs. "I'm here assigned to interview you. We'll have to take it from there; I don't know what my next assignment will be."

"Okay," I say, yawning. "Well, this was nice, and please tell the navy boys that I really appreciate the ride. But we've still got a demon king to stop. Am I being detained here?"

Agent Crane pauses for a long moment.

"Surely you know that you're not going to be able to hold me against my will," I point out. "Unless you're willing to take quite drastic actions."

"No, we're not detaining you. We just want information. I'm here to help you, Bryce."

"I know that you are, Agent Crane," I say. "And I also know that the government is sometimes very helpful, and sometimes not. And not always good at keeping secrets. But most of this is out in the open now. And you have a right to know what you're up against."

I explain to her everything that I know about the current situation, focusing on the fact that Demon King Rex has broken out of his cage and is a huge threat to the world. I explain how he's recovering from the Caesar Special that was shoved in his back and that the Leviathan was part of his playbook of destabilizing human governments and sowing chaos so that he can take over.

"Do you have a plan to stop him?" she asks, the color draining from her face.

"We have some ideas," I say, "But not a full plan yet."

"Would you even tell me if you did?"

I shake my head. "No, there's a very good chance that Rex already has spies in the MSA and other government agencies. I'd have to ask you to trust us, and to not try to figure out what we're working on. It could be leaked."

Agent Crane sighs and nods. "This battle has helped a lot with that trust. Let me know how we can help, and I'll do my best to get you what you need."

"Thanks," I say. "And I'm glad to see that they've given you some responsibilities back."

"I appreciate that," she says.

"Am I free to go?" I ask.

"As you point out," she answers with a thin smile, "us holding you captive would not go well for anyone. I'll have one of the naval staffers show you out. Thank you, Bryce."

And just like that, a few minutes later, with nothing but a cracked phone and a standard-issue navy T-shirt, shorts, and coveralls, I'm deposited at the bus station outside the main gates of the Joint Base Pearl Harbor-Hickam. I guess if I'm not giving them intel, there are no free rides in SUVs. But I'm pretty pissed that we saved all their butts, and we get nothing but suspicion and political nonsense in return.

I use my phone to call a car and head to the spot where Zambrano's teleportrait will land. It's on the north side of Oahu at a secluded little beach that is pretty empty now that night has fallen. It's really, really nice. So nice that I can ignore for a moment the drone that I occasionally spot overhead, definitely keeping tabs on everything I do.

I let Zambrano know that I'm here and ready, and I take a minute to stroll along the beach, admiring the waves in the moonlight. I love the New York/New Jersey area, but I have to admit . . . compared to this, our beaches are utter trash. It's peaceful and warm, and the trees are swaying in the perfectly salty breeze, and for a few minutes I can almost pretend that the world isn't about to be taken over by an ancient demon king. I really wish I could stay here for a few hours. Or maybe a week. Or a lifetime, if I'm asking for impossible things.

Finally, Zambrano pops into existence with a whoosh, and I jog back up the beach to meet him.

"I didn't mean for things to go like that," Zambrano says. "I was hoping I could drain that monster of its power. That spell I used was one of the oldest there is, from prehistoric times. We don't even know what language it's in. But it wasn't designed for monsters that have spent thousands of years gaining strength. They were all much younger and less powerful back then."

I shrug. "We figured it out, we won. I think there were some injuries on the destroyer, but I don't think anyone died. Let's chalk it up as a win."

"Agreed." Zambrano nods. "We live to fight another day." He pauses for several long seconds. "Thanks for pushing me to ask for help."

"I'm glad that—"

"No therapy nonsense," he grumbles. "We did it, it was good. Hip, hip, hooray, the old sorcerer isn't totally insane yet—let's move on. We should get back to the warehouse and try to plan out our next steps. We need to be ready with something when Liao Ling shows up with her demon-weakening spell prepared. I don't want to be there empty-handed. Come on," he says, holding out the teleportrait with the lab in the warehouse painted on it.

He grabs my neck, and the beach disappears. There's that strange warm feeling, and a split second later, we're standing in the lab. Seraphex is sitting on one of the tables—she must have gone to the beach pickup location and gotten transported while I was sleeping at the naval base.

"Welcome home," Seraphex says.

"You're a good friend, Sera," I say, smiling at her.

"A part of me resents every moment of this forced friendship," she answers. "But also . . . you're welcome. And I'm sorry about your sword."

"Yeah, what happened to it? Is it stuck at the bottom of the ocean? Could we use the amber nexus to go down and get it?"

"No," Seraphex says. "The second explosion was the sword. When the Leviathan exploded, it wrecked the enchantments on the Sword of Wayland as well, and it unleashed its magic in a second burst of energy."

"Well, that sucks," I say. "I got to be the hero of destiny with a cool sword for, like, less than an hour. I didn't even get to use it to slaughter wave after wave of orcs or anything."

"You do have a pretty neat pair of gauntlets!" Zambrano says, patting me on the shoulder. "And orcs aren't real, don't be ridiculous."

I stand for a long minute, eyeing the big wall of teleportraits that line the far wall. So many locations around the world, all accessible by teleportation in the blink of an eye. And every single one of them finds a way to humiliate me one way or another when we actually go there.

"Where do we go, when we use a teleportrait?" I ask.

"What exactly do you mean?" Zambrano says, looking at me like I'm an idiot, as if I didn't just help defeat an incredibly powerful and ancient monster. "We go to the place that's shown on the painting. That's the whole point of the magic. It takes you where you want to go."

"No, I mean when we're in transit. Is it instant? It feels instant."

"Basically, it's instant," Zambrano says, looking at me and raising a quizzical eyebrow. "In that moment, you're . . . you're just, well, nowhere. It's instant for you. But I've actually tested it, it's not instant for the rest of the world. It happens at the speed of light."

"Right," I say. "Because it would violate the laws of physics otherwise?"

"Yes, exactly," Zambrano agrees. "If you could travel instantaneously, that would let you travel back in time, violate causality, generate free energy—physicists would be super pissed. So you disappear in one place, and after the time that it takes light to travel between departure and arrival locations, you appear on the other side. But during that interim . . . I don't suppose you're anywhere at all."

"I wish we could just teleport Rex away, so that he could never come back," I say. "Like, could you just teleport with him somewhere a thousand light years away? Then he would, basically, not exist in the universe for a thousand years. And it would take him a thousand years to come back, even if he could teleport."

Zambrano sighs. "That wouldn't really work. The amount of arcane energy required to teleport someone goes up exponentially the farther you want to go. If I had the ability to cast and power that type of spell, I could probably just defeat or imprison Rex in some much more straightforward way. Sending him far away won't work."

"We just need to get him to be teleporting forever," I say wistfully. "But that probably takes, like infinite energy, huh?"

"Oh." Zambrano glares at me. "Oh!"

"The arcane conduit," Seraphex says, leaping up onto her webbed feet.

"Didn't we send half of it into the sun?"

"Yes, yes, we did," Zambrano says. "We certainly did that. But we only need half of it for this."

He and Seraphex start bouncing all sorts of arcane knowledge back and forth. The parts I'm able to catch involve things like "nonzero time in transit," "infinitesimal distance teleportation takes infinitesimal energy," and "continuous activation, no exit point." The other parts are even less comprehensible.

"Okay, what does it all mean?" I ask.

"Since one half of the arcane conduit is destroyed," Zambrano says proudly, "the other half won't teleport objects to it. Anything that it teleports will simply be teleported back to its location of origin. But since you return to the point where you departed, you are never re-instantiated. We can make it so he just keeps getting teleported back and forth. Rex stays in transit indefinitely as long as the conduit is powered."

"How much energy does it take?"

"Nothing a volcano can't generate," Zambrano says with a shrug. "It's incomprehensibly huge numbers multiplied by inconceivably tiny numbers—so it comes out to boring normal numbers."

"Okay, that's great," I say. "Only one problem—we don't have the remaining half of the arcane conduit."

"Well, two problems. As exciting as this is, we also don't have the spell that activates the conduit," Zambrano points out.

"Does Liao Ling know it?" I ask.

"No, unfortunately," Zambrano says. "Merlin created the arcane conduit while she constructed the Caesar Special and created an alliance of sorcerers and wizards. And she was trapped in the prismatic prison when it was finally activated, so she wouldn't have seen it cast."

"Zuzanna should remember it," Seraphex says. "She locked away her magical abilities, so she can't cast it. But she can teach it to you."

"She's alive?" Zambrano and I both say at the same time.

"I feel bad, as your friend, for not having told you sooner," Seraphex says. "Which is a very uncomfortable feeling, I must tell you."

"So then we have the bones of a plan to take down Rex," Zambrano says while I'm just sitting there dumbfounded.

"Why do I have the feeling this is going to be another one of those plans that I hate?" I finally say, coming back to the reality that we're constructing a campaign against a dangerous enemy.

"In order to do this, we shall need to accomplish two things," Seraphex explains. "First, we need to find your mother in order to get the details of her spell. Second, we must go to Mars to fetch the arcane conduit. Does that sound acceptable?"

"Okay, sure, yeah that's fine," I say, using that ancient advantage that humans have over demons—the ability to lie. I'm not okay with finding my mother or traveling across space to the home world of the demons.

And, honestly, I'm not sure which scares me more.

**DIRECTOR SCOTT:** Just landed at Dulles. Have to give a briefing to the Joint Chiefs tomorrow morning. Do we have anything new?

**AGENT CRANE:** None of my contacts have anything solid, I'm sorry.

**DIRECTOR SCOTT:** It's been eight weeks, and we still don't have any information. Nothing from Bryce Alexander?

**AGENT CRANE:** I think they're working on something, but he's not sharing details with me. They don't trust us to keep it secret, given the unknown capabilities of our likely adversary.

**DIRECTOR SCOTT:** Is there anything you can give me? There were those disturbances in the Pacific, crazy arcanometer readings, and then a giant sea monster appeared and got blown up. Everyone says this demon king is here, but there's no actual sign of him. It's been eight weeks! Where is he?

**AGENT CRANE:** My low-level demonic contacts have all gone silent. The Irish druids have relocated their children and won't tell me where. The Chilean mystics have disappeared into the mountains. The Indonesian auction houses are trading protective items and spells at a huge premium. China has shut down all exports of magical artifacts. Sorry, I know I told you all that last week.

**DIRECTOR SCOTT:** What the hell do I tell the Joint Chiefs? Something is wrong, but we have no news. There's military conflict in east Asia, a drought in central Africa, rioting in European capitals, stock market collapses in India and Pakistan, but none of it is clearly related to magic. No demons sighted, not even rogue wizards causing problems. But things on the world stage are looking dire.

**AGENT CRANE:** That's good though, right? No demon sightings, no sorcerers blowing things up? No collateral damage from their fights, no property damage, no California arcades or Chicago office buildings getting blown up. Can you spin that as a positive?

**DIRECTOR SCOTT:** It's something, I guess. But things are getting really tense over here. Something is clearly off. But nothing magical or demonic is happening, and everyone is freaking out. Is this demon king really out there, or not? And is he behind all these conflicts and disasters?

**DIRECTOR SCOTT:** Never mind, the regular Joint Chiefs meeting is canceled.

**AGENT CRANE:** Canceled?

**DIRECTOR SCOTT:** You need to get here immediately, I'm pulling you off your current assignment.

**AGENT CRANE:** Okay, getting a car now. What's happening?

**DIRECTOR SCOTT:** New meeting in an hour. The Mars Reconnaissance Orbiter just detected significant tectonic and volcanic activity on the Martian surface.

**AGENT CRANE:** Tectonic activity? Isn't Mars mostly dead? Inert?

**DIRECTOR SCOTT:** Can't say more until you get here. Something just moved that the scientists tell me should NOT be moving.

# ABOUT THE AUTHOR

Gavin Brown is a novelist, video game director, and entrepreneur. His books *include Josh Baxter Levels Up, Monster Club: Hunters for Hire*, and installments of the 39 Clues and Spirit Animals series. He also created hit indie mobile game *Blindscape* and directed the 39 Clues, Spirit Animals, and Scholastic's Home Base video games. Brown lives in a former ice cream factory in New York City.

# JOIN THE FELLOWSHIP

*follow us on our socials*

podiumentertainment.com

@podiumentertainment

/podiumentertainment

@podium_ent

@podiumentertainment